P9-DXF-747

Searching for SILVERHEELS

ALSO BY JEANNIE MOBLEY

Katerina's Wish

Searching for SILVERHEELS

JEANNIE MOBLEY

MARGARET K. McELDERRY BOOKS

New York   London   Toronto   Sydney   New Delhi

MARGARET K. McELDERRY BOOKS
An imprint of Simon & Schuster Children's Publishing Division
1230 Avenue of the Americas, New York, New York 10020
MARGARET K. McELDERRY BOOKS is a trademark of Simon & Schuster, Inc.
For information about special discounts for bulk purchases, please contact
Simon & Schuster Special Sales at 1-866-506-1949 or business@
simonandschuster.com.
The Simon & Schuster Speakers Bureau can bring authors to your live
event. For more information or to book an event, contact the Simon &
Schuster Speakers Bureau at 1-866-248-3049 or visit our website at
www.simonspeakers.com.
Book design by Debra Sfetsios-Conover
The text for this book is set in Baskerville MT.
Manufactured in the United States of America
0814 FFG
10 9 8 7 6 5 4 3 2 1
Library of Congress Cataloging-in-Publication Data
Mobley, Jeannie.
Searching for Silverheels / Jeannie Mobley.—First edition.
p. cm.
Summary: In Colorado during World War I, a young, romantically minded
girl and an old, bitter woman suffragist debate a local legend and examine
the role of women in a time of war and prejudice.
ISBN 978-1-4814-0029-9 (hardcover)
ISBN 978-1-4814-0031-2 (eBook)
[1. Sex role—Fiction. 2. Colorado—History—1876–1950—Fiction.
3. World War, 1914–1918—United States—Fiction.] I. Title.
PZ7.M71275Se 2014
[Fic]—dc23
2013033485

For Leah, my beautiful, strong daughter,
who gives me strength and beauty
every day.

Acknowledgments

I would like to thank my family and many friends who have been so supportive through my writing career thus far: my mom, kids, husband, critique partners, agency siblings, and many others who have been there with advice, support, sympathy, and tough love as needed.

I continue to be awed and inspired by the wisdom of my agent, Erin Murphy, and my wonderful editor at McElderry Books, Karen Wojtyla. Annie Nybo, editorial assistant at McElderry Books, has been incredibly helpful, and as always a whole crew of behind-the-scenes people at Simon & Schuster have worked their mysterious magic that turns a stack of pages into a beautiful book. I may not know all their names, but I certainly appreciate their efforts.

Searching for
SILVERHEELS

CHAPTER 1

It's strange how sometimes, even though the whole world is changing around you, everything can feel so much the same. President Wilson had declared war on Germany just two months ago and had called upon every citizen to step up and help out with the war effort. Women were planting victory gardens, and young men were talking of enlisting. My own father had gone up onto the mountain to mine the zinc needed for shell casings. But here in the Silverheels Café, life just moseyed on, same as always. Each morning, the old-timers gathered at their table in the corner and talked at length about nothing in particular. My best friend, Imogene, hovered by the counter, trying to flirt with my big brother, Willie, who only had eyes for his breakfast. And I was spending my days taking orders, hauling plates, and refilling cup after cup of coffee, without anything new or interesting crossing my path.

"Order, Pearl!" Mother called from the kitchen. I went to retrieve the plates of eggs and bacon for the old-timers. Mother fed them nearly every morning, come rain or shine, whether or not they had money to cover their bills. Neighbors do for neighbors, she always said, and it seemed to be true.

Those who never had the cash always seemed to find other ways to pay—fresh fish or game for the kitchen, or a load of firewood for the stove.

I stepped from the kitchen back out into the café just as George Crawford and his mother walked through the front door. Imogene glanced at them, then turned a pointed stare at me, her eyebrows bobbing. I tried to ignore her and offer a polite good morning to George and his mother, but I'm sure George noticed the rush of blood that flooded my cheeks.

"Good morning, Pearl," he said with a smile. George had the most stunning smile in all of Park County. Even girls who had no interest in him said so, not that there were many of those. Possibly the only girl who claimed no interest was Imogene, and that was mainly because she was my best friend and knew how I felt. Besides, she was sweet on Willie.

Mrs. Crawford directed George to the table in the opposite corner from the old-timers and began to peel off her kidskin gloves. Why she bothered to put them on at all mystified me; Crawford's Mercantile was only just across the street and a block down, but Mrs. Crawford was always a lady. At least, in her appearance.

"Coffee, please, Pearl," she called, even before she sat down. I carried my load of plates to the old-timers' table, then I went behind the counter to retrieve the coffeepot from its warmer. Imogene leaned across the counter toward me and whispered, "George is watching you."

"Shh!" I said.

She sat back and spoke in a voice loud enough for everyone in the café to hear. "We have some tourists at the hotel, Pearl. They came in last night and reserved a room for four nights."

I paused, waiting for her to go on. This was good news. Tourism was likely to be down this summer with the war on, and that meant less business for our café as well as for Imogene's family, who ran the hotel.

"They look like the type that might want a tour," Imogene continued. Most years this would have been good news too. My father and I made a few extra dollars in the summer taking folks on excursions. This year, though, with Father away, I wasn't sure if I'd be able to do that, no matter how much I wanted to.

Oblivious to my dilemma, Imogene kept talking. "There are three of them. A fashionable young couple, Mr. and Mrs. Robert Fischer, and a fellow about our age named Frank. Frank is *mightily* handsome!" She said the last with a hopeful glance at Willie, but he showed no sign of jealousy. Imogene sighed.

"Where's that coffee, Pearl? And George might want a cinnamon roll, when you are done with your little chat," said Mrs. Crawford.

"Yes, ma'am. Sorry," I said, snatching up a cup and the pot and hurrying to her table. George did want a roll, so I cut the very biggest one from the pan, as I always did when it was for George. I don't know if he ever noticed, but he always gave me that stunning smile when I placed it before him, which was worth more than the biggest cinnamon roll in the world.

I reluctantly turned from George's smile when the bell on the door clattered. Everyone in the café looked up to see the three tourists step inside.

Imogene was right when she had called them fashionable. The lady's skin was lily white, her fingers long and delicate, and her corset was cinched so tight that her waist was as thin as a wasp's. No one in Como had hands so soft, a waist so thin, or clothes so fine, not Mrs. Crawford or even Mrs. Engel who ran the millinery and yard-goods shop. The lady's hat angled jauntily on her smooth dark hair, the ostrich plume sweeping elegantly behind her. She wore a starched white shirtwaist, all ruffled up the front, and a blue skirt that reached just to the tops of her pearl-buttoned boots, according to the latest fashion. She was exactly what I imagined the ladies in my dime novels looked like. I could easily see her in distress, being rescued by a brave hero.

The man who escorted her, however, struck me as more of a dandy than a brave hero. He wore his hair parted neatly in the center and slicked down tight against his head. From his crisp pin-striped traveling suit and polished leather shoes, I could tell he hadn't stepped off pavement very often in his life. Nor did he want to, judging from the sneer on his face as he took in the locals in their work clothes and sturdy boots.

The boy Frank tagged along behind the couple. He was close to my age or a little older, perhaps fourteen. Though he looked good natured, Imogene had exaggerated when she called him mightily good-looking. Unlike his companions, he hadn't bothered much with his clothes and was a little disheveled. His hair needed a cut and a comb. The top button was missing from his shirt, and his collar, where it rubbed his neck, was brown with dirt. He walked with his hands crammed into his pockets and glanced around as if he were eager to see new things. I gave him a warm smile of welcome. *Exactly the sort of person who would want a tour,* I thought. Surely I could do it on my own if we didn't go far.

As soon as they were seated, I fetched the coffeepot to their table. The young lady smiled up at me. She was not old enough to be the boy's mother. She had to be an older sister, or at most, a youthful aunt.

"What smells so good?" she asked.

"My mother's cinnamon rolls," I said. "Fresh baked. And there's hotcakes, eggs with sausage, fatback, or hash. Oh, and oatmeal."

The gentleman laughed. "That's the whole menu? No wonder it's not printed up."

My face colored. I didn't have anything against city folks, even if most of them couldn't tell a pine tree from a horse's rear end, but I didn't think they had a right to come to our town and make fun of us. Still, they might want a tour, so I smiled. My politeness paid off, too, because after they ordered, the woman said, "We plan to explore today. Can your kitchen prepare a lunch basket?"

"Yes, ma'am," I said. "It's going to be a fine day for a picnic." I glanced out the window as I said it, only to have my hopes plummet to my toes. Old Josie Gilbert was stumping up the street toward the café. She wore her usual ragged miner's overalls and bulky men's boots. Her iron-gray hair was pulled back severely from her tanned and wrinkled face. As usual, she carried a stack of leaflets under her arm and a determined look in her black eyes. She was sure to drive away any visitors in no time if she was campaigning—and that look in her eye told me she was.

"I'll get your order in right away," I said hastily. I hurried into the kitchen even as I heard the bell on the door signal Josie's arrival.

"That's Josie, and she's campaigning!" I complained to my mother.

"Mrs. Gilbert," my mother corrected, without looking up from the eggs she was cracking into the big skillet on the stove. "Remember your manners."

"*She* never does," I grumbled. Mother gave me a sharp look.

"She's bad for business," I persisted. "Tell her she can't hand out her leaflets in here, Mother. Please? She scares away the tourists."

"You're exaggerating, Pearl."

"Well, she makes them uncomfortable."

"Perline Rose Barnell, she's your elder and you'll speak of her with respect. She's got the same right as anybody to say her piece. Now go serve her politely, and let me get on with my work."

I gave my mother the new order and returned to the front.

Josie had already swooped in on the tourists, and they were each gazing at a leaflet with polite disinterest.

"Women have had the vote in Colorado since 1893, but that doesn't mean we can rest. We have to keep up the fight for our sisters across this great nation!"

"Honestly!" said Mrs. Crawford at the corner table. She stood. "Come along, George. I won't sit here and listen to this." George rose, and with a polite nod and thanks to me, he followed her out of the café. I watched him go, mortified that Josie had driven them away.

Indifferent to my embarrassment, Josie's voice was rising in a self-righteous lecture. "The National Women's Party intends to send a united message to Mr. Wilson in the White House. The fight for liberty isn't just overseas. It is right here at home, in your kitchens and parlors. Everywhere women are found!"

The city folks set the leaflets down on the table and glanced at each other uncomfortably. Josie barreled on.

"Our forefathers said it best—no taxation without repre-sentation. It's high time that applied to every adult citizen of this country."

I looked desperately to the old-timers for help. Tom, Harry, and Orv bent over their coffee cups and pretended not to notice my look. Only Russell took pity on me.

"Sit down, Josie, and leave those poor folks alone. You're curdling the milk in their coffee," he said.

Josie turned a glare on Russell, and I used the opportunity to slide a chair over to the old-timers' table and fill an extra cup with coffee for her.

"Thanks a lot, Russell," Orv muttered.

Russell smiled at Josie and patted the chair I'd pulled up beside him. "Come have something to eat, Josie. Eggs and bacon, perhaps?"

She scowled, but lumbered over. She had a clumsy limp that made her broad frame roll back and forth like a ship in a choppy sea. She plopped down into the chair.

"I'll have the flapjacks," she said.

"With plenty of syrup," added Orv. "Maybe it'll sweeten her up a little."

"Sweet," she grumbled. "Why is it women have to be sweet for fool men like you? Mark my words, Orv. Someday women won't just vote; we'll do everything men do, and then we'll see who's sweet."

"In the meantime, you surely do put the sufferin' in suffragette," Harry said.

Russell fought down a smile and slid the cup toward her. "Drink your coffee and let's talk about the weather, like decent folks. I think we're in for a dry summer."

I hurried back to the kitchen to see if Mother had breakfast ready for the tourists. I carried their food carefully, smiling as I set each plate before the correct person, hoping to make up for any offense Josie might have caused.

"The man at the hotel said someone here named Pearl

could give us good advice about where to go on our outing. Is that your mother?" the lady asked.

"No, ma'am, that's me," I said eagerly. I could tell by the way her eyebrows raised that she wasn't sure about taking advice from a thirteen-year-old kid.

"Annie here would like a picnic," said the slick man. "And Frank probably wants an adventure, don't you, Frank."

The boy shrugged, but I could tell he did.

"I have maps, a penny a piece, that show all the sights in the valley, and I'd be happy to take you to any of them." If, of course, Mother would let me go without Father.

"Sounds like a penny well spent," Frank said. "Do you have a penny, Robert?"

Robert pulled a coin out of his vest pocket and handed it to me.

I scurried to the kitchen to retrieve one of my maps. In the winter months, when trains were few and far between and the stationmaster was glad for the company, I traced the old railroad land office map at the depot. Now that the tourist season was starting, I had a good supply of them.

"Let's see," Annie said, flattening the map on the table beside her plate. "What do you recommend? We have all day."

"If you want to try your hand at fishing, I'd recommend the Tarryall," I said, running my finger along the line of the river leading upstream from town.

"The only way I want to see a trout is sizzling on my plate," Robert said. Annie giggled and he looked pleased with himself.

"Where's a good spot for our picnic?" asked Frank.

"Good old Frank, always thinking with his stomach," Robert said. Frank looked embarrassed and I felt sorry for him, the odd wheel at the table.

"You might try Buckskin Creek," I said, pointing along another route. "There's a good buggy track as far as Buckskin Joe, if you like ghost towns."

"Are there real ghosts?" Frank asked, perking up. I smiled at his enthusiasm.

"It's what we call the empty mining camps," I explained. He looked mildly disappointed, so I added, "There is a cemetery at Buckskin Joe, though."

I was going to tell him more, but Robert interrupted. He was looking at the white-capped peak I'd drawn behind the town, his finger on the label *Mount Silverheels*.

"So did you name your café after the mountain? Or is this such a fine culinary establishment that they named a whole mountain after your café?" he said with a grin.

Annie smiled at Robert. Frank scowled at him. I liked Frank.

"The mountain is named for the most beautiful woman ever to set foot in Park County. She saved the town of Buckskin Joe, and some say she still walks its cemetery."

"Really?" Frank said, brightening again. "That sounds promising. Go on."

So I began.

ilverheels was a beautiful dancer who came in 1860 to the town of Buckskin Joe to perform in the dance hall. She was the most beautiful woman ever seen in Park County, and her dancing enchanted everyone who watched her. She was supposed to stay only a day or two, but the miners in Buckskin Joe fell desperately in love with her. They built her a cabin and begged her to stay, so Silverheels danced every night for them.

"But in the bitter winter of 1861, a smallpox epidemic hit the town. Most folks fled. The doctor telegraphed Denver for help, but none came. Only Silverheels stayed to tend the sick and dying—feeding them, nursing them, going tirelessly from bedside to bedside to ease their suffering. Some say she even wrote home to their families, or carried their bodies to the cemetery when they died."

"A real angel of mercy," Josie muttered from the next table, her voice thick with sarcasm. I ignored her and continued the story.

"Finally, when everyone thought the worst of the epidemic was behind them, Silverheels herself caught the sickness.

Covered with pox and burning with fever, she suffered terribly."

"Did she die?" the lady said breathlessly.

"No. But her lovely face was scarred and pitted and her legendary beauty was ruined forever! In shame, she shut herself in her cabin. But the miners loved her so much that they collected five thousand dollars in nuggets and gold dust for her."

Frank whistled. "That set her up pretty well for life."

"It could have. But when they took it to her cabin to profess their undying love, she had disappeared. They searched the mountains and roads and all the neighboring towns, but found not a trace. So they named the mountain after her, in hopes that wherever she was, she'd know they still loved her and she'd come back."

"Did she?" asked Frank.

"Years later, a veiled woman appeared in the cemetery, leaving flowers on the graves of the men who had died in the epidemic, but she fled when approached, and to this day, no one knows for sure what became of Silverheels."

"What a sad, romantic story," said Annie.

From behind me, Josie snorted again. "It's a load of cockamamie is what it is," she said. "Now where's my order of flapjacks, girl?"

I ignored her and smiled at the city folks. "If you are interested, I could show you around Buckskin Joe. The old dance hall where she used to dance is still there, and the saloon." I glanced at Frank. "And there's the cemetery, where some say the ghost of Silverheels still walks."

"We'll think about it," Robert said, before leaning toward me and whispering, "You better get granny her hotcakes before she gets any crazier, don't you think?"

I nodded and went back to the kitchen. The hotcakes were ready, and, as no one else seemed to be coming in for breakfast, Mother was rolling out the crusts for pies. I gathered the butter, jam, and syrup for Josie, but I wasn't quick enough. When I returned to the front she had pounced again. She was standing at the tourists' table, complaining about women only being remembered if they served men. Which led, of course, to her usual rant about the women's vote. I couldn't get a word in edgewise to suggest an excursion to the visitors. Not that they would have listened at that point. They were shoveling their food into their mouths, eager to get away. Without a glance my way, Robert dropped his money on the table, shot Josie a disgusted look, and offered his arm to his wife. She wiped her mouth daintily and rose to her feet. Only Frank met my eye and smiled when I called "have a nice day" after them as they left. Josie snorted and sat down at the old-timers' table where I had set her hotcakes.

"I don't see why a woman's worth has to be measured in her looks," she said.

"You wouldn't, you old boot," Orv muttered.

"It wasn't Silverheels's looks—it was her kindness," Russell pointed out.

Josie snorted again, sounding like an old pack mule. "Ah yes, womanly virtues."

"Ain't nothin' wrong with womanly virtues, Josie," Russell said.

"Well if you ask me," Josie said loudly, "it's not much of a story."

"No one is asking you, you old crank. The girl likes to tell it and the city folks like to hear it, so let it be," Harry said as he got stiffly to his feet. "Put it on my tab, Pearl," he called. The others followed suit and soon the whole crowd had shuffled out into the street, leaving only Josie, frowning as she ate her hotcakes.

I got my own breakfast and sat down at the counter beside Imogene.

"I told you that city boy was handsome, didn't I, Pearl?" Imogene said, glancing sidelong again at Willie. He still showed no sign of jealousy.

He pushed his empty plate back on the counter and got to his feet. "I'm going fishing," he announced. "Bye, Imogene. See you later, kid," he said, ruffling my hair. Then he headed out the door. Off for a day in the sunshine while I washed dishes.

Imogene sighed and watched him go. "Only a month until the Fourth of July picnic. When do you think Willie will get around to asking me to go with him?"

I didn't think he would, but there was no point in telling Imogene that. She was determined to catch him.

"Is George Crawford going to ask you to the picnic, Pearl?"

My heart sped up a little, but I only shrugged. Sure, I had spent hours dreaming of going to the picnic with George, dancing at a Christmas ball with George, strolling along the creek under a parasol with George. Not that anyone in Como ever had Christmas balls—or parasols for that matter. But that didn't stop me from dreaming.

"Come on, Pearl. You've got to start planning. You only have a month!"

"I can't plan anything until he asks me. It's the boy's job to ask the girl."

"You'll never get George to ask you with that attitude," Imogene said. "You don't think boys know what to do on their own, do you? You have to let them know you'll say yes before they're willing to ask."

I pretended there was a spot on the counter and scrubbed hard at it so I didn't have to look at her. "I'd rather wait for a boy to court me proper. I don't want to be forward."

There was an indignant huff from across the room, and I reddened. I had forgotten about Josie. Of course she was eavesdropping on our conversation.

"Honestly, until girls stop worrying themselves over boys and start thinking sensibly, we'll never make any progress in this country. Start thinking about making something of your-selves, why don't you?" she said.

Imogene tossed her curls over her shoulder and stuck her nose in the air. "My pa says the only women who care about politics are the ones who can't catch a man for themselves," she said. Then she flounced out of the café, leaving me alone with Josie.

I couldn't believe Imogene could speak so rudely! I expected Josie to explode, but she didn't. She just watched me over the edge of her cup, her black eyes cold and hard.

"Your head's full of drivel, girl. Waiting for a boy to court you and telling that mushy, cockamamie story to the tourists? Drivel and more drivel!"

"I think Silverheels was very heroic," I said.

"So a woman who stands up for her rights is a nuisance, while one who coddles a bunch of helpless men is a hero?"

"I suppose you think Silverheels ought to have just let the miners die?" I said.

"I think if the story's true the way folks tell it, she was a mighty stupid girl."

"Kindness isn't stupid," I said under my breath. She gave a little "hrmf" and my face flushed as I realized she had heard me. I knew better than to talk back to my elders, and if there was one thing Josie was, it was elder.

"I'll tell you what I think. I think the real reason she stayed was that she figured those dying miners would tell her where they had hidden their gold. Maybe they did, and that's why she lit out in the end. Why else would she risk everything and stay?"

"Because those men needed her. They were her friends," I said.

"Were they?" she said, her eyes more challenging than ever. "Her friends?"

"They loved her."

Josie drained her cup and got to her feet. "Then why, if they were her friends who *loved* her, didn't a single one of them know her real name?"

CHAPTER 3

I stared at Josie, my mouth hanging open. I couldn't think of a single answer. The truth was, I had never thought of it that way before. Josie's lips stretched in a grin of victory. I snapped my mouth shut and gritted my teeth, angry that she had gotten the better of me. As I gathered dirty dishes from the other tables, my mind kept turning the question over. There had to be a logical explanation. I was sure the men had loved her, but if they had, wouldn't they have known her name?

I carried the dishes to the kitchen, where Mother had a kettle steaming on the back of the stove. Willie had brought in a bucket of cold water from the pump before he left, so I filled the sink with a mixture of the two and began washing dishes. When I returned to the front with a tray of clean coffee cups, Josie was gone, but her question and her infuriating smile of victory lingered behind her. As soon as I thought of that smile, anger jumbled my thoughts all over again. There had to be a good reason—an answer to her question. There just had to be!

I wiped down the tables and swept the floor and was done

for the morning. I would have an hour to myself before the lunch train rolled through. Though tourists weren't coming to the mountains, the new zinc boom brought on by the war meant enough passengers on the trains to keep me rushed off my feet at lunchtime. Usually, I went outside, but today I climbed the back stairs to my bedroom above the café.

I pulled the handful of dime novels and penny dreadfuls from my shelf and spread them across the bed. There were a few that told tales of fur trappers, explorers, or sea captains, and I set those aside. The rest were tales of beautiful heroines, threatened by cruel men or dangerous animals. In their darkest hour, they were always rescued by a brave and handsome hero, and they would swoon into his strong, protective arms. I imagined what George's arms would feel like if I were to swoon into them. "Oh, George," I would say. "Oh, Pearl."

The fantasy slipped away and I frowned. The heroes always knew their heroines' names when they went to profess their undying love. Always.

Still, that didn't mean the miners didn't love Silverheels. But what did it mean? I picked up my favorite book and paged through it. The heroine had been an orphan who had fled a cruel orphanage. Only at the end, after being rescued, she learned who she really was—an heiress stolen at birth from her loving parents. She herself had not known her real name.

I set the book down, an idea forming in my mind. A woman

in trouble, on the run, would not reveal her true name, would she? A woman fleeing a cruel home or a dark past?

My thoughts were interrupted by my mother calling me back downstairs. I found her in the kitchen, her sleeves rolled up and beads of sweat on her brow as she sliced loaves of bread for the dozens of sandwiches we would be serving the lunch crowd. Behind her, heat radiated off the stove, where a ham sat cooling, freshly out of the oven, and a pot of stew simmered.

"Sorry, Pearl, but someone just came into the café, and I need to get these sandwiches made. Can you see to whoever it is?"

I stepped through from the kitchen to the café and stopped short.

"It's about time!" Josie barked at once from a stool at the counter. "Where have you been, girl? Off mooning over some boy?" She grabbed a cup from the tray I'd brought in earlier and set it pointedly on the counter in front of her. I plastered a polite smile onto my face and picked up the coffeepot.

"Has that been sitting there since breakfast?" she said, narrowing her eyes at the pot. Of course it had, since I hadn't yet come down to brew a fresh pot for lunch.

"I'm not paying my hard-earned money for the stale slop you couldn't foist off on someone else."

"Yes, ma'am," I said. I turned away from her to go dump the pot and refill it, but stopped when she clanged her cup against the counter.

"Well, don't waste it, girl. I'll take what you've got there while I wait for the fresh pot to perk. But I expect it on the house."

I bit the inside of my cheek to keep from saying something I shouldn't. She was a customer and my elder, and talking back to her would only get me in trouble. I poured her a cup of coffee, making sure the sugar bowl was on hand, and I turned again to take the pot into the kitchen to make fresh.

"Aren't you going to take my order? How long do you mean to make me wait, girl?"

"My name is Pearl," I said, my smile now gone.

Her eyes sparked with challenge. "It is, is it?"

"What would you like to eat, Mrs. Gilbert?" I asked.

"Apple pie. And make sure it's hot. And melt some cheese over it."

"Yes, ma'am." Maybe I could find a slice with worms in the apples.

"And don't forget the coffee. Fresh!"

Ignoring this last, I retreated to the kitchen.

Mother had slices of bread laid out across the big work table and was slicing the ham, so I refilled the coffeepot and set it on the stove. Then I took down the first of the apple pies from the baking rack near the open back door, and I cut into it. The sweet smell of apples and cinnamon floated to my nose as I lifted the first fat wedge out onto a plate. I smiled. Josie might complain about everything else, but she wouldn't complain about this pie. No one complained about my mother's apple pie.

"Who is it?" Mother asked, not looking up from her work.

"Jo—Mrs. Gilbert," I said, remembering my manners just in time.

"And she wants pie? Before lunch?"

"With a slice of cheese. And fresh coffee," I said. I was glad she hadn't ordered a full lunch. The less she ordered the sooner she'd be gone, and I wanted her out of the café before the lunch rush. It was hard enough serving the crowd off the train without Josie underfoot, ranting about her cause. The train only stopped for an hour, so our customers demanded quick service.

My mother's brow wrinkled. "She probably doesn't have enough money for lunch." Mother had been laying slabs of ham on top of the rows of bread slices. Now she pressed another slice of bread on top of one and put the finished sandwich on a plate. She held the plate out to me.

"Here, Pearl. Take her this and tell her it's on the house."

"Why?" I asked.

"Hmm," Mother said. "You're right. It will hurt her pride if she thinks it's charity." She glanced at the pie and smiled. "I know. Tell her we're out of cheese, and we hope the free sandwich makes up for it."

"But we're not out of cheese," I said, pointing to the big gold wheel under a cloth on the shelf.

"Never mind, Pearl. I'll not have that poor old woman

going without a decent lunch just because she doesn't have money and is too proud to ask for help. Neighbors do for neighbors. You know that."

I sighed, taking the pie in one hand and the sandwich in the other and returned to the front, where Josie was sitting at the counter, drumming her fingers impatiently and watching for my return. At once her eyes landed on the naked pie.

"Where's my cheese, girl? Did you listen to a thing I said?"

"Mother said to tell you we are out of cheese, so she wants you to have this sandwich on the house."

"It all should be on the house if you can't even get my order right. What kind of café runs out of cheese?"

I bit the inside of my cheek again, even harder than before, and turned back to the kitchen to retrieve the coffeepot. It wasn't ready, so I offered to help my mother, hoping to stay in the kitchen. She sent me to the front to lay out napkins and silverware on the tables in preparation for lunch. I refused to even look in Josie's direction, but it didn't matter. She swallowed her mouthful of ham and bread and said, "So, this boy you were mooning over, do you figure he knows your name?"

"No, ma'am," I said, then paused in my work. "I mean, I wasn't mooning over a boy."

"No? Not even the handsome George Crawford?"

"No, ma'am," I said again, though I could feel the prickle of a blush starting in the tips of my ears as the image of George holding me in his arms came back into my mind.

"Well then," she said, sounding satisfied, "maybe you aren't as big a fool as I thought you were."

I gritted my teeth, clanging the silverware down on the tables as I made my way around the room. I might have held my tongue until I could escape, if Josie hadn't given a gloating little chuckle. That was too much. She had complained about the food and service, and then complained again when my mother had found a gracious way to feed her. Now, on top of all that, she was heaping insults on me, for no reason at all. I still might have ignored it, if her insults had been directed at me alone, but I wasn't going to hear a word against George.

"George Crawford is a nice boy and a gentleman," I said. I didn't add handsome, charming, and the best catch in Park County. At least not out loud.

She snorted. "George Crawford is a slick-talking charmer, like every other male that thinks too much of himself. If it had been him back in 1861 it wouldn't have mattered whether or not he knew Silverheels's name. He's the sort who'd only see fit to name a mountain after himself anyway. Where's that fresh coffee?"

I retrieved the coffeepot and poured her a fresh cup, all the while trying to screw up my courage. At last, I just blurted out what I wanted to say without looking at her. I knew I'd never keep up my nerve if our eyes met.

"I think the miners didn't know Silverheels's real name because she couldn't tell anyone. Because she had run away."

There was a moment of silence before Josie spoke. "On the lam, huh? What did she do, rob the stage to Denver?"

"Of course not!" I snapped, offended both by the suggestion and the tone of mockery in her voice. I rushed on with my idea before she could say something else ridiculous. I had come up with an explanation that was such a perfect solution, I was sure it had to be right.

"She probably had a cruel father who sold her in marriage to a horrible old man she didn't love. She wanted to be a dancer—a ballet dancer—on the finest stages in Paris. But her father wouldn't hear of it, so he found a rich old miser for her to marry." I was warming to my story now as it unfolded in all its tragic beauty in my mind.

"She told her father she would rather die than marry the brute, but her father locked her in her room, vowing to keep her there until the wedding day. Just when she was giving up hope, a kindly maid took pity on her, and when her father was asleep, the girl let Gerta out of her room."

"Gerta?" Josie said.

I shrugged. I liked the name. "She snuck quietly out of the house and hurried to the train station, where she got a ticket to come west." As if helping me tell my tale, the train whistle blew, and across the street the lunch train came into the station, its wheels screeching on the rails as it braked. I continued, speaking quickly. I didn't have much time to finish before the lunch crowd arrived.

"She bought a ticket as far from home as she could get,

but she could never use her real name again. She knew her father was looking for her and would stop at nothing to get her back!" I felt triumphant as I finished my tale. I liked how the story sounded, tragic and beautiful. I was proud of the details I had created—an old rich suitor and a kindly maid. It was a perfect beginning for the legend I had known all my life. I felt so good about the story that I ventured a glance up into Josie's wrinkled old face and saw a strange expression there.

Could it be that my story had touched her bitter old heart? Had I reminded her of the joy and beauty of life and the tragic fragility of a young girl's dreams?

Her lips contorted and for a moment I thought she was about to cry. Instead, she burst out laughing.

CHAPTER 4

t's not funny!" I snapped. Then the bell on the door clattered and hungry travelers burst into the café. Within minutes every chair was taken, and I was in a scramble serving up sandwiches and stew and cups of coffee. Josie, in the meantime, sauntered around the café, handing out leaflets and extolling the virtues of her cause to anyone who would listen. It didn't make my job any easier. She was in the way, and she was putting folks in a bad mood that they took out on me. I ignored her as best I could and tried to soothe the customers with smiles and quick service, but inside I was seething.

At last the stationmaster, Mr. Orenbach, came into the café, clanging his handbell to announce the train would depart soon. There was a flurry of last-minute orders. Josie hurried out the door and across the street to the platform to catch any travelers who hadn't come into the café. The whistle blew its five-minute warning and the café emptied as quickly as it had filled, piles of dirty dishes and more than a few wadded-up *Votes for Women!* handbills left behind.

Across the street at the station, the train began to puff

more eagerly, preparing for the climb over the pass to Breckenridge. On the platform, only two battered trunks had been unloaded. That meant no tourists to take my tours. Luggage in that condition always belonged to miners or ranch hands, not tourists.

My mother came out of the kitchen, smiling, though her face gleamed with sweat. She helped me carry dishes to the kitchen and pile them on the counter, then wiped her forehead with the back of her sleeve.

"Let's eat something before we wash these," she said. She carried the leftover sandwiches to a table. She turned the sign on the door to read CLOSED, but she didn't lock it. Town folks often wandered by after the lunch rush to see if we had any sandwiches left over. If we did, mother would give them out free to old miners or ranchers who were down on their luck.

The door opened and Mr. Orenbach came in. "Anything left for a fellow's been worked off his feet the last two hours?"

My mother slid back a chair for him at our table, and I pushed the plate of sandwiches toward him. In exchange, he handed my mother a copy of the *Rocky Mountain News*, fresh off the train. He offered me a slightly battered dime novel that someone had left behind in the station.

"So, Pearl, what have you been saying to Sufferin' Josie?" he asked as he selected a sandwich. "She came by the station with her confounded handbills, and she was smiling. I'd never seen her lips curl up like that before—I thought she was having a spasm. I asked her what was the matter, and she said,

'It's that Pearl over at the café,' and then she actually laughed. I didn't think that woman knew how to laugh."

Both Mr. Orenbach and Mother were looking at me, expecting a response, but I wasn't going to tell them what I had told Josie. What if they laughed too?

I looked down at my plate and muttered, "I just told her a story."

"It must have been a real humdinger of a yarn to get her laughing," Mr. Orenbach said. "I'd sure like to hear it."

"It wasn't supposed to be funny at all!" I jumped to my feet and rushed off to the kitchen, stinging with humiliation. My mother let me be, at least until Mr. Orenbach left. Then she came back to the kitchen where I was scrubbing furiously at plates and cups.

"What was that about, Pearl?" she asked.

"Josie wasn't laughing at the story. She was laughing at me," I said.

"Why would a grown woman laugh at you?"

"Because she's mean to the core! I wish she wouldn't come in here!"

"Pearl," my mother said reproachfully.

"Well she is! Why do I have to be polite to her when she's so rude to me?"

"Because she's part of this town, and you, Perline Rose Barnell, are expected to do unto others as you would have them do unto you. I know Mrs. Gilbert is prickly and unpleasant at times. She's old, and I imagine she's had a hard life. She may well have her reasons for being as she is."

"She didn't have any reason to laugh at me."

My mother considered me for a long moment. "Maybe she laughed because your story gave her joy."

I scowled and kept washing plates. My mother took up a dish towel and began drying and stacking them.

"You give me joy, Perline. Every single day," she said. We continued to work in silence until everything was clean. Then I was free for three full hours, until supper time.

I left the café by the back door so I could avoid seeing anyone. I wanted to be alone in the fresh air and sunshine. That always made me feel better. I had planned to circle around, past the edge of our small town, across the railroad tracks, and down the short hill to the river, but I never made it. As I rounded the last house and turned toward the train tracks, I saw the last person I wanted to see. I tried to retreat back around the corner before she caught sight of me, but I was too late.

"Hey, there! Girl!" she called as I tried to disappear.

I sighed and turned back to face her. "Yes, Mrs. Gilbert?"

"Come with me," she said, and began straight up the center of Main Street in her lopsided seaman's gate.

I stayed rooted where I was. I wasn't working now; I could see no reason why I should do what she commanded, even if she was my elder. Maybe if I just stayed where I was she wouldn't notice I hadn't followed, and I could slip away.

That hope was soon dashed. She stopped, right in the middle

of Main Street and shouted, "Hurry up, Pearl!" loud enough for everyone out on the streets to hear. I couldn't escape her now. If I didn't do as she asked, word would certainly get back to my mother that I had been disobedient. If there was one thing my mother was strict about, it was manners in public. So, with another heavy sigh, I followed Josie. She marched up Main Street, directly to the old newspaper office where she lived. Not that it was a real newspaper office—not anymore. The paper had gone out of business over twenty years ago, when the silver crash of 1893 had closed the mines and emptied out most of the mountain towns.

Josie had come to Como just after the crash and bought the paper for a song, but she never published more than a single edition, or so my mother said. That had all been before I was born. For as long as I could remember, the place had looked as it did now. *The South Park Record* could still be read in peeling paint across the building's false front, but the large plate-glass window was boarded up, and the front door was locked tight. Josie came and went through the back door. As far as I knew, no one but her had ever gone into her house—after all, she wasn't exactly the sort to invite the neighbors in for tea. She was more like a hermit, right in the middle of town, so of course I was surprised when she led me around to the back and opened the door.

I paused a good ten steps away. I couldn't help it. When we were little, all the kids at the school had speculated in whispers about what she did in there. We had all seen the similarities between Josie and the witches of fairy tales like "Hansel and Gretel." Knocking on her door had been the dare that only the bravest boys had taken, and none of them had ever stood still long enough after knocking to know whether or not she ever answered.

"Well, come on, girl," Josie said, stepping through the door to the dim room beyond. "It's not as if I'm the kind of witch that eats children."

The ease with which she had read my thoughts was hardly reassuring. I swallowed hard and followed her inside, hoping she was telling the truth.

CHAPTER 5

Your shoes," Josie said, the second I stepped inside, pointing toward a pair of muddy work boots by the door.

"My shoes?"

"Take them off and leave them there. I won't have you tracking mud all over my house."

My shoes were clean, having come directly from the café, but I didn't argue. Even if I did notice that Josie hadn't taken her own boots off but clomped directly across the floor to her stove.

While she did that, I glanced around, my surprise growing everywhere I looked. I had expected to see squalor, but Josie's home was tidy, and strange. On the far side of the room, beyond a waist-high railing, the old newspaper printing press was still set up. Around it, *Votes for Women!* handbills were stacked in neat piles. Drawers of movable type lined an ink-stained worktable, where it looked like Josie had been laying out a new leaflet. I wasn't sure why. From the stacks around the printing press, it looked like she had already printed enough for a decade.

This side of the rail was the most surprising part of Josie's home. Even though it was a boarded-up newspaper office, she had filled it with elegant furnishings—a whole house worth all crammed into the single room. Beyond the stove, a fine mahogany bedstead and wardrobe made a bedroom. At the foot of the bed, a velvet-cushioned sofa with finely carved and polished claw feet divided the room and created a small parlor space, while nearest me, an elegant tea table and carved chairs stood beside a corner curio cabinet displaying fine crystal glasses and delicate china cups and saucers. Hardly what I expected from someone who came to the café for a free lunch.

"Close your mouth, girl. You look like a dead fish. I didn't bring you here to gawk at my things."

I snapped out of my reverie and closed my mouth, which I hadn't even realized had fallen open. I looked back at Josie, who was filling two chipped mugs from an old teapot. She set one on the table nearest me, which I took to be an invitation to sit down.

"Why did you bring me here, Mrs. Gilbert?" I asked.

"Well now, that's the question, isn't it." She pulled out the chair on her side of the table and sat heavily. I perched on the edge of the seat nearest the door. Just in case a fast retreat was in order.

"There are a few things we need to get straight, girl. First of all, this Mrs. Gilbert business. My name is Josie."

"My mother says that it's disrespectful to call you Josie."

"You call those old fools at the corner table by their first names," she pointed out.

"They're like family. They've been in the café every day my whole life," I said. Then I realized how that must have sounded to her. She had been there all that time too.

"Well, if you must, in front of your saintly mother, you can call me *Miss* Gilbert, but it's not missus. Unlike your lovely Silverheels, I've never let a man take away my name." She took a long, noisy slurp of her tea, then continued. "I'm proud to say that I have prospered for nearly seventy years without the burden of any man's laundry or his name."

"Yes, ma'am," I said, since she seemed to be expecting a response, but I had no idea what to say. And I still had no idea why I was there.

She smiled a little, with just the left corner of her mouth. "Tell me, how do you think Silverheels got to Colorado Territory in that story of yours?" she suddenly asked, surprising me yet again. I had to blink at her for a moment before I could turn my mind the right direction to find an answer.

"I told you, she took the train."

Josie shook her head. "Don't they teach you anything in school? The train didn't come to Colorado in 1860. In fact, it didn't come any farther west than St. Louis."

"Well then, she joined a wagon train," I said.

"All by herself? Your pretty, sweet, innocent dancer who wanted to dance ballet in Paris? Why would she go west at all? Why didn't she catch a boat to Europe right off?"

35

My mind was racing now. I was determined to come up with answers. I wasn't going to let her laugh at me again. "She didn't have enough money."

"Ah," Josie said. "And of course, the gold rush was on in Colorado. 'Pikes Peak or Bust!'"

"That's right," I said. "She hoped to strike it rich and be able to go to Paris to study ballet."

Josie nodded and took a long sip of her tea. I watched her, hardly daring to believe I had won the point. She set her cup down again and looked at me. Now both corners of her lips were curling up in a way that made me want to bolt for the door.

"So it was greed that made her come out west."

"Not greed," I protested.

"Just the desire to get rich quick," Josie said. "Call it whatever you like. But I don't think your pretty little dancer had any intention of shoveling ore for a living—not when her beauty was so precious to her. There were only a few women who came west in the gold rush, and most of them had their own plan of how to get rich." Her eyes glinted wickedly, and I knew she was suggesting something bad.

"She was a dance-hall girl," I said. "She performed for the lonely miners."

"I bet she did," Josie said. "Let's see, if, as you said, she took the train, she would have stepped off in St. Louis. Now—what did you call her? Gertie?"

"Gerta," I corrected.

"Right. So Gerta stepped off the train at its western-most terminus. And as it happened, just as that little blossom of innocence stepped into the den of hustlers and profiteers that was St. Louis, the cry came from the west—Gold! In the Pikes Peak country! And every red-blooded American man with a shovel and a hankerin' for money lit out for the territories.

"But there were red-blooded American *women* in St. Louis too, clever enough to know how to make a fortune without grubbing in the dirt. Of course, an innocent like Gerta wouldn't know of such things. Fortunately for her, Gerta was taken under the wing of a shrewd business woman, Lou Bunch. Madam Lou knew that with a few crates of whiskey, a wagonload of pretty girls, and a piano that could plunk out something close to music, she could make more gold in a night than a miner could make in a week. And who better to take along than a pretty young runaway who liked to dance."

"But—" I tried to object, but was silenced by a glare from Josie.

"Hush, girl. This is my story now. Silverheels must have known that what Lou was proposing wasn't respectable. But Gerta wasn't one to let that stand in the way of making her fortune. She threw away her name and her honor, bought a pair of silver-heeled dancing shoes and a skirt barely longer than her knees, and she set out west, to make a fortune at any cost."

"That's not right!" I protested. "She was good, and loving!"

"She was a dance-hall girl. And a conniving one at that. I imagine she started her own scheming the minute she signed on with Lou. Figured a pretty face like hers could convince fellas to tell her their secrets. Secrets worth a pretty penny, like where they had struck it rich, or where they kept their gold hidden."

"No! She had a good heart. She cared about folks. She wasn't after their gold!" I insisted.

Josie brayed with laughter again, and I sprang to my feet.

"Why do you have to spoil everything nice?" I said.

Her laughter sputtered to snorts and snickers. "Why do you want to sugarcoat everything? I'm just trying to get you to see sense."

"No you're not! You're trying to make everything rotten for everyone else, just because you're a sour old grump yourself."

She raised her eyebrows. "Sour old grump, eh? Careful there, girl. You'll be disrespectfully calling me Josie next."

I wanted to shout at her, but I took a deep breath instead. I was likely already going to be in big trouble when she told my mother what I had said.

"I'll tell you what," Josie said. "I'll make a bet with you."

"My mother doesn't approve of gambling."

"Well then, it's a good thing I'm making a bet with you and not her, isn't it."

I said nothing, only waited to hear what else she had to say.

"You don't like me talking to your tourists in the café, do

you. If you can prove to me that Silverheels was the sweet angel of mercy you say she was, I won't say another word to anyone there."

"How am I supposed to prove it?" I asked.

"Use your head for something other than drivel, girl. If you can't come up with a way, I can say whatever I please in the café. And if I can prove to you that I'm right—that Silverheels was a con and a thief—then you will help me give out handbills on the platform for a whole week. How about it?"

I chewed my lip, considering. I wasn't worried about losing, I knew she would never convince me of her version of the story. But I didn't think it was any more likely that I would convince her of my version of things. And there was a chance I'd be in trouble with my mother if she found out. Plus, I didn't trust her.

"Why do you even care about Silverheels?"

"I don't," Josie said, and the scorn in her voice proved her point. "I don't care one whit about her, and it's high time no one else did either. She's a symbol of everything that holds girls back in this country. Girls like you who need to stop sighing and moaning about love and make something of themselves. Then again, I should have known a girl like that wouldn't take my bet. You have no spine at all, do you, girl."

I scowled at her, my hands balling into fists. I wasn't going to listen to one more insult. I straightened my spine, just to prove I had one, and lifted my chin. "I'll take your bet, and I will prove Silverheels was good and kind and that those men loved her."

"You do that," she said with a smirk. "Now get, and let me get some work done in peace."

I left by the back door we'd entered by, my head full of the bet. I had no idea how I'd prove anything about the story, but I was determined to try. Anything to get Josie out of the café! Maybe some of the old-timers could remember something helpful. At least it was a place to start.

I was still thinking about the possibilities when I stepped out into the street, which is why I didn't see George and Mrs. Crawford until I nearly ran into them. They appeared to be walking back from the millinery shop, because George was carrying a large hat box for his mother.

"Good afternoon, Pearl," he said with a smile, shifting a little to avoid colliding with me.

"Oh!" I said in surprise, stepping backward so suddenly that I turned my ankle. George reached a hand to my elbow to steady me. His hand felt strong and warm. I was sure that if I swooned right there he would catch me, but I wasn't feeling woozy, and besides, his mother was there, spoiling the moment.

Mrs. Crawford glanced at me, then back the way I had come, the dirt path along the side of the newspaper building that only led to Josie's back door. When her eyes darted back to me, her expression was severe.

"Honestly, Pearl. What would your father say if he knew

you were running wild like this while he's away? What were you doing back there?"

"I wasn't— I'm not—"

"Come along, George." She lifted her nose in the air and strode away.

I couldn't look at George, for fear I might see the same disapproval on his face.

He took his hand gently from my elbow. "Never mind, Pearl," he said. "I'll see you later, okay?" Then he followed his mother, while I nearly collapsed with relief and gratitude.

That evening, the Crawfords came to the café for supper. Mr. Crawford was handsome like his son, but I never saw much of him. He was always working at the store in the mornings when his wife came into the café for coffee and gossip. And when he occasionally came in the evenings, as he had this evening, he generally retreated behind the evening paper. Tonight, however, he looked me up and down when I stepped to the table to take their order. I supposed he knew how I felt about his son and was sizing me up, deciding if I was suitable.

"What's on the menu tonight?" he asked, without any hint as to what his verdict was.

"Shepherd's pie, fresh-caught trout, or sausages and fried potatoes," I said.

"Not *German* sausages, I hope," Mrs. Crawford said with a frown.

I shrugged. "Just the same sausage we always get from the butcher."

"Perhaps I should speak with your mother. Run along and fetch her, please, Pearl."

I went to the kitchen and told my mother what Mrs. Crawford had said. Mother sighed heavily, but she wiped her hands, arranged her face into a smile, and went out front. She left me to watch the sausages sizzling in a skillet on the stove, but I snuck to the doorway and listened.

"Maggie, dear, you know we all have to do our part for the war effort. I'm only thinking of our boys over there," Mrs. Crawford was saying in a honeyed voice.

"You know full well we Barnells are doing our share," Mother said with a little catch in her voice. I understood. I missed Father too.

"But sausages, Maggie? From *Schmidt's* Butcher Shop?"

"Rest assured, Phoebe, that our butcher's sausages are as American as my apple pie," Mother said. "Mr. Schmidt is a good man. Now what would you like for supper?"

Mother came back into the kitchen a few minutes later with the order, but without the smile. Mrs. Crawford wasn't smiling either when I returned to the front with plates of food. She was talking to her husband and son, but plenty loud for everyone in the café to hear her.

"I'm only trying to do what's best. Heaven knows, our boys have it hard enough over there. It's every citizen's duty to keep the home fires burning. That's why I'm organizing the

Fourth of July picnic this year, and making sure it's the most patriotic we've ever had. People talk, you know, and I won't have folks saying that Como isn't doing its part!"

Mr. Crawford retreated as usual behind his paper, leaving George to listen to his mother. I felt sorry for George, and I tried to show my sympathy by smiling as I refilled their water glasses and coffee cups. George gave me a brief smile in return, then went back to nodding at what his mother was saying.

When Mrs. Crawford finally finished her supper, she instructed her husband to leave the money on the table and stood.

"Come along, George," she said as she turned toward the door. George stuffed his last bite of pie into his mouth and scrambled to his feet. His hat, which he had hung on the corner of his chair, had fallen on the floor. I picked it up and handed it to him with another sympathetic smile.

"Thanks," he said. He glanced at his parents, now almost to the door, and hesitated. "Whatever you're doing with Josie Gilbert, be careful, Pearl," he said quietly. "My mother says she's un-American."

I frowned as my cheeks warmed. "What do you mean? I'm not doing anything with her."

"Come along, George!" said his mother again, stepping out into the night.

"Good, because Sufferin' Josie says things that are going to get her in big trouble someday." George looked into my eyes and smiled, a smile that made my knees go a little wobbly. "And I'd sure hate to see her get a sweet girl like you into trouble. If she ever bothers you, just let me know, okay? I'll come to your rescue."

"Okay," I managed to choke out as he walked away. But in my mind, I was already swooning into his arms.

CHAPTER 6

After George offered to save me, I couldn't think of anything else for the rest of the evening. I was dreaming both before going to sleep and after. I woke the next morning more determined than ever to get Josie to leave me and the café alone. If I was going to have any chance at all with George, I couldn't let him think I was up to anything with her. I could call off the bet, but that would probably just inspire her to come into the café and needle me more often. If I wanted to get her to leave me alone for good, the best way—the only way—I could think of was to prove my version of the Silverheels story correct.

So early the next morning, I sat down with the old-timers before the café got busy, to find out what they might know. I asked if any of them knew anything more about the story than what they had heard me tell a few days earlier.

"I think you know the story as well as anyone," Orv said.

"And you do a mighty fine job in the telling, too," Harry added.

"Thank you," I said. "But is there anyone around who really

knows what happened? Maybe someone who was around back then?"

Orv shook his head. "Back in '61 prospectors were panning free gold out of the creeks. When the nuggets dried up, they moved on. It wasn't till hard rock mining got going in the seventies that folks put roots down. The early prospectors were all gone by then."

"But someone must know more about it. Like the names of other folks in Buckskin Joe?"

"Well, let's see," Tom said, rubbing the white bristles on his chin. "I believe there was a fellow owned a dance hall. His wife was one of the only other women in town in those days. I think his name was Jack. I can't quite recall her name."

"Lou Bunch?" I asked.

As soon as I said the name, all four men looked alarmed, then glanced around at each other in that way adults do when they realize a kid knows something she shouldn't.

"What on earth made you think Lou Bunch had anything to do with Silverheels, Pearl?" Russell said. Being the youngest of the old-timers, he had stayed quiet until then. Orv, Harry, and Tom seemed relieved to have him jump in now, though.

I could feel the heat of a blush prickling up my neck and into my cheeks. I couldn't think of any answer except the truth. "I thought I heard Josie mention her."

Russell scowled. "Did you, now. That just figures."

"Why? Who was she?"

All the old-timers glanced at each other again. "No one

you need to worry your sweet head about, Pearl," Orv said.

I frowned at them. I wasn't a little child anymore. I wanted an answer. I wished Father was there—he always gave me an honest answer without beating around the bush.

"Lou Bunch didn't know Silverheels," Russell said. "Josie was playing a trick on you. Mrs. Bunch runs—um—a parlor house over in Central City. She never came here, and Silverheels was long gone before she was even born."

"Oh." My face was on fire now. Josie had known I would ask around, so she had picked a name that would make a fool of me when I said it in public. I vowed right then that I wouldn't trust anything Josie told me again. And I would certainly think twice before blurting out any more names she gave me!

I stood and hurried to get the coffeepot. As soon as I disappeared into the kitchen I could hear the old-timers snickering. It was kind of them to spare me, but I heard it all the same. Josie had gotten the better of me for sure.

I loitered in the kitchen, hoping the old-timers would move on to some other gossip before I headed back out with the coffee, but the bell on the door jangled. With a sigh, I took the coffee and returned to the front.

Frank, the city boy from the day before, was standing alone just inside the door, his hands thrust into his pockets. I smiled and gave him a nod in greeting.

"Sit anywhere you like," I said.

"Are you all alone this morning?" Orv asked as Frank sat down at a nearby table.

"Yes, sir."

"Where are your friends?" Harry asked.

"They aren't my friends. Annie's my sister. They're on their honeymoon. Annie was pretty nervous about it. She hasn't known him that long, you see, and he's signed on for the war, so he asked her to marry him. I guess Annie got over her fear after the first night, though, and changed her mind about wanting me around. So they left me here."

"Left you?" Russell said in alarm.

"Just for a few days," Frank added quickly. "They went on to Breckenridge. They'll be back."

"Will you be lonely?" I asked.

"Lonely? I'm glad to be rid of them. All they wanted to do was moon about. I want to explore. Besides, I don't like Robert much."

"Well there's your ticket, Pearl," said Harry. "If you want to know more about Silverheels, take young Frank here up to Buckskin Joe and explore. If you want names of folks that were around back then, there's plenty of them in the cemetery."

"That's a fine idea!" Frank said, before I could even respond. "I wanted to go there yesterday, but Robert wouldn't. Would you take me up there, Pearl? We could make a day of it. You said you take folks on tours, and I can pay."

"I'd love to, but I'll have to ask my mother," I said.

I took Frank's order and retreated to the kitchen to ask Mother's permission.

She hesitated when I told her it would only be me and

Frank. "I don't know, Pearl. Things are different this summer without your father here. I don't know about you going off alone with him."

"What if Willie went with us?" I suggested.

She considered, then nodded. "If Willie will go, I suppose it's okay."

Willie was out back chopping wood for the cookstove, so I went to ask him. Last summer, he would have been quick to agree, but I wasn't sure what he'd say now that he had decided he was too old for my games.

Imogene was sitting on top of the woodpile, her chin in her hands, watching Willie and chattering away as usual. From the cheerful way she welcomed me into the conversation, I could tell she wasn't getting anywhere with Willie.

"That boy Frank is in the café and he wants to go to Buckskin Joe today," I explained to them both. "Mother says I can take him if you will go along, Willie."

Willie paused in his chore and looked at me. "What's in it for me?"

I sighed, even though I had expected it. "He's paying. I'll give you half."

Willie smiled. "Okay, then. But you can't go until after the lunch rush, can you? We won't have much time at Buckskin Joe if we go that late."

I bit my lip and looked up at Imogene. "I had thought of that too. Maybe Imogene could wait tables for me at lunch? You could have the other half of the tour money. And of course, some folks leave tips. You could have those, too."

Imogene sat up straighter. With so few tourists staying in her family's hotel, she wasn't getting much pocket money this summer. "Can I have a piece of pie, too?"

"After the lunch train pulls out you can have anything left over."

"It's a deal! Let me go tell my mother." She jumped down off the woodpile and ran to the hotel's back door, just a few yards away from ours. I went back into the kitchen and told my mother the plan. She wasn't thrilled to have Imogene take my place. Imogene had helped before, but she wasn't as quick as me. Seeing how eager I was to go to Buckskin Joe, however, Mother agreed.

I served until the last of the breakfast stragglers drifted out of the café. Then I hurried to wash all the dishes and lay out the fresh napkins, silverware, and coffee cups on the tables and counter so all would be ready for lunch. When that was done, I ran upstairs for a paper and pencil. I would write down every name I saw in the graveyard. I didn't know what I might gain from it, but it was the only place I knew to start. Maybe some name up there would jog a memory for someone.

Back in the kitchen, I grabbed my old straw hat and a canteen. My mother was making sandwiches and she let me take three. I wrapped them in waxed paper and put them along with three apples in my apron pocket. It was a glorious day, with clear skies and comfortable temperatures, and I figured a day like that called for a picnic.

Willie and I stepped out the front door and turned toward the hotel. Strawberry, the best horse money could rent at Johnson's Livery, was hitched to a trap and waiting in front of the hotel. Frank grinned and waved from up on the seat, then quickly jumped down and offered me a hand to step up into the buggy. I didn't need it, but it was a sweet and gentlemanly gesture, so I smiled and took the offered hand. It was soft and uncalloused, not like the hands of folks around here. Willie scrambled up from the other side, squishing me in the middle. Willie offered to drive, but Frank was eager to take the reins, and he snapped them smartly on the horse's croup to get us started. We jolted along at a trot, a merry party all the way to the track that turned up Buckskin Creek. Here the road got steeper and rockier, and Strawberry slowed to a walk. Even so, it was rough going. We were all glad to get to the old ghost town at last. We climbed down from the trap and stretched our muscles. The boys rubbed their jolted backsides. Being a girl, I remembered my manners and refrained.

Buckskin Joe was as picturesque as ever. The buildings stood silent, their windows empty, their weathering boards gray and rough. Grass and wildflowers grew up around them and in the open spaces that had once served as roads and alleyways. Aspen were sprouting here and there between the old cabins, their shimmering leaves the only movement in the deserted town. Aspen were always the first trees to come back around the mining towns, and as Buckskin Joe's last residents had left it nearly twenty years before, they had a good start here.

Frank was drawn at once toward the old dance hall. It was the largest and finest building in the abandoned town site, a two-story structure crowning the top of a low hill. With its milled clapboard walls and well-finished door and window frames, it sat like a stately queen overlooking the cluster of log cabins and crooked shacks that made up the rest of the town.

"That's where Silverheels herself danced," I told Frank, hurrying to keep up as he climbed the hill with long purposeful strides. Willie had stayed behind to secure the brake on the trap and put rocks behind its wheels.

Frank reached the door of the dance hall and stepped through without hesitation. I liked him for that—so many city folks declared the old buildings too dirty or unsafe. That was certainly true of the empty mine shafts and riggings that dotted the mountainsides, but the dance hall was still a fine building and I loved going into it.

"The piano must have stood over in that corner," Frank said as he looked around the big downstairs room. "And maybe they had a bit of a stage over there." When he had turned three-fourths of the way around, he was facing me. "And right here where we are standing is where all the men would line up to dance with—what did you call her? Silver Shoes?"

"Silverheels," I corrected.

"Right. Her." He suddenly bowed to me and said, "Silverheels, would you do me the honor of this dance?"

Before I could answer, he grabbed me around the waist with one arm and took my hand with the other, and we were off swirling around the room in a lively polka as he hummed accompaniment for us. I couldn't help laughing when my old straw hat flew off and landed where we had imagined the pianist to be.

We had circled the room once when Willie stepped through the door. He watched us make a second circuit, then stepped into our path as we came past him again.

"Excuse me, but I must cut in," he said. "You dance so charmingly, Silverheels, that I must have the next dance!"

Frank and I stepped apart. To my surprise, Willie grabbed Frank's hand instead of mine and the two of them resumed the crazy polka around the room. Still dizzy from my spin, I fell over laughing. It was like the old, fun Willie had come back as soon as we had gotten away from Como. Frank proved himself a good sport by doubling the tempo once he got over his initial surprise, and they wheeled so crazily around the room that I just knew they would crash into something and hurt themselves. At last they broke apart. Frank spun past me by himself, then collapsed beside me, laughing and breathing hard as he stretched his long legs out on the boards. Willie did one last jig, apparently having now become Silverheels instead of her suitor. He kicked his bulky boot heels up in several silly steps, pranced toward us on his toes, then dropped into a clumsy curtsy, holding imaginary skirts wide with both hands. Frank and I clapped enthusiastically, and Willie plopped down beside us. We sat in silence in the cool room while they both caught their breath. Then Frank got back to his feet and retrieved my hat from the corner.

"So that's the dance hall," he said, grinning. He extended a hand and pulled me back up to my feet. "I can't wait to try out the saloon."

We walked through the rest of the town site, poking our heads through cabin windows or pantomiming the lives of the people who had once lived there. At the saloon, we passed around the canteen and offered toasts to everything we could think of. At the old mercantile I went behind the counter and "sold" Willie and Frank the cheese sandwiches from my pockets, a little worse for the wear from the day's activities. We found a sunny patch beside the creek and sat to eat them.

"What's that over there?" Frank asked, pointing across the water. From where we sat we could see a leaning picket fence amid a grove of young aspen.

"That's the old cemetery," I said.

"Where the ghost of Silverheels still walks," Willie said in a low, mysterious way. He was trying to give Frank a shiver, but his mouth was too full of cheese sandwich for his voice to sound ominous.

Frank chewed, considering. "She wouldn't have to be a ghost, you know. She didn't die in the epidemic, right?"

"Right."

"So say she was eighteen—Annie's age. She'd be about seventy-five now, right?"

Willie laughed. "Well, when people see the veiled woman in the cemetery, they never mention her having a cane."

"Have either of you ever seen her?" Frank asked.

Neither of us had. The story had always finished with the suggestion that people had seen her, or her ghost, but I'd never put much stock in that part of the legend.

"Let's go over and see if she's there now," Willie suggested.

We pulled off our shoes and socks and waded across the cold creek. On the other side, we climbed the slope to the cemetery, where the picket fence leaned crazily, first one way, then another. There was no gate, or if there had been it had disappeared years ago, so it was easy to enter the little graveyard. Many of the graves had no markers, consisting only of a rectangular outline of stones nearly hidden among the weeds. Others had simple wood crosses made of two weathered boards nailed together. Names and dates had been carved or painted on the cross boards. Only a handful of graves had actual headstones. I took the paper and pencil from my pocket and began writing down the names I could read.

"What are you doing that for?" Willie asked.

I wasn't sure what Willie would think if he knew I had a bet with Josie, so I just shrugged. "I'm just curious, that's all," I said.

"Curious about dead people?" Willie scoffed, as if it was

the craziest thing he had ever heard.

"Curious about who might have known Silverheels," I said. "Maybe some of them still have relations around here."

Frank's face lit up. "Do you think so? That there might be people around who remember her?"

"Maybe," I said with another shrug.

"I'll help you," Frank said. Willie stuffed his hands in his pockets and watched, while Frank began reading names off crosses for me to write down.

Though it was early in the year and the grasses and weeds were not yet tall enough to completely hide the graves, the place looked overgrown and forgotten. In places Frank had to push aside snarls of weeds or thorny raspberry thickets to read the names. Gradually, we worked our way toward the back corner of the cemetery, to the very oldest graves, the names and dates getting harder to make out as we went.

"This is where the victims of the smallpox epidemic are buried," I said when we reached the very back corner. Frank nodded as we examined the tilting wooden crosses. Few of the names were legible, but here and there the dates still stood out.

"They were all so young," Frank said in a quiet voice as he moved from grave to grave. His playful mood from earlier had become subdued here in the most overgrown and forgotten part of the cemetery. "Imagine coming here thinking you'd get rich, and dying of smallpox instead."

"Maybe they would have died of smallpox at home, too,"

Willie said. He was leaning against a tree nearby, watching but refusing to help.

"But if they'd stayed home, they would have had their families around them. Their wives and mothers to take care of them," Frank said.

"That's why Silverheels was so beloved," I said. "She gave that feminine comfort to ease their suffering."

Frank nodded as he moved from cross to cross. "Why do you suppose she stayed?" he asked.

"She knew they were far from home and needed her," I said.

"Maybe she was hoping for a big reward," Willie said. "After all, some of those miners must have had a big stash of gold."

Frank frowned at Willie. "That spoils the story, don't you think?" He squatted down beside the last cross in the row.

"Hey, look at this."

I bent over his shoulder. The cross had recently been straightened and supported by a fresh pile of dirt at its base, and someone had scratched into the shallowly carved name on the cross slat so that the fading words were once again clearly visible:

BUCK WILSON 1840–1861

Frank looked up at me and our eyes met.

"Why do you think Silverheels stayed?" Willie asked from

his tree across the little graveyard. He couldn't see what we were looking at and was still thinking about Silverheels.

Frank ran his fingers lightly over the name that someone had so carefully preserved. "I think," he murmured, "that she did it for love."

CHAPTER 7

We were quiet in the trap on the way back to town. I imagined Frank was thinking about Silverheels, and about love that endured all. Willie was probably thinking about going fishing. I was thinking about my first good clue, and how I might use it to convince Josie my version of the story was right. I had to find out more about Buck Wilson and who in Park County remembered him, and I was delighted to have found both an ally and an alibi in Frank. After all, he wanted to know the truth about Silverheels as much as I did. I could enlist his help investigating her and no one would suspect I had a wager with Josie. And I liked Frank, even if he wasn't as handsome or charming as George. Searching for Silverheels with Frank would be fun.

As we arrived back in town, Willie said he wanted to stop in at the mercantile, so we dropped him off. Normally I would have gone into the store too, in case George was there, but I had an idea of how Frank might help me, so I went on alone with him.

"Would you like to come by the café tonight and talk to the old-timers?" I suggested. "They can remember back to the mining boom days. They might be able to tell us more about Buck Wilson and who tends his grave."

"Do you think any of them remember Silverheels herself?" Frank asked, his voice eager.

"I asked this morning. They didn't think anyone was still around from back then, but someone must be. Otherwise, who would have tended that grave?" I reached into my pocket and pulled out the paper on which I'd written down the names from the grave markers. "Maybe if we show them this list they will recognize the family name of someone still around."

"Okay, I'll come by after supper. Maybe you could save me a piece of your mother's pie."

"Sure. Mother makes the best pie in town," I said.

Frank pulled the horse to a stop at the hitching rail in front of the hotel and we climbed down. I was brushing the dust out of my skirt when Imogene came bursting out of the hotel.

"Hello, Pearl. Hello, Mr. Frank. Did you have a nice buggy ride in the park?"

Frank smiled back. "It was a very pleasant day," he said politely.

Imogene gave him a little curtsy, then linked her arm through mine and began walking me toward the café. When we were just a few steps from Frank she started talking again, her voice lowered.

"George came by the café looking for you earlier today. I thought he might be coming by to ask you to the picnic, so I didn't tell him you'd gone off on a buggy ride with another boy. You should be extra sweet to George next time you see him. You don't want to miss your chance because of Frank, do you? He's just going to forget you the minute he gets on the train, you know."

I pulled my arm out of hers. "Imogene, we dropped Willie off at the mercantile. I bet you could catch him walking back to the café if you hurry," I said.

Imogene's face lit with a smile so big I thought her teeth might fall out. "Thanks, Pearl!" She hurried off up the street to pester Willie with her feminine charms and left me to continue on into the café. She was my best friend, and I knew she was right—I didn't want to give George Crawford the wrong impression. But I had to keep working with Frank to gather information about Silverheels. I'd rather George had the wrong idea about me and Frank than know the truth about me and Josie. After all, as Imogene had said, Frank would be gone in a few days. Surely George wouldn't think I was doing anything improper. I spent time with tourists every summer, and Willie had accompanied us the whole way.

When Frank arrived in the café later that evening, I took him to the old-timers' table and introduced him all around. "Frank would like to know more about Silverheels and the mining days, and I told him you all remember a few things."

"That we do, lad. A few things," Orv said, sliding back an empty chair and inviting Frank to sit down. As soon as he did, they all launched into stories of the glory days, when gold and silver flowed out of Park County like water, and everyone dreamed of getting rich. As they talked, the nuggets seemed to get bigger and the saloon girls prettier. Frank listened eagerly to everything. Either he was truly interested or a very good sport.

"What about Silverheels? Did anybody stay around who knew her?" Frank prompted after hearing several of their personal stories.

"Most all of the fifty-niners were gone a long time ago," Russell said.

"But there must still be someone around who knows people buried in that cemetery. Relatives, or old friends? Pearl and I made a list." Frank retrieved the list from me and started running his finger down it, reading out names:

"John Gordon

Theodore Birchum

Elijah Weldon

Zachariah Stuart

Edwin Carlisle . . ."

Russell snapped his fingers. "Carlisle. That's Mae Nelson's family name. Her father and one uncle are buried up there. She moved down to Fairplay when everything closed down in Buckskin Joe. She'd be the one to talk to."

"That's right," Orv said. "She's one of the ones who saw the Veiled Lady in the cemetery."

A prickle of goose bumps broke out along my arms. "And she's in Fairplay?" I asked.

"Is that far?" Frank asked.

I shook my head. "We could go in the afternoon tomorrow."

"Does she still go to the cemetery to tend the graves?" Frank asked.

"Don't rightly know," said Orv. "Old Mrs. Carlisle, her mother, moved on down to Denver a few years back. Couldn't take the mountain winters in her old bones anymore."

"Why?" asked Harry. "Have the graves been tended lately?"

"Maybe it was the Veiled Lady, come back tending the grave of her lost lover," said Orv, mischief in his eyes.

"Well if it was, she'd be in the back part of the plot. That's where the smallpox graves are," Russell said.

"There was one fella back there she was supposed to have been sweet on, right?" Harry said.

"Buck Wilson," said Orv. "I remembered after you asked this morning. Some folks say they were engaged to be married, but he was one of the first to die from the pox."

Frank looked at me, his eyebrows raised. "Did you know that?" he asked.

I shook my head. I had heard versions of the story in which she had been in love or engaged to various miners, but if I had ever heard the names of the men, I'd forgotten. Tourists only needed enough to get interested in a tour.

"Where did you hear that?" I asked Orv.

He shrugged. "Don't rightly recall, but that's what I've heard. Why so interested? Did you see the Veiled Lady?"

"No," Frank said, "but someone has cleaned up Buck Wilson's grave recently. We saw it when we were there today."

The old-timers all stopped talking or eating and stared at Frank.

"Buck Wilson? Really?" Russell said.

"Do you know who around here might have known him?" I asked.

"I don't rightly know," Russell said. His brow wrinkled and he looked like he was thinking hard, but he didn't say anything more.

"Well, I'll be," said Harry into the silence that followed. "Maybe the Veiled Lady's been to the cemetery, tending her beloved."

"You ought to talk to Mae Nelson. She can tell you if it was the Veiled Lady or not. She's seen her," Orv said.

"Who knows," Harry continued. "You two may be the ones to find Silverheels at last, after all these years."

The goose bumps I had felt rising on my arms spread with a little shiver all over my body. It looked like we had a new mission for tomorrow.

CHAPTER 8

I was in a good mood the next morning, looking forward to another outing with Frank. I was just sure Mae Nelson would be able to tell us something useful. I was refilling coffee and daydreaming about my triumphant return from Fairplay with all the proof I needed to win my bet, when Josie walked into the café. I tried to ignore her, but she stumped to the counter and banged a coffee cup against its saucer so hard I was afraid it might crack. Her idea of a polite request for coffee. I hurried to her and filled the cup before she could do it again.

"Well, girl, are you ready to help me pass out leaflets today?" she said, loud enough for everyone to hear.

"You haven't proven anything," I said. "In fact, I happen to know your story was all false."

"And how do you happen to know that?" she said. She was smirking in a most unpleasant way, waiting for my answer. Waiting for me to admit that I had fallen into her trap and made a fool of myself by asking about Lou Bunch. I glanced around the café to see who was listening. At least the Crawfords weren't there, but I could tell the old-timers were pricking up their ears. I leaned in close to Josie and answered in a whisper.

"Because I found out who Lou Bunch is, and she couldn't have known Silverheels. Which you knew."

Josie waved a hand in the air, as if my point was a pesky fly that could be waved away. "Lou Bunch doesn't matter. My version of things could still be true."

"How could it be, when we both know you put someone into the story who couldn't possibly have been there? You can't just put anyone into the story willy-nilly."

"Can't I? I don't remember that rule being made when you took the wager."

"I've got work to do," I said. "Do you want hotcakes this morning?" I hoped no one took note of what she said. If word got back to my mother that I had taken a bet, I would be in big trouble.

"Of course. And hurry up with it," she said. Then she took a long noisy slurp of her coffee and opened a newspaper as if I wasn't there. That was fine with me. I didn't speak to her again until she finished her breakfast and demanded another cup of coffee. By then most folks had cleared out of the café, but I kept my voice down all the same.

"We didn't make any rules, but you won't prove anything by making up stories and characters that we both know aren't true."

"You made up a cruel father for her," Josie pointed out.

"That was different," I insisted. "That was just a possibility.

I was trying to show you that there could be a logical reason why a girl would keep her name a secret, even with those who loved her."

"And I was showing you that the kind of women who strike it rich in gold camps have their own methods. Being a sweet, addle-headed romantic didn't get them anywhere. And it won't you, either."

Being called addle-headed stung, but I refused to rise to the bait. Instead, I tipped my nose up with an air of superiority, and I spoke as haughtily as I could.

"Anyway, I don't have to make up names or people any more. I know Silverheels was in love with Buck Wilson, and I know I can prove it. Real proof."

At this, Josie's face changed. Her smirk disappeared and her eyes narrowed into a glare. "Buck Wilson?" she growled. "You are going to bring Buck Wilson into this?"

It was written all over her face—I had hit a cord. I was onto something important with Buck Wilson's story, and she knew it.

"What do you know about Buck Wilson?" I asked.

"None of your business, girl. If you want to find out about Buck Wilson, don't come bothering me about it. I'm not giving you any help in this."

Now it was my turn to smirk. "I know exactly how I'm going to learn all about Buck Wilson. And from someone who really knows."

"And who exactly would that be?" she demanded.

I only smiled at her and went to clear plates from a table, pleased to have gotten under her skin for a change.

A few minutes later, Frank arrived and took a seat at the counter, a few stools down from Josie.

"I was talking to Mr. Sorensen at the hotel and he says there's a train coming through around one thirty this afternoon that takes on water here before going on to Fairplay. He says that's the best way to get there, if you can afford a ticket."

"I can work out a trade with the stationmaster, Mr. Orenbach," I said.

"Do you think Mrs. Nelson will see us if we just drop in unexpected?"

"I hope so. Mother says she's a widow, so I'm hoping she'll be glad of some company. Mother is making a raisin cake for me to take to her."

Josie gave a sudden loud bray of laughter. "Mae Nelson? That's where you plan to learn all about Buck Wilson?"

I lifted my chin defiantly. "Russell says she grew up in Buckskin Joe and remembers a lot of what happened up there," I said.

"And they say she saw Silverheels in the cemetery," Frank added. I wished he hadn't. That fact wasn't going to make her seem one bit more credible in Josie's eyes.

"Mae Nelson makes her living selling postcards and candy on the platform while the train takes on water," Josie said. "She'd say anything to sell another nickel's worth of her wares."

Frank smiled at Josie politely, something only my mother and strangers did. "What about you, Mrs. um—"

"Gilbert," I said.

"Mrs. Gilbert. Have you lived here all your life?"

"I've lived in Como for nigh on twenty years. The lovely Silverheels was long gone by the time I came here."

"But that's long enough to have heard people say they've seen her in the cemetery up there," Frank said.

"You only have to be in Park County a few hours to hear that," Josie said. "Especially if you happen to run into Miss Perline Rose Barnell at the Silverheels Café. The sooner you meet her, the sooner you'll hear the story."

Frank glanced at me, but was gentlemanly enough to pretend he couldn't see my irritation.

"But have you met folks who say they have actually seen her up there?"

"There are plenty of crazy folks in the world. I don't have time to listen to what they are saying." She slid off the stool, dropped a nickel on the counter, and left, throwing open the screen door so hard it banged against the wall.

Mr. Orenbach was happy to let Frank, Willie, and me ride the train to and from Fairplay in exchange for my sweeping and dusting the station every evening for a month. It seemed to me that Willie should do his own work for his ticket, but he refused. He was only going because Mother insisted Frank and I couldn't go alone, so I had no choice. If I didn't work for Willie's ticket, he'd refuse to go, and then Frank and I couldn't go either.

After the lunch rush, I changed into my Sunday best and we set off on the train to Fairplay. As soon as we arrived, Willie gave us a wave and headed for the drugstore—and the only soda fountain in Park County. Hardly the chaperone Mother had sent him to be, but I was glad to be rid of him.

The stationmaster in Fairplay knew where Mrs. Nelson lived and Frank and I were soon standing in front of her little clapboard house. It was tiny, but neat as a pin, painted bright yellow and surrounded by a picket fence. Geraniums bloomed in pots on either side of the front steps, cheerfully welcoming us.

Still, Frank and I approached the door a little nervously. I clutched the small raisin cake with both hands as Frank knocked.

The woman who answered the door was not the old woman I had expected. She was no older than my own mother.

"Mrs. Nelson?" I asked.

"Yes?" She was drying her hands on her apron as if she'd just come from the kitchen. I hoped she would have time to talk to us.

"I'm Perline Barnell, from Como," I said.

"Maggie Barnell's girl?"

"Yes, ma'am. And this is my friend Frank."

"How do you do, Mrs. Nelson," Frank said with a stiff little bow, very formal and gentlemanly.

I held out the cake and continued politely. "Frank is visiting from Denver and he's curious about Buckskin Joe. We were wondering if we might ask you a few questions about when you lived up there."

Frank smiled. His smile went a little higher on his right cheek than his left, making his dimples lopsided. It wasn't dazzling like George's smile. It was the kind of smile that put a person at ease. Mrs. Nelson smiled back.

"Well, of course I would. I'd be happy to. Too few young-sters care to hear about the old days now."

She took the cake and held the door wide for us. We stepped inside the tiny house and she waved us to the right, into a sunny alcove just big enough for a stiff-backed bench and two horsehair chairs.

Frank took charge of the conversation as soon as we sat down.

"How long did you live in Buckskin Joe, Mrs. Nelson?"

"Well, I was born there," she said. "By then there weren't many folks left, so we kids went down to Como to school." She paused and smiled at me. "I went to school with your ma. We moved down to Fairplay when I started high school. That was the fall of '92, just before the big silver crash. And of course, that was pretty much the end of Buckskin Joe."

"So you grew up there? And you heard all the stories of Silverheels?" Frank asked.

"Everyone in Park County knows the story of Silverheels," she said. "But I think I saw Silverheels two times in the ceme-tery there."

71

"Really?"

"Are you sure?" Frank and I spoke at the same time, but it was okay. I could tell by the twinkle in her eye that it was just the reaction Mrs. Nelson had wanted.

"That's right," she said. "The first time I was about your age, I suppose. There were rumors, you know. Everyone said the ghost of Silverheels haunted the cemetery there. So, my sister, Marjorie, my brother, Charles, and I decided we would stay overnight in the cemetery to see her. It was a dare, really. The older kids thought we'd be too scared.

"And of course we were. Marjorie, she was the youngest and mother's little pet, she ran home as soon as it got dark, but not Charles and me. We stayed, but we didn't sleep. It was round about midnight, I think, when we saw her."

"What did she look like?" Frank asked.

"She was straight and tall, very lean. She was dressed all in black, just like they say in the stories, with a heavy veil over her face."

"What was she doing?" I asked.

"She was walking among the graves when we saw her, but Charles shouted and she fled, and Charles and me were so scared we froze up, so she got away." She laughed at the memory, but a shiver went up my spine.

"You think she was a ghost then?" Frank asked.

"I did at the time," she admitted, "but I don't think so now. Because I saw her again, some years later, shortly after I married. My father and uncle are buried there in the cemetery, so I took my mother up every year in the spring to tend the graves."

"Do you still do that?" Frank asked. I'm sure he was thinking of what we had seen the day before—I know I was.

Mrs. Nelson shook her head. "Momma moved to Denver about four years ago and I haven't been up there since."

"So when exactly did you see her the second time?" Frank asked.

"Oh, it would be maybe fifteen years ago, maybe a little more. Momma and I had made a day of it, tending the graves and then having a picnic a few miles farther down Buckskin Creek, in the big meadow there. It was getting on toward evening when Momma realized she had left her new gloves back in the cemetery. I went back by myself to fetch them. I was looking for the gloves, so I was walking along, my eyes on the ground, when I heard a sound. I looked up and there she was, no more than twenty feet from me."

"So you got a good look at her that time?" Frank asked.

"Certainly. It was toward dusk, but not dark yet. She was dressed all in black, as before, and wore a broad hat with a black veil. I couldn't see much of her face, but our eyes met for a moment. There was something about those eyes . . ." She paused and shook her head. "Then once again, she fled. I called out to her to wait, but she kept right on going."

"Did you chase her that time?" I asked.

Mrs. Nelson shook her head. "Momma was waiting for me, and we had to get off the rough part of the roads before it got too dark. But I did see what she had been doing. She had been there for the same reason as us. She had cleaned off a grave and left a neat bouquet of flowers."

"Which grave?" I asked, goose bumps already rising in anticipation of the answer.

Mrs. Nelson smiled. "Buck Wilson's. That's how I knew it was Silverheels. She was sweet on him, you know."

"So why did you think she wasn't a ghost?" Frank asked.

"I suppose by then I was a little too old to believe in ghosts. Besides, she seemed perfectly solid. I figure she'd been alive and living in these mountains all along."

"Do you think she's still alive now?" I asked.

Mrs. Nelson shrugged. "Who's to say? No one knows her name or just what she looks like. I'm not the only one who ever saw her in the cemetery, but no one's ever caught her or gotten a good look at her face."

"But you saw her eyes. What were they like?"

Mrs. Nelson got a faraway look and shook her head again. "I can't rightly put it into words. Sadness, regret. And something more, too." She sighed and looked tired all of a sudden, so I changed the subject.

"What about Buck Wilson? What do you know about him?" I asked.

"Nothing, really," she said. "He must have been a dashing fellow to have won the heart of the beautiful Silverheels, though. So sad to think of a young love, dying so tragically like that."

"Is there anyone else around that might remember him?" Frank asked. "Anyone who still goes up to the graveyard at Buckskin Joe?"

"I don't rightly know," Mrs. Nelson said. "Old Tom Lee had folks up there, but he's moved down to Denver. Can't think of anyone else, except that Veiled Lady who loved Buck Wilson." She paused and cocked her head in thought, smiling. "You know, I'm glad I never caught her. It's more romantic for being so mysterious, don't you think?"

I nodded. It was sad but very romantic to think Silverheels was still visiting his grave all those years later, and all the mystery made it a finer story. Even so, if I could find her, it was just what I needed to prove that Josie Gilbert was wrong. And that would be sweeter still.

CHAPTER 9

George Crawford was sitting on the steps of the mercantile when we arrived back in Como, and as we crossed from the platform to the café, he came to meet us. He was frowning as he approached, and I thought I saw a jealous glint in his eye when he glanced at Frank. My heart beat a little faster.

"Good afternoon, George," I said. I thought about batting my eyelashes like Imogene always did with Willie, but I didn't want to flirt with George in front of Frank. Besides, I wasn't any good at it.

"Can I talk to you for a minute, Pearl?" George asked.

"Sure."

He turned and started back across the street toward the mercantile, so I excused myself from Frank and Willie's company and followed. Once we were out of earshot of Willie and Frank, George spoke.

"Pearl, what's going on between you and Josie Gilbert?"

My stomach twisted. "What do you mean?"

"You know I saw you with her in the café yesterday morning, and then you were coming out of her house. And folks say you were whispering with her at the café this morning."

"I wasn't whispering." I thought fast, searching my mind for a reasonable excuse for talking to her so much. I settled on something that wasn't exactly a lie, though not exactly the truth, either. "I'm trying to convince her to stop campaigning in the café, that's all," I said.

I was afraid I would look too guilty to believe, but George looked relieved. "Good. Because I like you, Pearl, and I've been worried about you." He took my hand and squeezed it. "With the war on, folks have to be a lot more careful about what they say, and how they say it. We've got to support the boys over there. Josie's one of those who criticizes the president, our commander in chief. It's our duty to stand behind him, for the sake of victory."

I nodded. I wanted to reply, but I didn't know exactly what to say, and even if I did, I couldn't trust my voice now that my hand was enfolded in his.

"You will be careful, won't you? Be a true patriot?"

"Of course."

"Good." He smiled just a little, crinkles forming at the corners of his green eyes, bringing out their sparkle. "Then will you go to the Fourth of July picnic with me?"

"Oh! Yes! Thank you, George!" He gave me a true smile then, dazzling me. For a moment, I feared I might collapse, my knees went so weak. I, Perline Rose Barnell, was going to the Fourth of July picnic with the most handsome boy in Park County!

George brushed his hand gently along my cheek. "Good. See you later, Pearl," he said, and with a wink, he departed.

Willie and Frank were sitting at a table right inside the door when I floated back into the café a moment later.

"What did George want?" Willie asked.

"He asked me to go to the Fourth of July picnic with him."

"You? With George Crawford?" Willie said. "I hope you said no."

"Why?"

"Honestly, Pearl. You know what the Crawfords are like."

"I know what his mother is like, but I'm not going to the picnic with his mother. I'm going with George!" I insisted.

"If you're going with George, I promise you, you're going with his mother," Willie said.

"Just forget it," I said, and I brushed past their table and into the kitchen to help Mother.

By the time I came back out to the front, the old-timers had started to gather. They were eager to hear what Mae Nelson had told us. Of course I had work to do, but I kept an ear on their conversation as best I could as I served the handful of other customers or wiped up tables.

"I believe Mrs. Nelson did see someone up there," Frank said after he'd recounted all we had learned. "For one thing, it matches what we saw. Someone cleans up the grave of Buck Wilson in the spring. A woman in a black veil, apparently."

"Must be Silverheels, then," Orv said.

"Unless Buck Wilson had other family around, right?"

Frank said. "I mean, Mrs. Nelson was up there because she's got family buried there. Maybe Buck Wilson had a sister or niece or someone like that too. Does anybody know anything about him?"

"He was just another bachelor gold seeker," Harry said. "They were all the same—when they weren't digging up gold they were spending it on whiskey and women. The miners were a greedy, dirty lot."

I felt my hackles going up. How could Silverheels have loved a man like that? Like Mrs. Nelson had said, it had to have been a powerful love for her to still pine at his grave so long after.

"Surely they weren't all so bad," I said. "Some of them might have been decent fellows just trying to make enough money to marry their sweethearts."

"I can't really recall many miners that fit that description," said Harry.

"Well, my father is working a mine right now, and he's not like that!" I said.

"Of course we didn't mean your pa, honey," Harry said quickly. "I was talking about the fifty-niners."

"If someone was to go up to the cemetery to watch, like Mae did as a little girl, I bet you could catch old Silverheels sneaking around. Find out for yourselves," Orv said.

"Say, there's a fine idea," Willie said, grinning at Frank and me. "We could spend the night in the cemetery."

"But do you think she'd show up? She's already tended the

grave. Maybe she just comes once each spring," Frank said.

"You won't know until you try," said Orv.

"Unless you're too chicken to spend the night in a grave-yard," Willie said, his eyes daring Frank to do it.

Frank smiled up at me. "I'll go if you two will go with me."

"Pearl can't go," Willie said. "Mother will need her here in the café. Besides, she'd just run off at the first crack of a twig, like Mrs. Nelson's little sister did."

"I would not! And Mother might let me go, if I could be back in time for lunch," I said.

Willie called to my mother, asking for permission to take Frank camping the next day.

Mother appeared in the doorway. "What about Frank's companions? Aren't they due back in Como tomorrow?"

"We aren't planning to leave for Denver till the day after. We'll be back by then," Frank said.

Mother considered. "You will have to do your morning chores before you go, Willie, and chop enough wood to keep my cook stove working till you get back."

"I will," Willie promised.

"Can I go too? If I'm back before lunch?" I asked.

Mother's brow knitted. "I don't think I can spare you, Pearl. Not with your father and Willie away."

"That's not fair. Why can't Willie stay and I go?" After all, I was the one who needed to find Silverheels, though I couldn't tell my mother why.

"Pearl, you know you can't spend the night up there alone

with a young man! We'll go on a family outing later in the summer." She disappeared back into the kitchen.

"See? I told you," Willie said. Then he and Frank put their heads together and started planning.

I turned my back on Willie and went to fill cups at the other two tables still occupied by diners. Everyone said women were the weaker sex, but once again I'd be hard at work while the boys would be off having fun.

CHAPTER 10

At last, the only folks left in the café were the old-timers, Frank, and Willie lingering over their coffee and pie. Mother had tidied the kitchen and gone to join them, which meant that I could quit too. So as soon as the plates were all dried and put away, I left through the kitchen door and went to sweep the train station, as I had promised.

Mr. Orenbach was just closing out his books for the day when I entered. He locked his cash register for the night, handed me the broom, and after I assured him I didn't mind, he crossed the street to join in the coffee and conversation at the café. I was alone in the station and glad for the peace and quiet. Living and working every day in the café as I did, peace and quiet were rare.

I began sweeping and thinking about Silverheels and Buck Wilson, and what their love must have been to have endured so long, even after his death. A love like that must have been extraordinary, and was surely enough to have brought Silverheels to Colorado. Josie was wrong; women hadn't just come to the camps to get rich. At least not women with true loves like Buck Wilson.

In my mind, I could see them, the beautiful young Silverheels and her lively young gentleman. He was tall and charming, but not in a trim, neat way like George Crawford. Buck had been a prospector, risking hard and dangerous work every day to make his fortune so he could marry his sweetheart. A man like that would have been handsome, but a little rugged, too, his hair always needing a trim and his shirt collar and fingernails a little dirty. Despite all that, though, he'd have gentlemanly manners, a kind heart, and a friendly smile. Not dazzling, but the kind of smile that put a person at ease.

By the time I'd worked out Buck Wilson's details, I'd swept the whole waiting area and ticket booth in the depot. I had a good-size dust pile, but I couldn't find the dustpan, so I picked out the ticket stubs and cigarette butts and threw them away. Then I opened the door out onto the platform and I swept the dirt out and off the platform edge, onto the ground.

The moon was nearly full and the stars were glittering as the cool evening air settled down on us from the mountain tops. It was a glorious evening to be outside in the moonlight. I smiled to my broom and curtsied.

"May you have this dance? Why of course, Mr. Wilson," I said. I held the broom in front of me with one hand and gathered up my skirt with the other. Then I swirled around as if I was waltzing across a grand ballroom.

I was brought up short by a disgusted snort from the other end of the platform. I hadn't seen Josie sitting there alone in the dark, waiting for me to make a fool of myself, but I had obliged her all the same. Blood rushed to my face, as it so often did when Josie showed up.

"Well, I see you've met old Buck Wilson at last. Doesn't look like he's all that loyal to Silverheels if he's sneaking away to dance with you under the stars."

"What are you doing here?" I demanded.

"Just being neighborly. I saw you were all alone here at the station. Thought you might want some company. I didn't know you had a rendezvous with the handsome Buck. Careful, girl. A charmer like that can sweep a girl right off her feet."

"Ha-ha," I said, and began sweeping the platform again, angrily raising a cloud of dust that I hoped would drive her away. She stayed where she was, sitting on the edge of the platform, her stout legs dangling over the edge.

When I finished sweeping, she spoke again. "I suppose Mae Nelson told you she and the Veiled Lady sat down and had a nice cup of tea together and talked all about Buck Wilson's many virtues."

"She didn't know Buck Wilson. But I'm sure we'll find someone who did."

"And what makes you so sure?"

"I have my reasons. And when we find the person, and she—"

"She?"

"—she tells us what she knows, you will see you are wrong. Silverheels didn't come to Buckskin Joe to get rich off the miners!"

"That's the only reason dance-hall girls came, Pearl. Surely even a romantic ninny like you can see that much. I don't see how you can argue it any other way."

"I think she came to Park County with her true love."

"Her broom, you mean?"

"Of course not," I snapped. I took a deep breath. If I was going to survive this bet with Josie, I was going to have to learn not to let her get under my skin. So she'd seen me dancing with my broom. So what. I had to think back before she'd embarrassed me and recapture the feeling of romance I had felt. I sat down on the edge of the platform a few feet away from Josie and closed my eyes, letting the cool air cleanse the heat from my face.

"After Silverheels fled her cruel father, she went to St. Louis as you said. There she met Buck Wilson."

"How'd she meet him?" Josie asked.

I thought for a moment. "She would have had to take a job, since she had fled her father's house with little more than the clothes on her back. And her only skill was her dancing. Buck saw her on stage in her debut performance. She was so beautiful and graceful that he fell madly in love with her at once. Love at first sight."

"Don't make me laugh," Josie said. "There's no such thing as love at first sight."

"There was for Buck and Gerta. There must have been," I said, remembering again the well-tended grave.

Josie snorted. "So then what happened?"

"Well, he asked her to dance with him that first night, but she refused. She'd been brought up a lady, after all, and had no chaperone. Night after night Buck came back and asked, until at last one night, after her work was done, he asked and she agreed. And she, too, fell in love as she spun around the floor in his arms."

"Oh, of course. His strong arms, no doubt, that enfolded her," Josie said, scorn and sarcasm dripping from her words.

I ignored her and continued. "Buck and Gerta wanted to marry right away, but Buck was a poor boy."

"An orphan," Josie said. "Make him an orphan."

"He was a poor boy who had nothing of his own to offer Silverheels. She had spent all her life in luxury, and Buck could not marry her until he made his fortune."

"Aw, so she was after money. You admit it."

"No!" I said quickly. "Silverheels would have married Buck right off, but he insisted he would not have her living in squalor. When word reached St. Louis of gold in Colorado territory, Buck knew that was the answer! Gerta begged him not to go, but he was determined. He packed up all his belongings and set out, promising his beloved Gerta that he would make his fortune and return to marry her and sweep her off to Paris."

"Which of course, he could do, being a broom," Josie said. I didn't laugh.

"How did she get to Colorado?" Josie asked. "Most women didn't come west in the gold rush with their men. And why was she dancing in dance halls for all those other men if her virtuous heart belonged only to the stalwart Buck Wilson?"

"She couldn't wait in St. Louis! Imagine, he was away in the wilderness, where anything could happen. She couldn't bear to sit alone at home, wondering and worrying. So, she found a troop of dancers headed for the territory and she joined them."

"And how on earth did she expect to find Buck Wilson? After all, there were gold strikes from Denver to Telluride. Buck could have been anywhere."

"But they shared a bond of love," I said. "True love. And a bond like that can never be broken. It drew her to him, like steel to a magnet."

"Humph," she said. "A very pretty story. And where's your proof?"

"I don't have proof for all of it. Not yet. But I saw his grave. Just the other day, someone had fixed it up."

"That doesn't prove a thing."

"It proves that their love endured all," I insisted.

Josie snorted again. In the dark, it was easy to imagine I was talking to an old donkey. A very stubborn old donkey.

"Your story's nothing but a load of horse apples," the old donkey said.

"Well, how would you explain it, then?"

"I'd say that if your sweet ninny Silverheels was that madly in love with Buck Wilson, it was more likely because he was a fast-talking, high-rolling, silver-tongued swindler."

"That's not true!" I protested.

"Hush, girl. I let you string your cockamamie yarn; now it's my turn. I figure Buck Wilson came out west to get rich, same as every other man in the gold rush. They came pouring across the prairie with only one thing on their minds—an easy fortune. The thing was, once they got here, they didn't find the fortune to be so easily gotten after all. It was a life of hard-working days and cold, lonesome nights, and the gold wasn't nearly as plentiful as expected.

"The decent family men were quick to figure out the gold rush wasn't for them. They went back home. The bachelors and the desperately poor, who had nothing to go back to, labored on, scratching out a living. But there was a third group of men, ones who saw opportunity around them and took it. The gamblers, profiteers, and swindlers who could make their living without ever picking up a shovel. I figure Buck Wilson was among their number."

"Silverheels wouldn't have loved such a man! An undying love like hers was pure," I said.

"Maybe," Josie replied. "Maybe Buck Wilson was the kind of silver-tongued snake who could make women love him and men trust him with a single smile. And I figure he used that smile to break deals and hearts in equal measure. I figure he came to Buckskin Joe in the fall of 1860, in the hopes of swindling miners out of their claims. Of course, while he was at it, he was happy enough to swindle some women out of their virtue. Once a woman's fallen in love with a handsome man, he's in the lap of luxury. I'm sure he knew that quite well."

"And I suppose you think that woman was Silverheels," I said.

"Among others. I figure he wasn't the type to let any opportunities pass him by. He probably had every woman in town madly in love with him. Willing to do anything for him."

I smiled. She had trapped herself in the inconsistencies of her own story. "There were no other women, just the prospectors back then. You said so yourself—women didn't come west with their men in the gold rush."

"Women didn't *come* west, no. But there were the dance-hall girls. And there were the women already here."

I looked at her, confused.

"Most of the fur trappers took Indian wives, and they brought them to town when they came. Some had probably been married long enough to have daughters susceptible to Buck's charms too. And there were Mexican women down along the Arkansas River and in the San Luis valley that made their way up into the mining camps. For a strapping young charmer like Buck, I'm sure it was easy enough to win all their hearts with his smile.

"But Silverheels, now there was a prize he just had to have, no matter how many women already loved him. Her beauty was legendary. Plus, she was a kindred spirit."

"What do you mean by that?"

Josie grinned. "She was just like Buck—beautiful, charming, able to win anyone over with her smile. And ambitious for wealth. Yes, I imagine they were drawn to each other right away. Two swindlers with the same game and the same set of weapons. How could Buck resist such a conquest? All those other women pining for him were cast aside the minute he laid eyes on Silverheels. He swore he would have her at any cost."

"You can't prove any of that," I said.

She shrugged and smiled a superior smile, as if to say she could prove it. It made me uneasy. I waited for her to offer her proof, but she didn't. She just went back to watching the mountaintops in the dark.

Across the street, my mother stepped out onto the porch and called me. I'm sure she wondered what I could be doing that was taking so long, and I wasn't going to be able to tell her. I sprang to my feet and hurried into the depot to put the broom away.

Back in front of the café, Mother held out her arms to hug me. "I'm sorry, Pearl. I know you wanted to go to Buckskin Joe with the boys. Maybe we could all go up to the Lucky Fork for a few days later in the summer for a family campout. That way we could see your father. Wouldn't that be nice?"

"Yes, ma'am," I said. I did miss Father, but I wasn't getting my hopes up. We couldn't afford to close the café just to go camping.

Willie and Frank were still where I had left them, planning their outing. Frank got to his feet as soon as I stepped inside. He had been waiting for me.

"I'm sorry you won't be able to go with us, Pearl," he said. I just shrugged, wanting to pretend it didn't matter, but the tender regret in his voice made me want to cry.

"I'll tell you everything that happens when I get back, I promise. We're still in this together, you and me. Partners, right?"

I nodded. "Partners."

Frank gave me a quick flash of his crooked, enthusiastic smile and stepped out into the night. I went straight up to bed, leaving Willie to lock up and turn down the lamps, jobs that were usually mine. After all, I thought, I had nothing to look forward to tomorrow except hard work in the café, so I might as well enjoy a good night's sleep.

CHAPTER 11

The next morning, Frank was the first person to come into the café, eager as he was to set off on his adventure with Willie. I served them breakfast as cheerfully as I could, but I was relieved when they were gone and I didn't have to pretend I wasn't disappointed.

Josie came in with a huge stack of campaign handbills under her arm the minute they walked out. She thumped them down on the counter and demanded her usual order of hotcakes. I avoided her as best I could until the hotcakes were ready and I had to deliver them. When I did, she smiled at me like the cat that just ate the canary.

"Well, girl," she said, "have you seen sense yet? Are you ready to help me deliver these leaflets?"

I glanced down at the stack at her elbow. The one on top blared a new headline I hadn't seen before:

PRESIDENT WILSON,
IF WE FIGHT FOR LIBERTY OVERSEAS,
WE MUST FIGHT FOR LIBERTY AT HOME!

I looked back up at her, horrified, remembering what George had said. "You can't say that!"

Josie's eyes flashed in challenge. "Say what? Liberty?"

"You can't attack the president—he's trying to fight a war right now!"

"So you approve of hypocrisy, do you?"

"You'll get yourself accused of sedition, saying things like that. George Crawford says we have to be careful. We have to be true patriots now."

Josie cut me off with a louder-than-usual snort. "George Crawford? A word of advice, Pearl. Don't put too much stock in what a Crawford says."

"Whatever you think of Mrs. Crawford, it's not fair to judge George by his mother."

"I'd wager that George is as silver-tongued a schemer as your beloved Buck Wilson. That's the thing about men. The better they look, the less they can be trusted—especially by a quiet, well-behaved girl like you."

"That's not true. George is a gentleman."

"George is a handsome young man. And handsome young men take advantage of sweet girls like you, Pearl. That's the way of the world."

I gritted my teeth to keep my anger inside, but I could see from Josie's snide grin she knew she'd gotten the better of me. She picked up the jug of syrup and poured a hearty amount on her hotcakes.

"I've been thinking about what you said last night, Pearl,"

she said. Several heads turned our direction around the café. I fought down the urge to shush her, knowing it would only look more suspicious, so I had to let her continue.

"I've been thinking about those other women in the early days of the gold rush."

Russell got up from the old-timers' table and came to the counter stool beside Josie. "You're not going to be talking to Pearl about Lou Bunch and her kind again, are you, Josie? Because you know she's just a kid, and it's not right you telling her that kind of thing."

"Don't get your long johns in a knot, old man," Josie said. "I'm talking about the Indian wives of the trappers and traders in the early days."

"What about them?" I said. "If they were already married when they came to town, I don't see that they would have had anything to do with Buck Wilson."

"Buck Wilson? Are you still trying to figure out who cleaned up his grave? And you think it might be Indians? There haven't been any Indians around here in forty years," Russell said.

Josie ignored him and pointed to her cup. I refilled it.

"I was thinking of all those sick miners needing nursing, and those Indian wives who knew the lay of the land and all the healing herbs and plants. Seems more likely it would have been them to nurse those sick miners in the epidemic, not some dancing ninny who only knew how to kick up her heels and bat her eyelashes."

"There are no Indian women in the story," I said. "If it had been them nursing the sick, why don't we have a mountain named after one of them, too?"

"Maybe they just weren't as pretty as your lovely Silverheels."

"The mountain wasn't named for her because of her beauty. It was for her kindness to the sick men."

"That's the thing about being a woman," Josie said. "History doesn't have much use for you unless you look and act just how men want you to. If you're beautiful and work yourself to death for them, that's worth remembering. If you weren't much to look at to start with, well, feed them supper and be forgotten. When we have the vote, though, we'll change all that."

Russell rolled his eyes, drained his coffee cup, and stood. "I've got cattle to move today. Try to keep your nose clean, Josie," he said. He handed me payment for his breakfast and left the café, shaking his head. I looked around. He was the last of the old-timers to leave; the others had trickled out while we talked. It was down to just Josie and me.

I was putting Russell's money in the cash register when I had an idea. I pawed through the papers underneath the register until I found the list of names I had copied off the graves with Frank. I pulled out the paper and read through the list to check my hunch. Then, feeling victorious, I took my list to where Josie sat eating her hotcakes.

"Look, there were no Indian wives in town in the epidemic," I said, pointing to the bottom of the list where the 1861 graves appeared. "See? Frank and I wrote down the names of all the people buried in 1861, and they are all men."

Josie let her eyes slide down the list while she chewed. Her expression didn't change, but I knew I had her.

"If there had been other women in camp, at least some of them would have died along with the men, right?"

"As I said before, Indian women probably knew the medicines of the forest."

"But it was the dead of winter," I said.

"Maybe they fled the town when the epidemic hit. Men that had wives probably sent them to Fairplay to keep them safe," Josie said.

"Then the Indian women wouldn't have been there to tend the sick. Only Silverheels stayed when she could have gone. So she was the only one left to treat the men."

"When she could have gone, yes. But I figure some of those Indian wives of the old mountain men didn't have much choice. The way I see it, men take wives either as trophies or as workhorses." She stabbed her finger at the list, picking a name at random.

"Take Zachariah Stuart here. He probably traded a grizzly hide and three bottles of Scottish whiskey for a pretty little woman. That's how they did it in those days. And having paid such a high price for her, he would have wanted to protect her, so he would have sent her to Fairplay at the first hint of sickness. But this fellow"—she gave another jab at the list, landing on Elijah Weldon, 1815–1861—"he won his Indian woman in a card game, already carrying a papoose on her back. She wouldn't have been worth sending off. Unless she had given him sons. Then he would have sent her and the boys to Fairplay to be safe."

"Either way, there would have been no one left to tend the sick but Silverheels."

Josie thought for a moment. "You're forgetting that papoose that came with Mrs. Weldon. A baby girl, grown now to a child about your age. A sweet, obedient girl just like you, that old"—she glanced down at the name again—"old Eli Weldon wouldn't have cared one whit about saving. A workhorse that history could easily forget, quiet and polite as she was, and probably as homely as a mud fence. Probably madly in love with the dashing Buck Wilson, like the rest of them."

I opened my mouth to reply but, glancing up, caught sight of George and his mother across the street, talking to some of the other townswomen. In fact, there seemed to be a number of townswomen out and about. I folded the list of names and slipped it into my apron packet.

"If you will excuse me, I have work to do," I said.

I gathered the last few dirty dishes and cups from breakfast and wiped down all the tables. In the kitchen, I set to washing the dishes. I paid no attention when the bell on the door clattered, figuring it was Josie leaving. I was surprised, however, when it rang again a few minutes later. Usually we had these few hours between breakfast and lunch to ourselves. When I heard the bell a third time, I dried my hands on my apron and went out to the front. Josie was still at the counter, mopping the last of the syrup off her plate with her spoon and licking it off.

Townswomen were arriving in small groups—Mrs. Schmidt, the butcher's wife, with her two little boys, and Mrs. Johnson from the livery; Mrs. Engel from the millinery and yard-goods shop in one of her fine hats, with the postmistress, Mrs. Abernathy. I moved among them and took orders—coffee or tea mostly, but a few wanted coffee cake or bread and jam. Josie huffed a complaint about the crowd and left as six or seven of the railroad workers' wives arrived. They settled near the window with their knitting where they could watch their children playing in the street. Even a few of the ranch wives showed up in a wagon driven by Mrs. Larsen, who owned the meadow where the Fourth of July picnic always took place.

"What is going on?" I asked Imogene when she arrived with her mother.

Mrs. Sorensen raised her eyebrows. "You mean you don't know?"

"Should I?"

"Mrs. Crawford called a meeting. She's in charge of the Fourth of July picnic, and she wants it to be special, what with the war and all. I assumed since the meeting is here, she had talked to your mother about it," Mrs. Sorensen said.

I shook my head. I had heard nothing about a meeting.

Mrs. Crawford herself waited until every other woman in town had arrived before she made her grand entrance. She came striding into the café with crisp, purposeful steps, wearing a straw hat festooned with red, white, and blue ribbons and carrying a clipboard. George held the door for her, then stepped into the café behind her, looking as good as ever. His eyes danced around the crowd for a moment before alighting on Imogene and me. Then, with a dazzling smile, he winked at me.

"Mercy me!" Imogene said under her breath. I smiled back at George and hoped he couldn't hear my heart racing from across the room.

Mrs. Crawford's eyes also landed on me, but without any warmth. "Where is your mother, Pearl?" she demanded, as if I had misplaced her.

"Um—in the kitchen," I said, still reeling from George's wink.

"Well, go get her. You can fill the orders. We need her."

"Yes, ma'am," I said politely. I didn't see what right she had to boss me or my mother around in our own café, but I did as I was told.

"Mrs. Crawford is having a meeting for the Fourth of July picnic out front, and she wants you," I told Mother.

"Right now?" she said. She was rolling out pie crusts, getting ready for the lunch business that we relied on to make a living. "I've got to get these in the oven first. You go, Pearl. Tell her I'll be out when I can. Tell her I'll do whatever she needs."

I went back to the front room and relayed my mother's message.

"The rest of us are here, Phoebe, and we don't have all day. Let's get on with it," said Mrs. Sorensen.

Mrs. Crawford stiffened her back in displeasure, but she started the meeting.

"Very well. I've called you all together to plan the Fourth of July picnic. It's only two weeks away, you know. We need to get busy."

"Busy with what?" asked Mrs. Johnson. "We always have it in Larsen's Meadow, and it's never taken any planning before. We all just show up."

"But this year we have the war and our boys over there to consider. In honor of them, we are going to make this the most stirring patriotic event in Park County. This year we will be raising money for the war effort," Mrs. Crawford continued. "As you know, we are selling Liberty Bonds at our store. We've just received them. And Scotty Merino's store down in Fairplay has challenged all the stores in Park County to see who can sell out first. I shouldn't need to tell you that Mr. Crawford and I have taken that challenge. I think Como can outshine Fairplay any day of the week!"

There were some murmurs of approval and scattered applause. Then Mrs. Johnson asked, "What do Liberty Bonds have to do with the picnic?"

"Good question, Harriet. I know most of you will contribute, but there are some ne'er-do-wells in the county who won't, and folks who don't get to town very often. They will all be at the picnic. I propose we make the picnic a big fair.

We will set up booths, and all the proceeds will go toward our Liberty Bond drive. Subscriptions are fifty dollars."

"Fifty dollars!" said Mrs. Abernathy. "No one around here has fifty dollars to spare."

"Exactly," said Mrs. Crawford. "But it's a subscription— you don't pay it all at once. If everyone who runs a booth puts her proceeds toward her initial payment, you will have that much less to pay in the remaining months. You have till January to pay in full. George, here, will keep track of how much everyone has paid toward their goal. If we put our backs into it, ladies, we can make enough money at the picnic to pay it out much sooner. I'm sure everyone will have good ideas about how we can do that. To begin, I think we should have a bake sale. Pearl, your mother can bring pies. Say, a dozen?"

A dozen pies sounded like a lot, but my mother had told me she'd do whatever Mrs. Crawford wanted, so I nodded my head. Mrs. Crawford slid the clipboard to George and he wrote the contribution down.

"I'll bring my *pepparkakor*," Mrs. Sorensen said. There was another stir of approval. We had all had her spicy Swedish cookies at Christmas time, and everyone loved them. George wrote and Mrs. Crawford nodded and looked around. "What else?"

At once other contributions were called out—breads and cakes and cookies. George busily recorded them all. I thought everyone in the room was being very generous, but as the offered contributions died down, Mrs. Crawford shook her head.

"This isn't going to raise enough money to fulfill your subscriptions."

There was a moment of silence. "We've been knitting socks and mittens," said one of the railroad workers' wives. "We could sell our knitting." The other women at the table nodded in agreement.

"And I've got fine new summer hats in at the millinery shop," said Mrs. Engel. "We could raffle one off. A quarter a chance."

"Excellent," said Mrs. Crawford. "Every little bit helps. What else, ladies?"

"How about a kissing booth," Imogene piped up. "Pearl and I can run it."

All the women laughed and twittered at the idea.

"Imogene, I can't!" I whispered.

"Oh, come on, Pearl, don't be so strait-laced. It will just be a few pecks on the cheek," Imogene said.

"Yes, we will make sure it is perfectly innocent. A quick kiss on the cheek, no more," Mrs. Sorensen agreed.

"But George asked me to the picnic!" I whispered. I couldn't possibly let other boys kiss me at the picnic when I was going with George.

Imogene's face lit up. "Oh, Pearl!"

"Fine," Mrs. Crawford said. "George, put down Imogene and Pearl for a kissing booth. Say, a nickel a kiss."

"I—I'd have to get permission from my mother," I stammered.

"Nonsense, Pearl. It's a fine idea, and perfectly innocent. Your mother will approve. I will see to that personally," Mrs. Crawford said.

"And I'll make sure George has a pocketful of nickels," Imogene said, plenty loud enough for the whole room to hear. My face felt so hot I thought it must be steaming.

I glanced at George. He gave me another wink and a grin.

"I should have a new batch of strawberry jam by the fourth," Mrs. Larsen said. "I don't know how much, but I'll bring some jars to sell. And my boys could run a horseshoe toss."

All the ranch wives started chiming in with similar offers.

To my relief, George went back to writing and the conversation turned back to the picnic, and away from kissing.

"I'm sure Fritz could bring some of his fine frankfurters for folks to roast in the evening," said Mrs. Schmidt, the butcher's wife. "They fetch a good price."

Mrs. Crawford had been looking around the room, encouraging donations, but now her eyes narrowed as she turned toward Mrs. Schmidt. She smiled a stiff, icy smile.

"I don't think we can use frankfurters, Mrs. Schmidt," Mrs. Crawford said, pronouncing the name *Schmeedt*, and biting the *t* off sharply at the end, as if she were the kaiser himself. "After all, we're not in Frankfurt, are we? It's our boys we're trying to support, not the Huns."

A few women around the room drew in sharp breaths, but no one said anything. None of them seemed to be able to look at Mrs. Schmidt, or Mrs. Crawford either. Instead, they stared into their coffee cups, or at their knitting, though their needles had gone still.

I stole a glance at Mrs. Schmidt. She had gone white and her mouth was open. It seemed to take her a try or two before she could speak. "I— I didn't mean—"

"I don't think we want anything from Schmidt's for the Fourth of July event," Mrs. Crawford said.

"Don't be ridiculous, Phoebe," Mother said from the kitchen doorway. I didn't know when she had arrived, but she had heard enough of the exchange to know what was going on. "A wiener roast would be a fine addition to the picnic."

"I don't think so," Mrs. Crawford said, her voice so cold that the temperature in the café seemed to drop a few degrees.

Mrs. Schmidt stood. Her face, which had been so white a few minutes before, now flushed with color. "Never mind, Maggie, it's all right," she said. She fumbled in her pocket-book for a few pennies to pay for her coffee and set them quietly on the table. Then she whispered, "Excuse me," and taking her little boys by their hands, hurried out the door, her head down. The brief silence that followed was broken by Mrs. Crawford.

"Well, there's one in every crowd, I suppose," she said in a superior tone.

"There certainly is," Mother said, and she disappeared

back into the kitchen. Mrs. Crawford shuffled her papers, ignoring Mother, but George stared after her disapprovingly. My cheeks were burning. Why couldn't Mother have just stayed quiet, like everyone else in the café? I hoped George wasn't regretting having asked me to the picnic.

"Now, where were we. Ah yes, entertainment," Mrs. Crawford said.

The meeting continued, but subdued now, the excitement and fun gone. Mrs. Crawford told people what they would do and they quietly agreed. No one dared not to.

When the meeting finally broke up a few minutes later, the café emptied quickly. George didn't look my way as he accompanied his mother out the door.

Imogene volunteered to help me gather up dishes—her excuse for staying behind until everyone left so she could hear when and how George had asked me to the picnic.

"You'll be the envy of every girl there, showing up on George's arm," she said. "Every girl except me, that is. George is very good looking, but I prefer an older man. Speaking of which, where is Willie? I sat through this whole boring meeting because I thought he'd be here. He's only got two weeks left to ask me, you know."

My mood darkened another shade or two. "He and Frank went camping. They won't be back until tomorrow."

"Well, at least he's gotten Frank out of town."

"What do you mean by that?"

"Honestly, Pearl, use your head. It was okay making George

jealous to get him to ask you to the picnic, but now that you've got him, you want to hold on tight to George."

She flounced out of the café, knowing she was right. It was bad enough that my mother had just insulted his mother in front of half the town. I didn't need anything else to which George might object.

I began washing the dirty dishes and daydreaming about showing up at the picnic on George Crawford's arm. I would bring the most delicious picnic in the world for him, and after lunch . . .

My fancy, which had been taking flight, came crashing back to earth. After lunch, I'd work the kissing booth. My first kiss would be to whoever paid a nickel for the privilege—not exactly the way the daydream was supposed to go. Unless, of course, George stole a kiss before the kissing booth, and that wasn't likely with the whole town in Larsen's Meadow. No, my fist kiss wasn't going to be sweet or romantic. It was going to be my patriotic duty for the war effort. Real romance, it seemed, had left Park County, right along with Silverheels.

CHAPTER 12

By the time I had the café tidied up from the meeting, there was no chance for me to get away. The lunch train was due at the station in only half an hour, and my mother was scrambling to get ready. I sliced bread and made sandwiches until I heard the approaching whistle. Then Mother sent me out front with silverware and napkins to get the tables ready. Across the street the train chugged into the station. It released its huge, hissing clouds of steam and the doors opened. Passengers began to emerge.

I paused in my work and stared. These weren't the usual lunchtime tourists and travelers. From every car it was the same—young men in uniform.

"Mother!" I called.

She stuck her head out of the kitchen. "What is it now?"

"Look. The whole train is soldiers!" I said, pointing through the window.

Mother came up beside me. As she gazed, her hand went to her heart, not in a patriotic salute, but more as if to ease an ache there.

"Oh!" she said.

She stood like that, watching as they spilled off the platform into the street. The first wave of soldiers had almost reached our front door when my mother crossed to it and threw it open.

"Come in, welcome, come in," she said in greeting. "Your meal is on us today, gentlemen. Eat your fill, it's on the house."

"What?" I said in surprise from my place by the window.

"They're to have anything they want, Pearl, and you are not to take so much as a penny for it."

Soldier after soldier trooped inside, each taking off his hat and bobbing his head toward my mother with a "thank you, ma'am." Then they rushed to the seats, cheerful and boisterous—and hungry!

For the next hour I was scrambling more than usual, with the tables packed full and so many men at the counter that they stood two between each stool. I had no time or energy to think about anything but getting plates to the right table, refilling coffee cups, cutting pies, and wiping up spills. I got plenty of thank-yous, but collected nothing else, even refusing those who offered money. I had no time to dwell on it, though. The very moment I set down a load of plates in front of one group of soldiers, another group was calling out for more.

I was in the kitchen lifting the last pieces of fried chicken out of the grease when I heard a shout and a loud burst of laughter. Afraid trouble might be starting, I snatched up the plates and hurried up front to see what was going on. A big crowd had gathered at the window watching the scene unfold at the depot.

Josie Gilbert was standing on the platform, clutching her stack of new leaflets and shouting into the faces of two railroad security men. They were both shouting back. Even from this distance and through the wavy glass of our front window I could see the spittle flying.

One of the guards tried to take Josie by the elbow. She jerked free, a little flurry of leaflets scattering as she did. Another wave of laughter broke through the café crowd. I stood rooted, watching with the rest of them, the loaded plates forgotten in my hands.

The guard grabbed for Josie's arm again, and this time as her arm jerked away, whether by accident or intent, she caught the man with a right hook, square on the jaw. Another burst of laughter and a little applause sounded along with a collective "Ooh!" from the occupants of one table.

There was a pause of three blinks as the security guard recovered from the surprise punch. Then both men lunged for Josie. The stack of leaflets exploded from her grip and scattered across the platform as the men grappled for her arms. In short order they pinned them to her sides and marched her, still struggling, from the platform.

The show over, the still-laughing men returned to their places, and I remembered what I was doing. I took the plates to their tables, but I suddenly found I couldn't look anyone in the eye. Josie had ruined everything. Here I was, doing my patriotic duty, working without a penny's pay, but that's not what they would remember of our small town. They would leave here remembering the crazy suffragist with the fierce right hook, as one fellow at the counter was already saying. And to make matters worse, I was actually worried about Josie!

More than ever, it was a relief when Mr. Orenbach came through ringing his handbell, and the crowd began to thin. When the final whistle blew, the stragglers grabbed their hats and their half-eaten sandwiches and scrambled away. I let out a huge sigh. There had been no further sign of Josie, but the last group of soldiers to leave were still talking about her. They were still laughing, too.

Silently, I began to stack up plates, saucers, and cups. My mother came in to help me. She didn't know what had happened. She had been busy in the kitchen and had only heard the buzz of conversation and laughter. I did not tell her either. I just kept gathering the dirty plates and carrying them in heavy stacks to the kitchen.

There was very little food left, so Mother sliced a rasher of bacon and scrambled a big mound of eggs for us. She made extra, knowing that Mr. Orenbach would be along. The coffeepot was down to the gritty dregs, so I refilled it and set it on the stove to percolate while the bacon sizzled in the skillet. Sure enough, Mr. Orenbach arrived from the station just as we carried out the platter of eggs and bacon from the kitchen.

He was not his usual cheerful self. In fact, he looked like he was about to boil over.

"Why, whatever is the matter?" Mother asked.

"That troublemaker Josie Gilbert has a new handbill. It's downright seditious, that's what it is. And she had the nerve to stand there on the platform, shouting her 'votes for women' slogans and handing them out to all those brave young men being shipped off to war. The nerve! To soldiers!" He popped a forkful of eggs into his mouth and chewed angrily.

"The railroad guards got into a pretty big argument with her," I said. "I saw it from here."

"Everyone saw it!" Mr. Orenbach said. "They are going to be talking about it all up and down the line!"

"Good heavens!" my mother said. "What on earth did her handbills say?"

Mr. Orenbach pulled a crumpled paper from his pocket and handed it to my mother. She read it, a little crease nesting between her eyebrows as she did. She pursed her lips, but said nothing.

"She can't do this. She'll ruin me!" Mr. Orenbach said.

"Surely not," my mother said, handing the paper back to him. "It's a public platform. It's nothing to do with you."

Mr. Orenbach shook his head. "Every day the papers are saying how Germans shouldn't be in vital jobs like the railways."

"But you're not a German. No more than the Schmidts!" I protested. Sure, he had a faint trace of an accent, but he was proud to have become an American citizen, and he'd been in Como all my life.

"Wilhelm Orenbach isn't exactly an American name, Pearl," Mr. Orenbach said. "When Phoebe Crawford hears of this, she'll be writing the governor."

"Don't worry about Phoebe, Mr. Orenbach," my mother said. "There's plenty of folks in this town who would vouch for your character and your loyalty to this country."

Mr. Orenbach was glaring out the window. "But there's those who wouldn't," he said. I followed his gaze to see Josie Gilbert herself, striding angrily up the street. Russell was beside her, trying to talk to her, but she was ignoring him. I hoped the two of them would pass on by, but I was having no such luck today.

CHAPTER 13

Josie stomped straight up to our front door and right on through, looking madder than a wet cat. She tried to slam the door behind her, but Russell caught it before it closed and followed her in.

"Dagnabbit, woman! If you won't talk sense, you durn well better listen to it!" he exploded. Then the room fell silent. Russell snatched his dusty cowboy hat off his head and looked at my mother sheepishly.

"Begging your pardon, Mrs. Barnell," he said.

My mother jumped to her feet. "We're all out of our lunch specials, but I've got bacon and eggs. Sit down and I'll go fry them up. Pearl, pour everyone a fresh cup of coffee, would you?" She seemed to think anything could be fixed with coffee and a hot meal.

"Thank you, Mrs. Barnell. I'd be glad of a cup of coffee, but I've already had my lunch." Russell gave Josie a sharp glare before continuing. "I was mending fences just outside of town when I heard rumor that this stubborn old mule had gotten herself into trouble with the railroad. I came in to see if I could talk some sense into her. Should have known better than to try."

"Yes, you should have," Josie said, whirling to face him. "You are not my keeper!"

"Who's fault is that?" he muttered under his breath as he took the cup of coffee I filled for him.

I held a second cup out to Josie, but she only gave her usual donkey snort and plopped herself down at a table across the room from where we were sitting. Mr. Orenbach continued to glare at her.

My mother still stood by the table, looking from one to another of the folks in the room. "I'm sure this is all just a misunderstanding. I'm sure everything can be cleared up."

"Are you, Maggie Barnell?" Josie said. She had no right to talk to my mother in that sarcastic tone, but I held my tongue, knowing better than to get into the middle of this.

"You can't be causing trouble at my station like that," Mr. Orenbach said. "I won't have it!"

"It's not *your* station, and I didn't cause trouble. It was your railroad men that caused the trouble."

"You can't be saying those things there," Mr. Orenbach said. "And especially not when the train is filled with new soldiers. It's not right."

Josie straightened with self-righteous dignity. "I may not have the same rights to vote as you under the Constitution, but it seems to me I have the right to exercise my speech freely."

"Not in war time, I'm afraid," Russell said. "You know that good and well, Josie Gilbert."

"It's sedition!" Mr. Orenbach said. Splotchy pink patches

appeared on his cheeks in his otherwise pale face. Sedition was a word that scared him, but it seemed to have no impact on Josie.

"Defending the First Amendment is sedition, Mr. Orenbach?"

Mr. Orenbach started to puff and bristle like an old porcupine, and my mother stepped between them.

"Perhaps, Mrs. Gilbert, if you worded your informational leaflets more—more gently?" my mother suggested.

"I will not whitewash the truth!" Josie said.

"I didn't mean whitewash, I just meant . . ." Mother searched for words, and Russell stepped into the void.

"She means you could be civil, like everyone else. You don't have to be spoiling for a fight every minute of every day. You might even get a few folks to listen to you if you made an effort to be sociable now and then. Decent manners wouldn't hurt either."

"Manners!" Josie scoffed. "Oh yes, manners. Like Pearl here, she's got fine manners. All 'yes, ma'am' and 'no, ma'am' and not saying a word against things she disagrees with. No thank you!"

"I am proud of Pearl's manners," Mother said, smiling at me.

Mother's support took a little of the sting out, but not much. I couldn't believe Josie would drag me into this and insult me for what everyone else said I had to do. It was not my place to speak, though, so I bit my tongue and kept to myself.

"Too many women are silenced by their manners, and for their sakes, I will not be," Josie said.

"Mrs. Gilbert, no one's trying to silence you," Mother said.

"Oh yes they are!"

"Mr. Orenbach is worried for his job. He's from Germany," Mother said. "If the railroad or the government hears rumors of seditious activities at the Como depot, he could be blamed. You wouldn't want that, would you?"

"Of course I don't want that. I'm just fighting to better our country."

"And our country is fighting a war!" Mr. Orenbach exploded.

"What about a compromise," my mother suggested. She was the only one in the room still able to speak in a calm voice. "Mrs. Gilbert, you could promise to stay away from the train platform and to not give out your handbills to soldiers."

"You call that a compromise?" Josie said.

"You can come in here instead. We serve most of the passengers off the train. You can give out your papers in here so you won't be associated with Mr. Orenbach."

My mouth fell open. How could Mother *invite* Josie to campaign daily in the café! And at our busiest time! And when Mrs. Crawford might be writing to the governor!

"That's a very generous offer, Mrs. Barnell," Russell said.

Josie snorted again. "Yes, very generous to give an old woman the right to speak her mind in public."

Russell rolled his eyes. "Oh, yes. Such a poor old woman."

Josie gave him a nasty look, but then she glanced toward me and a little smirk came over her lips. "Very well, Mrs. Barnell, I'll stay away from the depot and I'll come in here instead."

Now it was my turn to glare. I suppose she was thinking that I'd never get her out of the café now that my mother had given her permission, but I didn't see that it changed anything. It only hardened my resolve to prove my story right and win the bet. And soon, before Mrs. Crawford found out about my mother's bargain with her.

Josie turned to Russell. "As for you, you can be satisfied I'm properly tethered and corralled and you can go back to tending your other cattle, thank you very much."

"Gladly," Russell said. "They aren't nearly so thick-skulled and stubborn as you, woman."

"Well, they will just have to try harder then," Josie answered.

Russell stomped out of the café, no calmer than when he'd arrived, and Mr. Orenbach soon followed. That left Mother, still standing in the middle of the room, me, still holding a lukewarm cup of coffee, and Josie, still sitting by herself at the corner table. She looked up at my mother.

"So?" she said. "What about that bacon and eggs?"

I washed plates and held my tongue as long as Josie remained in the café. I hoped that if I stayed out of sight, maybe nothing worse would happen. Already today I'd been roped into kissing strangers, been embarrassed in front of George, and seen two good people threatened just because their ancestors were German. I now had Josie Gilbert planning to campaign even more in the café, after I'd been working to get her out. And on top of all that, I'd worked twice as hard as usual to serve the lunch crowd and hadn't made a cent. Meanwhile, Willie and Frank were off somewhere whiling away the hours in the sunshine, not a care in the world.

"Well," my mother said cheerfully when she joined me in the kitchen after Josie went home. "Never a dull moment, is there?"

"Why did you tell her she could campaign in here, Mother?"

"I had to do something. You don't want Mr. Orenbach to lose his job, do you? Things can get bad for a German accused of sedition."

"And what if we get accused of it instead?" I said.

"I don't think anyone will pay too much attention to what's said in a small café in a small town. And we aren't German."

"George will pay attention. And what if Mrs. Crawford writes the governor—"

"Why would she write the governor?"

"Mr. Orenbach said she might. And you saw what she did to Mrs. Schmidt," I said.

Mother frowned. "Yes. We'll have to do something to show our support for the Schmidts too."

"I don't think we should get involved. It's bad enough you're letting Josie campaign in here so everyone will think we agree with her."

"Pearl, think about what you are saying! The Schmidts

are our friends and neighbors. They'd help us in a fix, and I intend to do the same for them."

"And what about Josie?" I said. "She wouldn't do a thing for anyone else, and yet you'll let her come in here saying things she shouldn't."

"I doubt she would agree with you on that, Pearl. She's trying to get the vote for women everywhere. She's trying, in her own way, to do something for every woman in this country."

"But what about business?" I said. "The locals won't come in if Mrs. Crawford decides to cause trouble for us. And if folks off the train see Josie campaigning in here, they won't come in either."

Mother sighed. "That's their choice, I suppose. I'm not going to deny Josie her rights, Pearl, wartime or no. Sometimes standing up for something, or someone, is more important than a few dollars' worth of business."

"What about our rights?" I was almost shouting with frustration now. "It's not fair, Mother. We did our patriotic duty and fed all those soldiers for free, and now we're going to risk losing customers so she can speak her mind? When do our rights—our *needs*—count?"

My mother stopped wiping plates and stared at me, but not in reproach. "Oh, Pearl. Patriotic duty had nothing to do with why we fed those young men. I thought you understood that."

"Understood what?" I asked, feeling foolish.

"I fed them because I know that every one of them is some mother's son."

The catch in her voice made me stop washing and look into her face. I had never seen my mother cry—not when Father left for the Lucky Fork mine for the summer, not even when she burned her whole arm with cooking grease. But there were tears in her eyes now.

"If it were my son, I would hope that somewhere out there other mothers would remember this is my precious child, and would help him remember it too."

I thought of Willie, and my heart went cold with fear. "But it won't be, right? It won't be your son. Willie's not old enough to be drafted, and you won't let him enlist, will you?"

"Who knows how long this war will go on. He's seventeen this summer. In another year—" Mother stopped and took a deep breath. "There's so little we mothers can do past a point, but I'll do everything I can when the chance comes. Those young men needed a mother's love." She went back to her chores, but I did not.

My heart seemed to have frozen, and my whole body with it. "Do you really think Willie will have to go to fight in the war?"

"We can only hope and pray he doesn't," my mother said. "But I can't bring myself to deny him a moment of his childhood this summer. I know that makes things harder on you, Pearl, but I just can't."

I thought again of Willie and Frank enjoying a sandwich in a sunny meadow while I was stuck here in this hot kitchen—but this time, like my mother, I couldn't begrudge them a minute of it.

CHAPTER 14

When the dishes were clean and put away, I thought I would finally have a quiet moment. I didn't want to think about the picnic or Josie or young men going to war, so I decided to think about Silverheels and winning my bet. I hoped Willie and Frank would find the person who was caring for Buck Wilson's grave! Thinking of the grave didn't conjure romantic visions for me this time, though. Instead, I found myself seeing the faces of the soldiers at lunch. How many of them would die young and alone, far from home? And what about Willie?

The eastbound train arrived at the station to refill water and coal, as it did every afternoon. Hardly anyone ever got off that train in Como, so I paid no attention. If I had, I wouldn't have been quite so surprised when Robert and Annie appeared at the café door and banged on it. Despite the CLOSED sign, I hurried to let them in.

"Where's your mother?" Robert demanded as he stormed in. Annie followed, wringing her hands.

"Now Robert—" she began, but he held up a hand to stop her.

"I told you, Annie, I'll handle this."

I was so surprised I just stood blinking and staring at them.

"Well?" he demanded. "Are you deaf? I asked where is your mother? Or better yet, your father."

This time I didn't have to answer him. His bellowing brought my mother out of the kitchen.

"Where's the boy?" Robert demanded as soon as he saw her.

"The boy?"

"My brother, Frank," Annie said.

Mother's smile warmed once again. "He's gone fishing with my son, Willie."

"Fishing where?"

"Up the Tarryall, I suppose. Or maybe up at the beaver ponds on Buckskin Creek. There's plenty of good holes around here."

Annie glanced out the window, looking worried. "I hope they haven't gone too far. It'll be dark soon."

"I don't think they were planning to come back yet tonight," my mother said.

"What?!"

"Oh, don't worry. Willie's an experienced camper, and they took everything they need. They will be perfectly comfortable and will be back for breakfast."

The color drained from Annie's face. "Robert! There are wild animals out there! There are bears!"

A little laugh escaped me, but Robert's glare silenced it quickly.

"How dare you send him out into the wilderness alone!" he said.

"He's not alone; he's with Willie. They are perfectly fine," my mother said. She was no longer smiling, but she was still calm and polite. "He was on his own here, so it seemed he had a right to choose what to do. Willie camps all the time. He knows how to stay safe."

"You cannot expect Frank to spend the night off in the woods," Robert said.

"Please, ma'am," Annie said, her pale brow knotted, "I couldn't live with myself if anything happened to Frank after I left him here. He's never been out alone in the mountains like this."

My mother smiled again. "As I said, miss, he's perfectly safe with Willie."

"But they're just boys," Annie said.

"And we should be on the morning train," Robert added.

"I'll see what I can do to get word to him that you're back in town," Mother said. "He didn't expect you back until tomorrow. Go on back to the hotel, and I'll let you know if there is any news."

Annie thanked my mother and pulled a still-muttering Robert toward the hotel.

Mother went back toward the kitchen.

"What are you going to do?" I asked, following.

"The boys were planning to camp at Buckskin Joe, so I suppose someone will have to go retrieve them. Maybe after supper you could ride up with Russell or Orv. I know you were anxious to get up there yourself."

This was the first good thing that had happened to me all day. I was glad when Russell arrived for supper and agreed to go, and I was impatient for the café to empty and for mother to say she could spare me. As soon as she could, I swept the depot for Mr. Orenbach, and I was free. Dusk was gathering as we rode out of town, me on a borrowed horse from the livery, Russell on his big bay.

The ride was pleasant. The twilight air felt cool and fresh on my skin after the whole day inside. The deer were moving out into the meadows to graze and we saw more than one doe standing watch over frisky fawns. Dusk in June was the perfect time to be out in the mountains, whatever city folks like Annie might think.

It was fully dark by the time we arrived in Buckskin Joe, but we had no trouble finding Willie and Frank. They had a bright campfire crackling away just across the creek, not far from the cemetery. They were hungrily watching two trout sizzling in a cast-iron skillet on the edge of the fire as Russell and I dismounted. Frank looked up from the skillet and his face burst into a big smile.

"Pearl! You came after all. Now I know we'll see Silverheels tonight!"

I was glad he was happy to see me, but I knew he wouldn't be when he found out why I'd come.

"Looks like you've got a mighty fine supper planned,"

Russell said, stepping up to the campfire and looking into the skillet.

"We caught them just this afternoon," Frank said proudly.

"Nothing's better than a fresh trout supper over an open campfire," Russell said, settling himself down on the ground. I took a cue from him and sat down myself, glad to delay the bad news as long as possible. Frank seemed content to believe we'd just come to join their adventure, but Willie glared suspiciously at me from across the campfire.

"Why are you here, Pearl?" he said.

I bit my lip and glanced at Frank. "Annie and Robert came back into town on the afternoon train, and they were upset that you weren't there, Frank. Annie is worried about your safety, spending the night out in the mountains."

Frank shook his head. "Annie's not worried about me. She's worried she'll get in trouble with my mother for leaving me here alone."

"Maybe, but she did seem pretty upset," I said. "And Robert says you have to leave for Denver on the morning train."

"You mean we can't stay the night?"

I shook my head. "I'm sorry, Frank."

"Well, I won't go!" he said, suddenly angry. "We're just settling in for the night. We haven't even eaten our supper."

"Well, now, there's no need to rush," Russell said. "We told your sister we'd bring you back safe and sound, and I figure that means we ought to let you eat your supper at the very least. If she's worried because she left you here alone when she shouldn't have, then I see no harm in letting her stew a little longer."

"Thanks, Russell," Frank said with a smile. To my relief, his anger faded as quickly as it had flared. Russell started telling of other nights around campfires and the shenanigans that fellas pulled out on the cattle drives. We all laughed until our ribs ached.

Eventually the fire burned down into glowing embers, and Frank flopped down on his bedroll and looked up at the stars. I lay back too, suddenly aware of what a romantic scene it all was, or would have been if I were here with George. The full moon was so bright it wasn't the best night for stargazing, but the big bear was visible, and the little bear as well. Russell pointed them out to us.

"I thought those were dippers," Frank said. "See, there's the handle and the cup."

"Some folks call them that," Russell said, "but I always like to think of them as a momma bear and her cub. Ain't nothing in this world safer than a cub when the momma bear is watching over it. I like to think we've got something like that watching over us, too. Makes me feel comfortable and safe when I'm out here under the stars."

"And Annie was worried about bears," I said.

Frank chuckled softly, and in the darkness, his hand moved to rest gently against mine, his little finger hooking through my own.

"I wish I didn't have to leave tomorrow. I wish I could stay all summer," he said quietly.

"Me too," I said, surprised at how much I suddenly wished it. I knew I should pull my hand away from his. Frank was leaving tomorrow, and I was going to the picnic with George, and that was all as it should be. And yet, I felt a tingle of electricity where our fingers intertwined, and a comfort and warmth all through me that I didn't want to give up. So I lay as I was, enjoying the feeling, telling myself no harm could come of it, since Frank was leaving tomorrow.

I closed my eyes, listening to the soft sounds of the night: the buzz and chirp of night insects, the rustle of field mice in the grass, the steady gurgle of the creek—and then the sudden, unexpected thump from the direction of the cemetery!

Willie, Frank, and I all sat up, our eyes alert and straining into the darkness. The moonlight was bright where we sat on the open creek bank, but the shadows under the trees were deep and played tricks on our eyes. Still, I thought I saw something moving. Frank and Willie were already on their feet, sneaking toward the cemetery in a stealthy crouch. I scrambled to my feet and followed.

They must have made a plan for catching Silverheels before I arrived, because without a word they separated, Willie going farther downstream. Frank waited a few minutes, then began moving up the short bank toward the level ground where the break in the picket fence allowed for easy entry into the graveyard. I followed behind Frank, trying to stay low and move quietly but craning my neck to look for whatever had made the noise.

Frank spotted her first. I knew he had because he abruptly stopped, and I bumped into him. Every muscle in his body felt rigid. I followed his gaze, and I went rigid too. A tall dark figure stood among the graves at the back of the plot, framed in a beam of moonlight that filtered through the trees. She wore a long black dress. A black shawl was draped over her head, obscuring any view of her hair or face. She stood there for only a brief moment before stepping again into the shadow, but it was enough to set my heart hammering harder than it ever had before. Silverheels! At last!

Frank grasped my hand and pulled me forward. Seemingly unaware of us, the dark figure walked among the graves at the back of the cemetery. Gradually, we crept closer. I was sure the pounding of my heart would alert her at any moment. Frank's hand was growing sweaty in mine. He was as nervous as I was.

We were still crouching low and moving forward stealthily, no more than twenty feet from her now. We could easily make out her shape, even in the shadows. I could hear the rustle of dry leaves under her skirt as she moved, so I knew she could not be a ghost. Then Frank stepped on a twig and it snapped. The Veiled Lady stiffened and turned her head in our direction.

"Now!" Frank shouted. He let go of my hand and leapt up.

The woman in black turned, gathered her skirts up, and ran. Frank was after her in a second.

"Wait! Stop! We just want to talk to you!" I yelled, but she kept on. I couldn't help but notice that she did not wear fine ladies' shoes, but sturdy boots. She was not nearly as small or delicate as I had expected either, but then many years had passed to change her figure.

She was making for the back of the graveyard where the fence had fallen down. She was nearly there when another figure stepped from behind a tree beyond the break, cutting off her retreat. He shouted, and I realized it was Willie! They had set up a trap, and now we had her!

The Veiled Lady hesitated for a brief moment, then veered to the right and took a running leap at a higher portion of the fence. She cleared it, and I thought she would escape, but the hem of her skirt caught on one of the slats. She seemed suspended in the air for a long moment, then she came crashing down in a heap of black fabric and collapsed fence pickets. She landed in a position nearly as unfeminine as the string of obscenities that spewed from her mouth. The voice, too, was unfeminine. And familiar.

"Orv!" I said.

Laughter exploded from the forest a few yards away, and Harry and Tom emerged.

"Why, Silverheels!" said Harry, looking down at Orv, who was trying to untangle himself from the black blankets they had made into a dress. "You are just the picture of beauty and grace!" Then he doubled over with laughter again, slapping his knee.

I wasn't laughing. I felt much too foolish for having been taken in by their trick, so I was surprised when Frank began to laugh too.

"Those miners must have been pretty hard up if you were the prettiest thing they had to dance with," he said, and he offered Orv a hand up. "You okay?"

Orv had gone down hard and his lip was swelling, but he didn't seem to mind. It was worth it, he said, to have seen the looks on our faces when we thought we'd been sneaking up on the real Silverheels.

"You kids are sharper than we expected though, I'll give you that," he said, clapping an arm around Willie's shoulder. "I'd have made a clean getaway if you hadn't have been there."

Together, we all started back toward the campfire. By the time we got there, we were all laughing. Russell still sat by the fire waiting for us. I wondered if he had been in on the whole thing too. I suppose he had. That's why he hadn't made Frank and Willie pack up and head back to town yet. Even though I knew the old-timers would give me a hard time about this for weeks, I was glad they had given Frank one more adventure to go home with. I wanted him to fondly remember his time here. And despite George's invitation to the picnic, I wanted Frank to remember me fondly as well.

CHAPTER 15

We rode back to town by moonlight, Frank behind Russell and me behind Willie on our two horses. At the edge of town Willie and Russell took my borrowed mare back to the livery. Frank and I walked on ahead, since we figured Annie wasn't going to relax until Frank got back.

"Pearl," Frank said suddenly as we neared the hotel, "if I gave you my address, would you write to me? Tell me everything that happens here?"

"Oh, yes!" I cried. Not that enough ever happened in Como to fill a letter, but it meant I wasn't saying good-bye for good. It meant he didn't want to say good-bye either.

"And look for Silverheels in the graveyard again—only next time, don't tell the old-timers beforehand."

We both laughed. Frank could have said good-bye then and gone in, and I suppose he should have, given how worried his sister was, but instead we stood shuffling our feet, not wanting to part. I'd only known him for three days, but being with him felt comfortable, like an old friend.

"Promise you'll write back?" I said.

"I promise," Frank said. "Wait here a minute." He turned and ran into the hotel lobby, leaving me alone in the street. I glanced around. Next door at the café, I could see my mother sitting alone at a table by the window, reading a paper. She was waiting up for Willie and me. I looked back at the hotel, anxious now for Frank to return. I waited for a full five minutes before he reappeared, and when he did, I knew something was wrong. He was no longer laughing as he hurried down the porch steps and into the street. When he reached me he stuffed a crumpled piece of hotel stationery into my hand.

"You should go home now, Pearl," he said, his voice anxious.

"What's the matter?"

Before Frank could answer me, the pool of light from the hotel doorway dimmed and I looked up to see Robert. He staggered forward to the front edge of the porch and bellowed Frank's name. The sour smell of whiskey reached me even at this distance, and I took an involuntary step back.

Frank stepped in front of me and turned to face him. "I'm coming," he said. "Go on back inside."

Despite his words, Frank stayed where he was. Robert lurched down the steps toward us and I took another step back. Frank did the same.

"Oh no you don't!" Robert growled. "You're not running away from me again. You've caused me enough trouble already, you little brat."

"You're drunk, Robert. You should go to bed," Frank said, his voice trembling a little.

Robert was still staggering toward us. I took another step back, grabbing Frank's shirt to pull him along with me. If we bolted for the café we might make it inside and lock the door before Robert could reach us. If only my father wasn't away on the mountain!

Before I could act, Robert lunged for Frank. Frank tried to dodge him, but I was right behind him. He bumped into me and I sat down with a thud in the street. Robert caught a fist-ful of Frank's shirt and started shaking him so hard his head snapped back and forth.

"You've caused us a lot of trouble today," he growled.

Then there was a sharp *crack!* as a wooden spoon came down hard on Robert's knuckles. With a curse he let go of Frank. Out of nowhere my mother was between Robert and Frank, pointing the wooden spoon at Robert as if it were a deadly weapon.

"Take your hands off him," she said in a low, steady voice that sounded every bit as dangerous as Robert's drunken growl had.

Frank staggered back beside me. I scrambled to my feet, scared of what Robert would do to my mother.

"Stay out of this, lady!" Robert growled. He moved to step around my mother, but she countered him and jabbed the spoon at him again. He stepped back.

"You'll not be laying a finger on this child again, so you may as well go off to bed. He'll be sleeping at my place tonight. I'll have him ready to be on the train in time tomorrow morning," my mother said.

Out of the darkness, Russell and Willie ran to us. They stopped a few feet away. The mean glare faded a little from Robert's eyes as they flicked from my mother to Frank and then to Russell and Willie. Then he staggered two steps backward toward the hotel. He gave us all one more look, spit in the street, and weaved his way back to the doorway.

Mother turned to Russell. "Thank goodness you came along when you did."

"I think you had everything well in hand. You and Josie," he said with a nod toward the newspaper office. Josie stood in the shadows, shotgun in hand.

"What about Annie?" Frank said. "I can't leave Annie with Robert when he's like that." He took a step toward the hotel, but Russell held him back.

"I'll get her," Josie said. "I'm not leaving a woman in that man's clutches." She cocked the shotgun and walked toward the hotel, back stiff.

"You all get into the café and lock the door," Russell said. "I'll go with Josie."

"I don't need your protection, Russell McDonald!" Josie said.

"Are you kidding? I'm going to try to keep Robert alive," Russell said, falling into step beside her.

Mother herded Frank, Willie, and me into the café and

upstairs and told us to get ready for bed, but we crowded into Willie's room instead. His window looked out over the street in front of the hotel, and we didn't want to miss a thing. Nothing this exciting ever happened in Como.

"How long do you suppose Josie was there with that gun?" Willie asked.

"She must have heard Robert shout, same time as Mother," I said. "No wonder he backed down so quickly."

"I don't know that Robert saw her either," Frank said. He gave a nervous little laugh. "He didn't have to. I never saw anyone be so threatening with just a spoon."

"It's like what Russell said about momma bears," Willie said.

We waited in silence after that, watching the street through the window. In the darkness, Frank's hand found mine and clutched it. I squeezed it back to tell him his sister would be safe, since it was all I could do for him.

At last, Russell, Josie, and Annie came out through the hotel door, Russell's arm reassuringly around Annie's shoulder. Josie walked a few feet behind them, her shotgun resting across her crooked arm. Instantly Frank's hand was out of mine and he was running downstairs. Willie and I followed.

Russell took his arm from Annie's shoulder as she came through the door and hurried toward Frank. Her face was pale and she looked as if she might swoon. Frank put a supportive arm around her and guided her into a chair. She burst into tears. If Frank had been a little older and not her brother, it would have been a scene straight out of one of my books.

"I'm sorry, Frank. This is all my fault. I shouldn't have left you here," Annie said, sniffling into Russell's hanky.

"Shh. Annie, don't cry." Frank said, his arm still tight around her shoulder. She dabbed at her eyes, then looked at my mother.

"I'm so sorry about Robert, Mrs. Barnell. I'm sorry he behaved so badly. He's just . . . With the war . . . And me so worried . . ."

"No need to apologize," Mother said.

"He's not really like that, you know. I've never seen him drink so much before."

My mother nodded but gave no further comment.

"He's not!" Annie insisted. "He's kind and funny, and such a good dancer!"

She paused as if she were only just hearing what she had said, then her hands went to her cheeks in alarm. "Oh, Frank, what have I done! I married a man I barely know, didn't I. But he was going off to war, and it was all so romantic!"

Tears rolled down her cheeks. Frank pulled her head gently to his shoulder. "Don't worry, Annie. I'm sure when we get home you can explain to Mother and Father it was a mistake, and—"

Annie lifted her head, straightened her shoulders, and dried her eyes. "No. I married him, I have a responsibility. A duty to him and to my country."

"But he's dangerous, Annie!" Frank said.

She shook her head. "He hasn't hurt me. He hasn't hurt anyone."

"But—"

"He's going to war. I married him so he wouldn't have to face that alone. I made a promise and I intend to abide by it. He won't drink when we get home."

"Can you be sure of that?" Frank asked.

"I can hope," Annie said. "Because I do love him. I love the man he was before we married, and if I keep loving him I believe he will be that man again. I suppose you think I'm a romantic fool, but that's how I feel."

A crease formed between my mother's eyes. "Well, they say love conquers all."

"If he ever lays a finger on you, Annie—ever—promise you'll tell me," Frank said. His hands were balled up so tight his knuckles were white.

"What about tonight—do you think we'll be safe?" I asked. "He knows where we are. And without Father here—"

"I'll stay, if you like," Russell said.

"Thank you, but I don't think that will be necessary," Mother said. She nodded toward the window and we looked out. In the shadow of the newspaper office, there was a glint of moonlight off of gun metal. "It's like I always tell you, Pearl. Neighbors do for neighbors."

"Do you think she would have shot him if he'd tried to hurt us?" I asked.

"I'm just glad we didn't have to find that out. Now off to

bed all of you, and don't worry. We'll be safe."

I climbed the stairs, ready to put the long day behind me, but I couldn't get to sleep. I crept to the window again and looked out. Josie was still out there, keeping a silent vigil. I was more confused about her than ever. She'd been the last of our neighbors I had expected to come to our rescue. I felt a small twinge of guilt that I had so often wished her away from the café, but I knew I'd continue with the wager anyway. I wanted to know the truth, and to tell Frank when I found it. I wanted to win, too, and not just for the sake of Silverheels's reputation, but for my own. I knew that Josie would think less of me if I gave up, and I realized, surprising as it was, that that would be the biggest defeat of all.

CHAPTER 16

The next morning, we said good-bye to Frank on the platform. Annie had already gotten Robert aboard and I could see him through the window, his head flopped back and his mouth open in a snore. Frank was distracted, worrying about Annie as he was, so our parting was brief. With a reminder to write, I gave him my address. It was just "General Delivery, Como, Colorado," but I wrote it out for him anyway.

"Don't forget to write me, too," he said. He gave my hand a quick squeeze before he stepped up into the train. He waved through the window as the train pulled out. I waved back, and I kept waving until the train was nearly out of sight.

When it was finally gone, I turned back, only to see George leaning against the depot, watching me and looking a little hurt. Guilt swept over me.

"That was Willie's new friend, headed back to Denver. They went camping yesterday," I said quickly. "I suppose that's the last we'll ever see of him."

"Would you be sorry if it was?" George asked.

I hesitated, then forced myself to shrug as if I didn't care. "He was a nice enough kid, and he paid well for a tour of Buckskin Joe," I said.

"Would you prefer him taking you to the Fourth of July picnic, instead of me?" George asked, frowning.

I hurried to his side and wrapped my arm through his. "Of course not, George. I barely know him. He's a tourist, that's all. I want to go to the picnic with you."

"I just thought if we were going together, you'd have more time for me, that's all," George said. "I came by the café after supper to see you last night, and you'd gone off with him again."

"I'm sorry. If I'd known you were coming to the café, I wouldn't have gone," I said, wondering even as I said it whether or not it was true. He looked skeptical, so I added, "I'd rather spend time with you, George."

He gave me just a hint of a smile, like the sun gleaming around the edge of a cloud. "I'd like that, Pearl. But I have to be able to trust you. You spend all that time with that city boy, and now I hear your mother's invited Josie to campaign in the café every day at lunch, too."

"She was just trying to help Mr. Orenbach," I said.

"A German?"

"He's a neighbor. You know he's been here for years, and he's never done one bad thing to anyone."

"My mother says that's the way the enemy works. They gain your trust and then they use it to spy for the kaiser."

"Why would the kaiser want to spy on Como?" The idea was ridiculous.

George patted my cheek. "You're so sweet, Pearl. You see the good in everyone. It's just that sometimes, it's easy for an innocent girl like you to be fooled. That's why I want to look after you."

I smiled back, relieved that he had forgiven me for seeing off Frank's train. We began walking away from the depot, and I tried to assure myself that his concerns were romantic. I'd always dreamed of a man who would want to protect me and take care of me. It should all feel perfect, shouldn't it? He wanted to be with me, and thought I was sweet, and that made me the luckiest girl in Park County.

"What would you like for your picnic?" I asked. "Fried chicken, maybe? Or cold sliced ham, if it's a hot day? What is your favorite?"

"You are, Pearl."

I blushed, despite myself. He smiled as the blood filled my cheeks, the full beam this time. The smile that made it hard for me to think.

"Surprise me," he said. "I'm sure I'll like anything you cook." He stopped walking, and turned to face me.

"I have to go, Pearl. I have to help my father in the store today. But I'll be thinking about you. See you later, okay?" He smiled and gave both my hands a warm squeeze right there in the middle of the street, where everyone could see. I hoped they were all looking.

I watched him go, caressing the warm spot where his lips had touched my skin. He was so handsome, I didn't deserve him, but here he was, walking with me and kissing my cheek.

Back in the café, the breakfast crowd had all gone and mother was hard at work in the kitchen. She was lifting one batch of golden-brown pies out of the oven and putting another batch in. The sweet tang of rhubarb filled the air. Mother smiled when she saw me.

"Frank got off without a hitch?" she asked.

"Yes, ma'am. He seemed to think Robert would sleep most of the way to Denver."

"I should imagine," Mother said, her mouth tightening at the corners at the mention of Robert.

"You've made extra pies," I noted.

"Yes. Mrs. Larson brought me fresh rhubarb from her farm, but not everyone likes rhubarb, so I'm making apple, too. Next week, Mrs. Larsen said she'd bring us fresh strawberries."

She knew my favorite was fresh strawberry, with thick whipped cream on the top.

"Let's just hope the sugar supply holds out through cherry season. There's talk of rationing, you know, for the war effort. I can sweeten cakes and sweet rolls with raisins, but I need sugar for a good pie."

I nodded. I couldn't imagine this town without my mother's pies. Half of the business and most of the gossip in Como took place over pie and coffee in the Silverheels Café.

I was still thinking about it when Mother placed a warm apple pie in a basket and set it in front of me. "I want you to take this to Mrs. Gilbert to thank her for her help last night. Oh, wait."

She cut a wedge of cheddar cheese off the big ring on the counter and tucked it into the corner of the basket. I looked at the whole thing with apprehension. George had already heard about Mother letting Josie campaign here—what if he caught me going to or coming from her house again? How would I explain the gift of a whole apple pie and still maintain that my mother and I wanted nothing to do with Josie?

"Maybe we should let the pie cool a little longer before we take it over," I suggested. Maybe we could wait until Josie came in at lunchtime and we could let everyone think she had just bought the pie.

"Nonsense, Pearl. An apple pie is best when it is fresh out of the oven. I sent one home with Russell this morning, but Mrs. Gilbert didn't come in, so I want you to take this one to her while it's still warm."

I sighed. There was no way around it. I took the basket and slipped out the back door. I made my way around the back as best as I could, avoiding Main Street where the whole town could see me.

Josie answered her door in her usual grubby miner's overalls and a heavy leather apron. Her fingertips were black with ink. She looked neither surprised nor pleased to see me. She just gave a little grunt, as if that were a sufficient greeting, and turned back into the room. I followed, but was only one step past her doormat when she barked, "Shoes!"

Glancing down at her own feet, I saw she wore only thick wool socks, her rolling gait more awkward than ever. I found myself staring. One of her feet was noticeably shorter than the other, and the end of the sock, where her toes should have been, flopped loose and empty. No wonder she walked the way she did—the toes on her left foot were missing!

"Stop gawking and get over here!" she barked again, even sharper than before.

"My mother sent you an apple pie to thank you for your help last night," I said as I unlaced my shoes. "It's still warm."

"I don't have time for pie, girl. Set it on the table and get over here."

I took the basket to the table and lifted the pie out, so the crust wouldn't get soggy. There wasn't much room for it on the table. Josie had stacks of newspapers there—the *Rocky Mountain News* and *Denver Post*, but more than that—the *New York Times*, *Washington Post*, and *Chicago Tribune*. I had never seen newspapers from big cities before. They were twice as thick as any paper I'd ever seen, and I wondered how so much could be happening that they could fill papers that size. I wanted to open one, read it, and look at the ads for the fashionable city clothes, but before I could ask, Josie barked at me again.

"I haven't got all day, girl. What's keeping you?"

"I only came to deliver the pie for my mother," I said, edging back toward the door.

"You already said that. Now stop lollygagging and give me a hand."

I crossed the room and entered the area behind the rail, where the printing press stood. "A hand with what?" I asked.

"Stand there," she said, positioning me on the opposite side of the press from her. She snatched a piece of white paper off a stack and deftly inserted it into a binder that hinged down over the inky plate of metal type that would produce the printed page. In the brief moment it was visible I could not read the plate, as all the letters and words were backward. Once she had the paper in place, she pointed.

"Pull that lever," she said.

I did, and the platform holding the paper and plate slid smoothly forward until it was directly beneath a massive steel slab in the machine's center.

"Now pull that one there," she said, pointing upward to another lever above my head. "Good and hard."

I pulled the arm downward, and a series of gears turned. The heavy metal slab clamped down, pressing the paper into the typeset plate.

"Good. Now release it and pull it out," she said, pointing back at the first lever. I reversed my actions. The press opened and the papers slid out. Quick as a wink, Josie had the printed sheet out, a new sheet in, and had me pulling the levers again.

While I did, she lay a sheet of blotting paper over the freshly printed page, rolled them up, and slid the roll into one of the many little cubicles on the wall. Even as she stowed it, she was reaching for a new sheet.

It was fascinating to see the blank pages going in and the printed ones coming out, and the rhythm of Josie's movements that kept the process from coming to a standstill. She commanded me to pull the levers again, and I tried to match her rhythms.

"Frank left on the train this morning," I said, once I felt it was going smoothly and getting a little dull.

"Hush, girl. Keep your mind on your work."

I thought of telling her this wasn't my work, it was hers, but instead I did as I was told. The next sheet of paper went in faster, and the next faster still. We had settled into a rhythm, our movements slotting in against each other, like all the other parts of the machine.

We continued until the stack of papers was gone and all the pigeonholes on the wall were filled with rolled papers.

"Well," she said as she rolled the last page and slid it into the last little space on the wall, "that should hold me through the lunch rush."

I let go of the lever as if it was a hot coal. How could I have been so stupid? I had been so fascinated by the machine, I hadn't thought about what we were printing. "These are your handbills?" I said.

Josie smiled with that look that said she'd been waiting for this moment. "What else would I be printing? And since you helped me so willingly, I assume that means I've won our little wager and you've finally seen the light?" She walked past me, ignoring my angry sputtering, leaving me alone by the machine. She cleared the stacked newspapers off the table and put the kettle on the stove top.

"Tea and pie?" she asked.

"You haven't won," I said, hurrying after her.

She went on about her business, putting tea leaves in a pot, setting two mugs on the table, getting out forks and plates for the pie.

"The real work of curing those miners was done by Mrs. Weldon and her daughter," she said.

"Who?" For one horrible moment, I thought she had found some kind of new proof, but she pointed at my apron pocket where I had put the list of names from the graves after our last conversation.

"Wasn't that the name? Elijah Weldon, and his Indian wife? What's a good Indian name?"

I thought for a moment. Indian women in my penny dreadfuls were always named after pretty flowers or gentle animals. "Prairie Rose?" I suggested.

"Okay. Prairie Rose Weldon and her daughter." She paused and thought. "Sefa." Josie paused again to pour the boiling water into the teapot.

I didn't know what she meant to accomplish, making up these characters, but I was curious. "And how do you propose Prairie Rose and Sefa did that?" I asked.

"I figure Eli Weldon stuck around for the same reason most of the other men did, to protect his claim. Leaving a claim unwatched or unworked for even a few days was inviting claim jumpers. With news of the sickness, claim jumpers were no doubt circling like vultures. If a man didn't show up to work his sluice in the morning, it would have been taken over by lunchtime."

"But they would have to give it back once the owner got better and came back to it, right?"

"Possession, as they say, is nine-tenths of the law, girl. And the other tenth, a sheriff or district court, didn't come to Buckskin Joe till much later. The only way to get a claim back was to shoot the claim jumper, provided he didn't manage to shoot you first. So to men like Eli Weldon, the only reason to risk smallpox was to protect a claim that was producing or to steal one from the dead or dying. It was a dangerous gamble. Every man on that list of yours is one who took it and lost.

"There were a few who contracted smallpox at the very beginning who never had a chance to flee, but there are too many men on that list for it to simply be ignorance. Some of them must have figured they could cheat death. They stocked up on elixirs from snake-oil salesmen and thought they'd be protected.

"Now Eli Weldon had been a fur trapper, a mountain man, and a gambler all his life. He was a natural born risk taker, but he wasn't a fool. Fools didn't survive in the mountains, and he'd been there for years. What's more, he'd sired two or three strapping young sons with the Pawnee wife he'd won in that card game years ago. And having a woman of his own and a few little boys had domesticated him. He liked the comfort of civilization, and he'd decided to strike it rich, build a mansion in Denver for his family, and retire to a life of luxury like a proper gentleman.

"He couldn't do that if someone got at his claim, though, so he sent his wife and sons to safety and kept his stepdaughter with him to administer the herbal cures of Prairie Rose, should he get sick. And little Sefa was a good obedient child who did as she was told without a thought for herself. She was tearful as she said good-bye to her mother and brothers, the only people in the world who loved her."

"Why didn't she go with them? I mean, if Prairie Rose loved her, she would have insisted that Sefa go with her to safety too."

"Because wives must do as their husbands demand," Josie said.

"Sefa could have run away," I said.

"Sefa was a good obedient child that did as she was told. Just like you."

I shook my head. "I don't believe even a stepfather would have been that cruel, and if it meant risking her own life, I don't believe the girl would have stayed," I said. "Why would she?"

"Why will Frank's fool sister stay with that no-good Robert?" Josie countered.

I frowned. I wanted to say that was different, but I knew Josie would demand to know how it was different, and I didn't have an answer.

"Maybe you're right. Maybe Sefa needed another reason to stay." She thought a moment, then snapped her fingers. "I know—she, too, had fallen victim to the handsome, swaggering Buck Wilson. She harbored a secret love for him, like every other woman in town. And Buck, never one to leave a woman uncharmed, gave her just enough encouragement for her silly, romantic imagination to carry her away. So she stayed to be near him, maybe even to save his life with her mother's cures when the smallpox hit."

"But she didn't save him. No one did. He's in the graveyard," I said.

"Best laid plans, Pearl. That graveyard is full of their failures. Sefa Weldon stayed to save her beloved and her stepfather, but when both were lost, she turned her attention to the rest of the camp to save who she could. Silverheels probably never cured a single man. She just took the credit for it."

"Then why would she have stayed?"

Josie gave a little laugh. "Remember those claim jumpers, circling like vultures?"

"That's ridiculous! How could a dancer have been a claim jumper?"

"She was a *beloved* dancer, Pearl. Who better for a dying

miner to give his gold to? Who better to ask to send his money off to his family? She didn't need to set finger on a shovel. She just smiled and batted her lashes, and raked in the gold. But she had competition in Buck. Not that any of the miners fell in love with him, but they trusted him, thought he was an honest, upstanding man. He'd generously helped more than one of them whenever they needed it, so he knew where everyone's strikes were, and what was producing. All he had to do was wait.

"I wonder if Silverheels and Wilson were working together or against each other. Perhaps you are right and they were sweethearts. Perhaps they joined forces, though it's hard to imagine two such slippery and greedy grifters having a true partnership. More likely, they were competing. Maybe they even had a wager, as you and I do, to see who could take the most. Buck Wilson probably thought he had an edge over the dancer, because he had that cow-eyed Indian girl in love with him, ready to protect him with her medicines. All he had to do was smile at Sefa and she would do anything he asked."

"No," I said. "Buck and Silverheels were in love. True love. He wouldn't have led Sefa on, not even for life-saving medicine. Maybe that's why he died. He gave the medicine meant for him to Silverheels to keep her safe. He sacrificed his life to save her."

"I'll grant there was probably a mutual attraction between Buck and Silverheels. To someone like Buck, Silverheels would have been the ultimate conquest. There's no victory sweeter to a con man than to con another con. No doubt she saw the same in him.

"That's why they both stayed. To get the gold before the other could. To outdo each other, maybe even to win each other. If you want to call that true love, Pearl, be my guest."

I shook my head. Josie's story was full of flaws. If Sefa Weldon had had the cure, why did both Eli and Buck die? And where would Prairie Rose Weldon have gotten the cure to give it to her daughter in the winter, when there were no plants to be gathered? And I had learned in school that Indian tribes had been destroyed by smallpox epidemics. Indians had no resistance to it and died by the hundreds, so how could Prairie Rose have had a cure for it from the plants of the forest? I was getting ready to drill Josie with these questions, when I heard a train whistle far off across the park.

The lunch train! I'd lost track of the time with Josie, leaving my mother alone to prepare at the café, and the lunch train was approaching. I jumped up from my seat.

"I have to go. Thank you for the tea and pie," I said, and I hurried to the door. I pulled on my shoes and ran back to the café, expecting my mother to be cross with me for being gone so long. But when I told her where I had been, she smiled.

"That was very neighborly, Pearl. I think Mrs. Gilbert is a very lonely woman, but too proud to admit it. You've done a very kind thing."

That was all the time we had for conversation before the train rolled in and the rush began.

Mother was right, I had been neighborly. And to my surprise, I had even enjoyed talking to Josie, even though I was sure she was wrong. I liked the challenge of trying to outwit her in the storytelling, even if it was all made up. Eventually, I would find the solid proof to prove her wrong. At the very least, I knew someone in Park County knew Buck's true character, since someone was still cleaning up his grave. And if that someone was Silverheels herself, I could prove it all.

In the meantime, I would let Josie tell her story and make up her characters like Prairie Rose and Sefa Weldon. I could tell she wanted me to see myself in the girl. Sefa was well-mannered and obedient, and was sweet on a handsome fella with a glamorous smile. All things that Josie had criticized in me. I didn't care. The more she made up to make Silverheels and Buck look bad, the more she would be proven wrong when I found the truth.

I smiled to myself at the thought. I had never gotten much pleasure out of an argument before. Then again, I had hardly ever argued with anyone before. Not sweet, well-mannered, obedient me. Is this the way Josie felt when she was arguing for her cause? A little shiver went through me at the thought that I was turning into Josie, just a little bit, but to my surprise, it wasn't an unpleasant realization. I was going to enjoy the shock on Josie's face when I defeated her. When she discovered that I was not the obedient ninny she thought I was, after all.

CHAPTER 17

When we had cleaned up the lunch mess, Mother announced that she was going to the butcher shop. I was surprised. The Schmidts usually delivered our meat.

"Don't we already have pork chops and chicken?"

"I just feel like doing something different. And I want to have a word with Mrs. Schmidt about the picnic," Mother said, taking off her apron and tidying her hair.

I didn't like the sound of that, and I certainly didn't want any part of it. I wanted to do things that would please George, not upset him. Fortunately, Mother was still pleased with me for being neighborly with Josie that morning, so she didn't insist. Instead, she asked me to go to the post office to pick up our mail.

This was a task I was happy to do. The post office was in the back corner of Crawford's Mercantile, so I might run into George while I was there. Plus, this was my chance to continue my search for someone who knew Buck Wilson. If anyone named Wilson had ever lived in or around Como, the postmistress, Mrs. Abernathy would know and would be happy to tell me about them. Knowing everyone's name and address was her job; knowing their business, and sharing it, was her favorite pastime.

The store was a long narrow building, with a counter and shelves lining one wall and the post office in a small booth in the opposite back corner. The floor in between was filled with various shelves, barrels, crates, and racks of goods. Mr. Crawford was behind the counter, stacking cans of beans on the shelf. Mrs. Crawford was near the door, talking to Mrs. Johnson. She gave me a suspicious look and stopped talking when I entered. I gave her a polite smile and walked to the back corner. Once I was past them, Mrs. Crawford resumed her conversation in a whisper, so I knew they were gossiping.

"Good afternoon, Pearl," said Mrs. Abernathy cheerfully, handing me our mail—a single bill and a copy of the *Fairplay Flume*, the weekly paper that carried all the local news.

I thanked her, then posed my question. "Mrs. Abernathy, I was up at Buckskin Joe a few days back—"

"With that handsome city fella. I know." She winked and smiled at me. Mrs. Abernathy was an older lady whose children were all grown up, and when she winked, the wrinkles of her face bunched up until it looked like she had no eyes at all.

"Yes, with Frank," I said, relieved that George wasn't within hearing. "And when we went over to the cemetery, we saw that the grave of a Buck Wilson had been tended recently."

"So now you're wondering if Silverheels receives her mail here?"

"Actually, I was wondering if you know any Wilsons around here. Any friends or relatives who might go up there and tend the grave."

She shook her head. "No Wilsons get their mail here. There's a Wilson family over in Leadville, or used to be. Then again, Wilson is a pretty common name."

I nodded and thanked her, trying to keep the disappointment out of my voice, but not quite managing it. I turned to leave.

"Wait a minute," Mrs. Abernathy said.

I turned back.

She tapped her chin. "It just occurred to me. Mrs. Engel's maiden name was Wilson. And she's been in Park County a good long while."

"Thank you, Mrs. Abernathy," I said. A new lead, and one I could follow up on! Mrs. Engel's millinery shop was just across the street. I turned, meaning to go directly there, when George came through the front door.

"Hello, Pearl. Where are you headed?" he asked.

Funny, but now that he was here, I couldn't quite recall. In fact, I didn't want to go anywhere at all.

"Nowhere, really," I said.

"Do you have to get back to work?"

"No, I have the afternoon off." I gave him a little smile and hoped he would take it as an invitation for an invitation.

"Well, then maybe we could go for a walk along the creek," he suggested.

"I'd like that. Very much." I couldn't think of anything more romantic than a walk along the creek. Maybe my first kiss wouldn't be at the kissing booth after all. Maybe it would be a perfect, romantic kiss, amid wildflowers and sunshine and twittering birds. Maybe it would be today.

George held the door for me and we stepped out of the store. Just outside, he slipped his arm around my waist. I liked the feel of it there, strong and protective. I liked being out on the street, too, where everyone could see handsome George Crawford claiming me as his own.

The moment was ruined a few seconds later when I looked up and saw Josie Gilbert stumping up the street toward us, a scowl on her face. George saw her too, and the arm around my waist tightened. Her eyes were on the ground in front of her, and for a moment, I hoped she might not see us and we could just go the other direction. My hope was shattered when George spoke, plenty loud enough for Josie to hear.

"Well, look who's here. The kaiser's handmaiden."

Shocked by his words, I pulled away, but his hand at my side held me firm. I looked up at his face. His beautiful smile had slipped into a sneer as he looked at Josie.

Josie didn't acknowledge his words, not exactly. She looked up at him, then at me, and her eyebrows raised.

"Come on, George. Let's just go for that walk," I said.

"What's your rush, Pearl?" George said. We were still standing in front of the mercantile's front door, and now Josie had come to a stop right in front of us.

"Get out of the way, boy. I need to get my mail," Josie said.

"You might want to get a newspaper, too," George replied, not moving. "There's an interesting piece about those National Women's Party friends of yours. Arrested and sent to jail. And it's about time."

Josie pushed past him and through the front door without a response.

"Come on, George, let's just go, before she comes back out," I said again.

"You have to stand up to seditionists, Pearl. My mother says true patriots have to fight the war here at home, too."

"I thought we were taking a walk," I said.

"You think taking a walk is more important than protecting our country?"

"Of course not! But arguing with Josie—"

"You're not defending her, are you?"

"No! George, I—"

"Then prove it," he said. "Here she comes."

I looked through the doorway into the store. It had been open the whole time. Josie—and everyone else inside—had heard our whole conversation. The blood rushed to my face as Josie raised her eyes to mine. Her gaze was filled with as much challenge as George's voice had been.

"I— I—" I couldn't think of a thing to say. Instead I jerked out of George's grasp and backed three steps out into the street. "I just remembered. I have to help my mother," I said. I spun around and ran for the café.

I didn't look back when I got home. I rushed inside and straight up to my bedroom, where I threw myself onto the bed and burst into tears. I had been on the verge of the best moment of my life; why did Josie Gilbert have to come along just then? Now George might never kiss me. He might even decide he didn't want to go to the picnic with me!

I stayed in my hot, stuffy bedroom all afternoon, until my mother called me down to help serve supper. I felt miserable, but I tried to smile and be polite to the customers. I was relieved that neither Josie nor the Crawfords came in. I wasn't sure how I was going to face any of them, and I was in no hurry to find out.

After supper, Mr. and Mrs. Engel arrived in the café. Mrs. Engel was showing off the hat that she was donating to be raffled at the picnic. It was a broad-brimmed summer hat, festooned with a navy-blue ribbon embroidered with white stars. Two enormous blue ostrich plumes swept from the front along either side of the crown in a glorious arc. It was so lovely that all the ladies in the café that evening bought raffle tickets at once.

When the fuss over the hat settled down, Mr. and Mrs. Engel chose a table and ordered coffee and pie. I was cutting the pie for them when I remembered what the postmistress had told me that afternoon.

So, when I delivered the pie, I asked, "Mrs. Engel, when I was up at Buckskin Joe earlier this week, I saw that someone had tended the grave of a fellow named Buck Wilson. Would you know anything about that?"

She gave me a puzzled look. "Why would I know anything about that?"

"Mrs. Abernathy at the post office said your maiden name was Wilson. I thought he might have been a relative of yours."

"Mrs. Abernathy's memory isn't what it used to be. My maiden name was Wilkins, not Wilson," Mrs. Engel said.

I suppressed a sigh of frustration. Another dead end. "You have been in Park County a long time, right? Do you know any Wilsons, or someone who might be keeping up that grave?"

"Let's see. Old Tom Lee knew all about that sort of thing. He even claimed to have known Silverheels."

"He knew her?"

"So he claimed, but he moved down to Denver." She thought for another minute, then snapped her fingers. "Mae Nelson, down in Fairplay! She grew up in Buckskin Joe. You should talk to her."

"Yes, ma'am. Thank you," I said. Excitement was building inside me as I returned the coffeepot to the stove. At last— someone who remembered Silverheels herself!

Tom Lee was in Denver—and so was Frank! Surely Frank would be willing to find him and talk to him.

I was impatient after that to finish my evening's work. When I had, I composed two letters. The first was a short note to Mrs. Nelson in Fairplay to thank her for helping Frank and me and to ask her if she had thought of any-one else who still cared for the graves in the Buckskin Joe cemetery. Perhaps with a little prompting she would think of something she hadn't told us and would write me back.

The second letter was the more important one, and I wasted two sheets of paper before I thought of just how I wanted to word it. After all, this letter was to Frank. I didn't want to sound like an ignorant hayseed, but I didn't want it to be too formal, either. I wanted him to feel a tender friendship for me as he read it, but it was hard to know exactly what words would make him feel that way. Especially since I was really writing to ask him to do me a favor. I was writing to ask him to find Mr. Tom Lee, the man who had moved to Denver. The man who remembered Silverheels. The man who was my best hope to prove Silverheels a hero, once and for all!

CHAPTER 18

Josie did not come into the café the next morning. I was glad. I knew I had to face her again eventually, and when I did, I would have to apologize, but I was in no hurry. First, I would apologize to George. Maybe see if he wanted to take that walk today. Praying he wouldn't tell me he was going to the picnic with someone else, I headed to the mercantile the first chance I got, with the excuse that I had to post my letters.

George was stocking shelves for his father when I entered. I smiled as I passed him on my way to the post office in the back corner. I slid the two letters across the counter to Mrs. Abernathy along with my four cents for the postage.

That done, I took a deep breath and walked directly to where George was working. He gave me his usual, knee-weakening smile.

"George, about yesterday," I began.

"It's okay, Pearl."

"It is?"

"Josie Gilbert scares a lot of people. But when you're with me, you don't have to be frightened, okay? I'll protect you."

"Thank you, George," I said, relieved but a little annoyed. I wasn't afraid of Josie!

George squeezed my hand. "I've got to help my father, but see you later, okay?"

I nodded and left the store, grinning. George was still mine! He even wanted to protect me, which, I reminded myself, was very romantic, even if I didn't need protecting from Josie Gilbert.

I was almost back to the café when Imogene burst out of its front door, skipped into the street, and, flinging her arms wide, twirled around like a little girl.

"What's gotten into you?" I asked.

She skipped over and threw her arms around me in a huge embrace. "He asked me," she said. "He asked me to the picnic!"

"Willie?" I couldn't believe it. I had never once seen him respond to Imogene's flirting or hinting.

"Of course Willie. Who else?"

"Congratulations, Imogene," I said as I recovered from my surprise. "Does this mean we won't be doing the kissing booth after all?"

Imogene giggled. "Of course we'll still do the kissing booth. That won't be until after we eat, anyway. And I'll give Willie a nickel and make sure he's first in line. You have a nickel for George, don't you?"

I smiled and nodded. I would be sure he had several.

Imogene, still floating on air, danced off toward the hotel. I watched her go, then floated in my own direction, into the café.

Mother was wiping down the tables, which was usually my job. I offered to take over from her, but she sent me to the kitchen to help Willie instead. I found him at the sink up to his elbows in suds. He glanced up at me as I came in, but said nothing and kept washing. He didn't look nearly as happy as Imogene had.

I took up a towel and began drying the stacks of plates and cups. When I had dried three or four items and he still hadn't spoken, I asked.

"Imogene says you asked her to the Fourth of July picnic."

Willie nodded. "Yep."

I dried two plates in silence.

"She sure is excited," I said.

Willie shrugged. "She's been angling for it for months."

"I didn't think you were going to ask her. You never seem a bit interested."

He chewed his lip and said nothing.

I gave him a hard look. "Willie, what's wrong?"

"Russell said he heard that a couple fellas in Fairplay have been drafted. And Raymond Buford and Oliver McPherson have both enlisted. Neither one of them is more than a year older than me."

"You're not thinking of enlisting, are you? You're only seventeen, and besides, we need you here."

He shook his head. "No, I can't enlist until I'm eighteen. Thank goodness." He glanced guiltily at me before he continued. "I don't ever want to go to war. I don't want to shoot the Huns and I don't want them shooting me, either. I ain't a coward, Pearl, but it makes a fella stop and think."

"What does this have to do with Imogene and the picnic?"

"I figure in these times, a fella's got to do all the living he can, because none of us know how long we've got. I want to try out everything. Just in case."

I didn't know what to say to that, so I held my tongue.

Willie washed the last few dishes and wiped the suds off his arms. "And don't you tell a soul I said any of this, Perline, or I'll give you a whupping. I won't have folks calling me a coward!"

"I won't. I swear!" I said, but he was already headed out the door. I saw him grab his fishing pole from where it leaned against the back wall. He'd disappear for the rest of the day. I couldn't blame him. I thought about Ray and Ollie going off to war. When I first started school, they had been the big boys at the back that gave the teacher headaches with their tomfoolery. I couldn't picture them with guns and bayonets. I couldn't believe, either, that the war had reached us here, in little, out-of-the-way Park County. Here we all were in our sleepy little town where nothing ever changed. Yet as I watched Willie walk away, I realized how very much this war changed everything.

CHAPTER 19

The week before the Fourth, the picnic was all anyone in town could talk about. All the ladies except Josie were baking, sewing, knitting, or making decorations for the fund-raiser. Someone had even taken out an advertisement in the *Fairplay Flume* to invite the whole county to our grand event.

Mrs. Crawford and Mrs. Sorensen met with Mother and together they approved the kissing booth, so long as Imogene and I only offered our cheeks and not our lips for kissing and bestowed kisses in the same manner. To decorate the kissing booth, Mrs. Sorensen gave us a sheet from the hotel's supply, and Mrs. Engel gave us some scraps of red felt. Imogene cut out hearts and cupids from the scraps, and we stitched them onto the sheet. Mother gave me a pickle jar to put the nickels in. We planned to curl our hair and wear our prettiest dresses, although I wasn't sure it would make a difference. Everyone at the picnic would have seen both of us a thousand times before, so looking fancy wasn't going to make much difference in whether or not they'd be willing to pay a nickel for a kiss.

As we worked, Imogene talked about who we might get to kiss and imagined that handsome strangers would appear out of nowhere. Listening to her made my stomach knot up. It was bad enough thinking about kissing the boys I knew from school. The thought of kissing strangers was too much.

"Imogene, I don't know if I can do this," I said.

"Don't be a scaredy-cat. We've got to see it through now. It's for the war effort. We've all got to do our part."

When we weren't working on the kissing booth, we were admiring the fine hat for the raffle, on display in the window of Mrs. Engel's millinery and yard-goods shop. All the ladies agreed it was the most elegant hat they had ever seen, and raffle tickets were selling at a brisk pace. Imogene herself had already bought ten tickets, and insisted she *had* to win it, since it matched her Sunday dress.

The day before the picnic, a filthy, bearded miner stepped into the café while we were eating our lunch. At first I didn't recognize him through the grime and the whiskers, but Mother leapt to her feet and rushed into his embrace at once. Father had come home for the big event!

We hugged and laughed and hugged again. Then he sat down and ate every single sandwich on the tray as he told us all about his work. Things were going well up at the Lucky Fork, and they expected to make good money when they brought their zinc ore down in the autumn. He figured he could stay on until August if we could spare him here in the café. Mother assured him we could. I agreed. I wanted my father to come home, but if mother was brave enough to be without him for the summer, I could be too.

After lunch he took a long bath, and by supper time he looked like my father once again, clean and shaved, his mustache neatly trimmed.

"I have to look respectable for the picnic tomorrow," he said. "I wouldn't want to embarrass my family."

I didn't want to either. But what if no one wanted to kiss me? Or what if fellas lined up to kiss me and I couldn't see it through? I'd never kissed anyone before except my parents. Did you kiss a boy the same way you kissed your parents, or was there something more to it? I figured if fellas paid a nickel, they would be expecting a good kiss. I should have thought to ask someone sooner, but I didn't know who to ask.

And then there was George. He'd be picking me up in the morning to take me to the picnic. That afternoon I had fried chicken and packed a basket for me and George. My dress was washed and ironed, but I still worried that I wasn't prepared. After supper, Mother washed my hair and rolled it up with rags so it would curl. I went to bed shortly after, but between my nervous stomach and the bumpy rag curls all over my head, I did not sleep well.

The morning of the Fourth dawned clear and bright. Mr. Johnson had every horse from the livery hitched to a wagon or a buggy, and folks were loading up tables and chairs, baked goods, picnic baskets, fiddles and guitars, and anything else needed for a day in Larsen's Meadow. For once, Willie had to work, loading tables and chairs from the café, while I did not. Mother said there was no point spoiling my curls or my dress doing hard work when there were men at hand to do it.

When the rags were all untied from my hair, I did not look like an elegant lady or a Gibson girl. I looked like I had a squirrel's nest on my head. At least that's what Willie said before he burst out laughing.

Mother shooed him away. She gathered up the hair around my face and pinned it back. Then she attached an enormous pink bow to the back of my head. It stood out on either side like wings, or elephant ears.

She helped me into my best clothes, a pale pink dress with a crisp white pinafore. When we were finished, I felt more like I was going to church than to a picnic. I thought, with a bit of regret, about past summer picnics, when Imogene, Willie, and I had thrown off our socks and shoes and splashed in the creek, or held melon-seed-spitting contests, the juice running down our chins onto our clothes. This year was different. This year, I was going with a boy, and I would have to be a lady.

Soon, George arrived to escort me. He was even more charming than usual, if that was possible. His wavy blond hair was combed smooth and shone with sunshine, even when he stepped out of the sun. In his fine suit, he could have passed for a city boy. He stunned me with his smile as he greeted me. I retrieved my picnic basket and we set out together, my arm through his, like a duke and duchess stepping out on promenade.

The meadow was already filling when we arrived. Along its southern edge, children were dabbling in the creek. On the north side, a barbed-wire fence divided the meadow from the Larsens' south pasture. In front of the fence line, tables had been set up and were arranged with baked goods, knitted items, canned pickles and jams, and at the end, our kissing booth table, decorated with its red hearts and cupids. I wouldn't have to go to the booth until after we ate lunch, so I tried to ignore it and give George my full attention.

People were already spreading their blankets in the best spots in the meadow. George picked a spot for us right in the middle, where everyone could see us. There was no shade here, but I didn't mind. Besides, puffy white clouds were building over the peaks to the west and would likely keep the afternoon from growing too hot.

Soon, the whole meadow was filled with a patchwork of picnic blankets, laughing children running carelessly between them and being scolded by mothers and young lovers alike. Mother and Father spread out their picnic not far from us. I knew they were keeping an eye on my first outing with a boy, which made me a little nervous, but a little relieved, too.

Imogene and Willie arrived soon after and spread their blanket next to ours. Imogene looked gorgeous, her long blond hair falling in perfect ringlets around her shoulders. She had the porcelain complexion of her Swedish ancestors, and the sun and fresh air were brightening her eyes and the roses in her cheeks. The four of us made a merry party, talking and laughing and sharing our food.

While most everyone was eating their lunches, Mrs. Crawford was strolling regally through the meadow, reminding us all of the many ways to support the war effort and urging everyone to be generous.

"Good afternoon, girls. I hope you'll raise a good sum for the Liberty Bond drive," she said when she reached us.

"Yes, ma'am, I'm sure we will," Imogene replied with her usual sunny smile.

Mrs. Crawford glanced at me. "You aren't eating onions or garlic, I trust."

"No, ma'am," I said.

Mrs. Crawford gave Imogene a smile and made her way on through the crowd to the blanket my parents shared. Her surprise at seeing my father was loud enough for us to hear from where we sat several blankets away.

"Why, Mr. Barnell! How lovely that you could make it down to be with your family for the holiday picnic!"

"Thank you, Mrs. Crawford. It's good to be here," Father said politely.

"And will you be staying for a time now?"

"I'm afraid not. We have to make hay while the sun shines, as they say."

"A pity," Mrs. Crawford said primly. "I don't wish to concern you, Mr. Barnell, but I worry about the upbringing of children without a father's guidance."

"Not to worry, Mrs. Crawford. Maggie has everything well in hand," Father said, patting Mother's knee. "Besides, it's only for the summer months. I'm sure they won't turn into wolves in that amount of time."

Willie snarled, wolflike, at Imogene, who giggled and gave him a playful shove. Mrs. Crawford's back stiffened.

"You may make light of it, Mr. Barnell, but as your neighbor, I feel duty bound to tell you that your daughter has been associating with Josie Gilbert in your absence. If she was my child, I'd put a stop to it!"

My father leaned forward and made a quiet response to Mrs. Crawford. I couldn't hear what he said, but she strode away, her jaw set and her eyes narrowed.

Around us, people who had heard the exchange were glancing in my direction. I looked at George, hoping he'd say something in my defense. He was pretending not to have heard as he gnawed on a drumstick. I pretended too as we sat in uncomfortable silence. I couldn't help remembering how comfortable I had felt with Frank as we picnicked at Buckskin Joe, and I wished today was more like that. I wondered what Frank was doing right now. Did they have Fourth of July picnics in Denver? Had he received my letter?

"Oh no, not her again," George said. I looked up to see what he was talking about. Across the meadow someone else was moving from blanket to blanket. Josie Gilbert, flanked by two well-dressed ladies, each wearing a purple-and-green ribbon across her chest, from shoulder to waist. The ribbons read NATIONAL WOMEN'S PARTY, and each woman carried an armful of leaflets.

They were moving our way. I stood up quickly. "Let's take a walk before I have to run the kissing booth," I suggested to George. He agreed and got to his feet. I grabbed his hand and started off in the opposite direction from Josie and her friends.

"Looks like we might get some rain this afternoon," George remarked, glancing skyward as we walked. The clouds had continued to grow and darken over the western peaks, and a curtain of rain could be seen on the summit of Mount Silverheels.

"It wouldn't be the first time we got a sprinkle or two at the Fourth of July picnic," I said. I had even heard that some young couples hoped for rain, so they could huddle together under their blankets, but I didn't mention that to George.

When we were nearly to the creek, someone called my name. Mrs. Nelson was picnicking with some of the old-timers and was waving at me.

"I was so delighted to get your letter, my dear," she said kindly. "Pardon me for not writing back, but when I saw there was to be this lovely picnic, I decided it was time I came in person and saw all my old friends in Como. And I've brought something for you too."

She reached into her picnic basket and pulled out a small bundle wrapped in a dishcloth. As she unwrapped it, I could see it was an old tintype photograph, its image hazy and faded with age. She held it out to me. I took it and examined it carefully. Two rows of school children posed in front of a two-story building, the smallest children seated in the front and the older ones standing behind them. In the back left corner stood a woman, undoubtedly the school teacher, holding the littlest child on her hip. Many of the children in the front row were blurred, as was the face of the woman and the child she held.

"This looks old," George said, looking over my shoulder.

"It was taken in the 1870s," Mae said. "It's my mother's school picture. Back then the little ones couldn't hold still long enough for those old cameras, so you can't see most of their faces."

I looked closely at the building in the background. "It's the dance hall at Buckskin Joe!"

"It sure is," Mrs. Nelson said. "They used it as a school in the daytime, since Buckskin Joe never had a proper schoolhouse."

Mrs. Nelson pointed to a round-faced girl, about nine or ten yours old in the second row. "That's my mother, Eliza Carlisle. And this is Tom Lee, who I told you about." She moved her finger to the boy next to Eliza. While everyone else in the photo was looking toward the camera, his head was turned a little toward the girl on his right. She was by far the prettiest girl in the photo, her sweet face framed by a cascade of blond ringlets.

"Tom's people are buried up at Buckskin Joe. And this here is Joseph Richards, and I believe his son's still in Park County.

I can't think of anyone named Wilson, though. Are you still trying to find out about Buck Wilson?"

I said I was, and she shook her head. "I'm afraid no one around here knows a thing about him. But if you want to borrow this photo, it might jog some memories. I have a few others from Buckskin Joe days too. Come back by the house another time and we can look through them."

A cloud moved over the sun and a gust of cool air made everyone around us look up.

"Put it somewhere safe. It looks like we might get rain," Mrs. Nelson said.

I assured her I would and thanked her before heading to our blanket. A second gust of wind hit as we walked back across the meadow, blowing men's hats off their heads and kicking dust into people's potato salad.

"Yep, it's going to rain for sure," I said, hoping to distract George so he wouldn't ask about my interest in the photo and Buck Wilson.

"Don't worry. A little rain won't hurt us," George replied.

By the time we got back to the blankets, Imogene had already gone to prepare the kissing booth. I carefully stowed the photograph in the bottom of my picnic basket and went to help her.

At our table, the decorated sheet was flapping in the growing breeze. Imogene was trying to hold it down, but it kept puffing up, tipping over the money jar. I borrowed some bits of yarn from the ladies at the knitting table and used them to tie the ends of the sheet to the table legs. Then I nervously sat down in the chair next to Imogene and steeled myself for the ordeal ahead.

All along the row of tables ladies were stationing themselves to sell their baked goods and craft items. Mrs. Engel's fine hat was proudly on display next to a jar that was nearly full of raffle tickets. People were already browsing along the tables, seeing what they might buy.

At once, a line began to form in front of Imogene, with Willie at the front. I watched as he dropped a nickel in the jar, then leaned across the table and kissed my best friend square on the lips. I was scandalized, but neither of them looked a bit embarrassed. In fact, they both looked like they enjoyed it very much. It was a long kiss, and when they finished, Willie looped his thumbs through his suspender straps and swaggered to the back of the line, a big grin on his face.

I watched two more boys kiss Imogene. She made them kiss her cheek, much to their disappointment. Then someone in front of me cleared his throat. Nervously, I turned my eyes to my own line. My father smiled down at me. He dropped a dime in the jar.

"I believe that's enough for a hug and a kiss from my little girl, isn't it?" He leaned forward and kissed me, then gathered me into his strong, secure embrace. "I sure am proud of you, Pearl, and everything you are doing this summer," he said. "You're a big help to your mother."

I squeezed him back in gratitude. Finally he let me go and

smiled. "Now, I have to go see about winning that hat for your mother."

I said good-bye to him and turned to look at the next person in my line. Unlike Imogene, though, whose line consisted of most of the boys a girl might look forward to kissing, the only boy of that sort in my line was George, and in front of him was an odd assortment. All the old-timers from the café stood at the front of the line, their hats and nickels in their hands. Behind them were the Larsen brothers, three farm boys who hadn't done much washing up before coming to the picnic. One of them, to my horror, had a thick wad of chaw bulging out his lower lip. As I looked, he spit a pencil-thin stream of juice onto the ground. My lunch churned in my stomach, threatening to come up.

I swallowed and smiled weakly up at Russell.

He dropped his nickel in the jar. "We couldn't stay away when we heard our favorite little waitress would be here," he said. Then he bent over the table and gave me a grandfatherly peck on the cheek. Harry, Orv, and Tom each followed suit. The tobacco-chewing Larsen boy was stepping up to the table when a huge gust of wind hit, bearing with it the first drops of rain. The wind billowed the sheet that I had tied to the table legs. Imogene and I leapt out of the way just as it pulled the table over. The pickle jar hit my chair and shattered, sending a spray of broken glass and nickels everywhere. A second mighty gust ripped the sheet from the table legs and sent it flapping and fluttering into the barbed-wire fence. In the chaos, I was vaguely aware of other tables tipping, and knitted socks and mittens sailing away. Then the rain burst upon us in an icy, wind-driven fury.

Across the meadow people shrieked and cursed as they scrambled after their belongings and ran for the shelter of the trees or their buggies. Other folks pulled their blankets over their heads like tents. I ran after the sheet, which whipped and snapped, trying to break free of the barbed wire. I was soaked to the skin, struggling to get it loose. Then George was there, saving me. He yanked the sheet from the fence and held it up to shield us from the worst of the rain—and from the eyes of the crowd in the meadow.

"Thank you," I said, smiling up into his perfect face.

"You're welcome." Then he wrapped an arm around my waist, pulled me tight against him, and kissed me.

CHAPTER 20

My first real kiss. I had daydreamed about it for years while reading dime novels and penny dreadfuls. The moment had been exactly what it should be—I was a damsel in distress, and the young handsome hero had rescued me, taken me in his strong arms, and kissed me. Exactly the moment I had desired all my life.

So why did it all feel so wrong? I didn't like feeling so helpless, and his strong arm felt constraining around me. He hadn't even asked my permission, just grabbed me and pressed his lips to mine. I tried to melt into his arms and kiss him back like all the ladies did in my books, but instead I was fighting the urge to pull free. As the kiss ended, Josie's words sprang to my mind—handsome men took advantage of girls who didn't stand up for themselves. Girls like me.

Once again, Josie had spoiled the perfect moment. She had poisoned my mind to romance. I couldn't let her take this away from me, so I took a deep breath and I pushed my lips back up toward George's, determined that the second kiss would make up for the first. George looked surprised, then pleased, as he obliged me with another kiss and smothering embrace. It felt worse than the first. I pulled back.

"We should make sure Imogene is all right," I said. Not waiting for an answer, I led the way back against the wind and driving rain.

We found Imogene crouched behind the fallen table. George threw the sheet over the table to form a damp tent for us, and we all huddled inside.

"Where is Willie?" I asked when we were settled.

Imogene rolled her eyes. "He ran off to make sure your mother was okay, and never came back. I don't see why he needed to do that when your father is here."

"Well, I'm sure he's somewhere much less cozy than here, and it serves him right," George said. "Besides, I don't think we'd have room for one more in our little fort."

Imogene giggled. "Fort Kissing Booth," she said.

George laughed, then leaned over and kissed Imogene's cheek, right in front of me. It stung my heart, but I knew it was my fault. If I hadn't pulled away from him earlier, he wouldn't be turning to Imogene now.

"That will be a nickel," she said with another giggle. He reached into his pocket and produced the nickel and a pair of dice. "Craps, anyone?" he said with a naughty grin.

"I don't have any money," I said.

"Then we can play for other stakes," George said. "This is Fort Kissing Booth."

"We can use the nickels from the jar, as long as we give them back afterward," I said quickly. I lifted the corner of the sheet and gathered the nickels with shaking fingers.

The torrent lasted a full fifteen minutes, followed by another fifteen of steady rain. We played our game throughout. George and Imogene were perfectly at ease, but I couldn't stop thinking of the disappointment of my first kiss. At last we realized that we no longer heard raindrops pattering on the sheet or the table. Cautiously, we lifted the sheet and ventured out, stretching our cramped legs and backs.

The meadow looked like the Hun himself had marched through. Blankets, hats, and spilled picnics were scattered everywhere amid little rivers of mud. Slowly, bedraggled townsfolk were emerging from beneath blankets, as wet and muddy as if there had been no shelter at all. I looked down at myself and saw that I was no different. My dress, which had been crisp with starch just an hour ago, now hung limp, and my white pinafore was streaked with mud.

I looked over at the row of tables with all the town's hard work. One table of baked goods had blown over and my mother's pies were now a sticky, gooey mess on the ground. The other goods hadn't faired much better. The ladies at the tables had done their best to save what they could, but the storm had been too sudden and fierce, and there had been nowhere dry to put anything.

The craft table had also gone down, and the railroaders' wives were emerging and searching the ground for socks and mittens. The wind had carried some things off, and not every sock or mitten had a mate.

Worst of all, the fine hat that Mrs. Engel had donated for the raffle was gone. One lady reported seeing it catch the wind and sail clean over the barbed-wire fence and away across the pasture. The Larsen boys quickly formed a posse to go after it, but we all knew they were more likely to bring it back dead than alive.

Imogene, George, and I stood our table back onto its legs and wrung out the sheet. We draped it back over the table, but the felt hearts and cupids had bled in long red streaks down the sheet, an effect that was more gruesome than romantic. I sorted through the broken glass from the pickle jar for the rest of our nickels. Between us, we had made eighty-five cents, but I could only find eighty. I put all the money in the pocket of my pinafore and set the chairs back in place, but I didn't think we would reopen for business. I couldn't see that anyone was looking for a kiss from muddy, bedraggled girls, and I was too wet and cold to sit there waiting to find out.

Across the meadow folks were coming to the aid of friends and neighbors, helping to wring out blankets, recover lost items, and tidy dirty children. Mrs. Crawford, however, took one look at the mess and was immediately overcome by a headache. She insisted that her husband and George take her home at once. George gave me a quick peck on the cheek and a smile, then left me to collect the blanket and picnic basket from the mire on my own. It wasn't very gentlemanly of him, but his mother didn't give him a choice.

On the opposite side of the meadow, the Schmidts were

gathering their wet neighbors together. They had loaded their wagon with firewood, which they now unloaded and set ablaze. At once, shivering children, who had been crying to go home, gathered around it. Before long, everyone was warming there, and as we talked, the event began to take on a hue of hilarity. We laughed at our soiled clothes, and at tales of folks falling into cream pies, or men ending up in their wives' hats by mistake. When the Schmidts set up a table full of frankfurters and unfurled a sign that read *Roast a Liberty Dog to Help Roast the Kaiser!—Ten Cents Each!* a big cheer went up from the crowd.

A few ladies gathered what could be salvaged of the soggy baked goods and brought them to the bonfire to sell, and a few gallant gentlemen bought them, although I didn't see anyone trying to actually eat them.

The ragged sunshine grew stronger and warmer, and soon folks ventured away from the fire. Fiddlers and banjo players brought out their instruments and the dancing started, despite the puddles and slop. My father and mother stepped out, and Willie reappeared to ask Imogene. She, however, gave him the cold shoulder.

"Why should I dance with you, William Barnell, when you ran off and left me in the rain? A gentleman would have sheltered me and kept me company."

She walked away from Willie, and while he watched she flirted with one of the Larsen boys long enough to get an invitation to dance.

"Well, sis, I guess it's just you and me," Willie said.

"She'll forgive you soon," I said. "She worked too hard to catch you to let you off the hook so easily."

"Then I better get a Liberty Dog now, to keep my strength up."

He bought three dogs from the Schmidts, stuck them on the ends of willow sticks, and handed one to me. We joined the crowd of people roasting them around the fire. When Imogene returned from dancing, Willie presented her with a roasted dog, and as predicted, she forgave him.

In the end, most folks in town declared the picnic a success, and one that would be talked about for some time. The bonfire and dancing went well past dark, and the Schmidts sold all of their franks, even after Mr. Schmidt went back into town and got some more. Folks were still throwing wood onto the fire when I left to go to bed. Willie decided to stay, so I retrieved my picnic basket, blanket, and ruined sheet from the kissing booth, and walked back with my parents.

It was the loveliest of nights, the sky clear and sparkling overhead. It was a very romantic setting, and yet I wasn't sorry to be walked home by my parents instead of George. I was too confused about my feelings to want one more romantic encounter. I was afraid I would never experience romance now that Josie had spoiled it all for me, and I wished I had never taken her bet.

It wasn't until we were back at the café that I remembered the picture Mae Nelson had given me. I had tucked it down deep in the basket to keep it safe. Nervously, I took the basket to the kitchen to unpack it, hoping the photograph was undamaged. To my surprise, the cloth-wrapped photo was not alone in the bottom of the basket. Beneath the dirty plates, napkins, and leftover remains of our lunch, nestled against the photo, was a large damp envelope, bursting with pages. It was a used envelope, with a stamp and postmark from Washington, D.C., and the address of the National Women's Party in the upper left-hand corner. It had been addressed to Miss Josephine Gilbert, but her name had been crossed out and my own penciled in. The envelope and its contents had absorbed a good deal of rain, and by doing so had probably saved the photograph beneath it, which was dry.

I took the dry tintype and the damp envelope upstairs to my room. I put the photo on my dresser, leaning against the wall so I could look at it. Then I gently removed the pages from the envelope. They were neatly typeset, like pages from a penny dreadful, with a large headline across the top of the first one that read A TRUE ACCOUNT OF SILVERHEELS AND THE EPIDEMIC OF 1861. The ink on the first few pages was smeared, but I could still make out the words.

I laid them out across my bedroom floor to dry, thinking I would read them in the morning, but of course I could not go to sleep. I was dying to know what Josie had concocted now. Whatever it was, she had bothered to print it, which meant she intended to distribute it. But to whom? In the café at lunch time? To the tourists at the hotel before they got a chance to talk to me and ask for a tour? Maybe she had come up with proof for her story, and to complete my humiliation, she would have me distribute these along with campaign bills on the platform.

It was no good lying in bed wondering. I got up and relit the lamp. Then, on hands and knees, I crouched over the wet pages and began to read the blurring words.

CHAPTER 21

A TRUE ACCOUNT OF SILVERHEELS AND
THE EPIDEMIC OF 1861

Buckskin Joe was an ordinary mining camp that might have lived and died without notice if not for the tragedy that struck in the winter of 1861; a tragedy for which one woman was to blame. That woman was the dancer Silverheels, who had come in the fall of 1860 with a troop of dance-hall girls. She so enchanted the men of the town that they begged her to stay.

To keep her with them, they built her a snug cabin and promised to take care of her every need. As winter closed in around the town, the spoiled Silverheels complained of the cold, hinting she might leave for warmer climes if the miners didn't do something about it. Buck Wilson, who desired Silverheels for his own, organized an expedition to get woolen blankets from the Mexican sheep camps on the southern end of South Park. The mission was successful, but a week after Buck and his party returned with blankets, news reached Buckskin Joe that the sheep herders had fallen victim to smallpox, and not one was left alive.

Sure enough, before long the first telltale signs appeared in town. Wilbur Hall and Stephen Smith, who had gone with Buck for blankets, appeared in the saloon flushed with fever. By the next morning, pox stood out on their faces.

A doctor arrived from Fairplay to examine them. "It's small-pox, all right," he announced to the gathered townsfolk when he emerged from their cabin. Then he mounted his horse and galloped away, as eager as anyone to escape the sickness.

Panic swept like floodwaters through town. Everybody with a wagon and a lick of sense got out. Jack Herndon, the saloon owner, sent his wife to Fairplay as fast as he could load her on a horse. The dance-hall girls all headed for Denver City. Mountain men like Zachariah Stuart and Elijah Weldon sent their Indian wives and children to camp in the forests nearby until the plague had passed. Only the men with claims producing gold stayed, fearing theft more than they feared sickness.

Eli Weldon, being somewhat more prudent than the rest, kept his stepdaughter, Sefa, with him, to cook and clean. After all, she wasn't his child, and besides, she was half Indian. In those days, and to a man like Eli Weldon, that meant she wasn't worth much, so her safety wasn't as important as Weldon's comfort. As for Sefa, she was frightened of the pox, but she was more frightened that she might never again see Buck Wilson, her heart's desire, if she left. So, trusting to her mother's remedies for fever, she stayed.

Silverheels could have left town too, but she had her own

claim to protect: a whole town full of love-struck miners with gold, all eating out of her hand.

All except Buck Wilson, who seemed to do less work and have more gold than all the rest of the men in town. He had to be running his own con, and she wasn't about to leave the whole town to him with so much gold for the taking.

When the flight from Buckskin Joe was complete, the town settled uneasily into waiting, to see what the epidemic would do. Sefa Weldon, though, did not wait. She set to work brewing up the bitter tea that would fight fever. Taking it to Stephen and Wilbur, she encountered Buck Wilson. Love nearly buckled her knees when he called out to her, but her joy turned to fear when she saw the flush of fever in his face.

"Sefa, go to Silverheels and tell her I'm sick," he said. "Bring her to me."

"Oh, Buck, you can't be!" Sefa cried.

He smiled a little, but it was a bitter smile. He held out an envelope. "Take this to Silverheels, Sefa. Please? For your old friend Buck?"

Sefa knew it must be a declaration of love for Silverheels, the last thing she wanted to deliver, but the lovesick little calf would have done anything for Buck. So she turned up the path toward Silverheels's cabin.

Flakes of snow were swirling through the air by the time she reached the door.

"Who is it?" Silverheels called without opening it.

"It's me," Sefa said. "I have a letter from Buck!"

Silverheels opened the door just a crack to take the letter.

"He wants you to come to him. He's sick," Sefa said.

"I don't want to get sick too," Silverheels said, and she slammed the door.

Sefa wasn't sorry that Silverheels wouldn't come. She planned to cure Buck with her medicine. Then he would love her at last, instead of the pretty dancer.

Buck didn't bother to mask his disappointment when he threw open the door to Sefa instead of Silverheels, but Sefa pretended not to notice. She fussed over him and gave him her foul-tasting tea. He took one sip and dumped the rest while she wasn't looking.

After tending Buck, Sefa visited the other sick miners. Wilbur beckoned her to his bedside.

"I ran away," he croaked in a dried-out voice. "And now I'm gonna die!"

He clutched at her hand, the fear of death turning his grip to iron.

"You gotta write my momma and sister. Send them my gold. I been saving it for them. It's in my trunk. Promise you'll send it. Tell them what happened to me."

"Send it where?" Sefa said.

His hand loosened on her arm, the strength running out of him like water. "There's a Bible in the trunk. Their names and address are there. Promise me, Sefa."

"I promise," she said, stepping away now that he had released her.

He smiled a little and closed his eyes.

Sefa returned to her cabin as darkness settled in over Buckskin Joe, bringing the coldest night in the town's history. A blizzard screamed and raged around the cabins, cutting the town off from the rest of the world.

Morning came and the storm slackened. Sefa brewed more tea and set out to visit the invalids. Buck was sprawled across his bed in his long johns and a filthy undershirt soaked with sweat. A tangle of blankets lay in a heap on the floor beside him.

Sefa gathered the blankets and covered him. "Buck. Buck, wake up. You should eat something to keep up your strength."

"No use," he muttered. "I'm dying. Sefa, bring Silverheels. I must have her here."

The tears froze on Sefa's cheeks as she made her way through the drifted snow to Silverheels's cabin, but she did as she was told. At first, Silverheels was reluctant to leave the comfort of her snug cabin. But when Sefa told her Buck was dying, she agreed to go.

Back in his cabin, Buck was drifting in and out of sleep. Silverheels bent over him and spoke sweetly. "Buck, darling. It's me, your Gerta. Buck, can you hear me?"

Buck opened his eyes and smiled weakly. "Lie here with me a moment, won't you, Gerta dear?"

Silverheels would have preferred to lie in a bed of eels rather than with this sweaty, filthy, fevered man, but she remembered his hidden gold and, kneeling beside the bed, bent her head to rest on his shoulder.

"You mustn't worry about claim jumpers or thieves," she said. "Tell me where your gold is, and I'll keep it safe for you until you're better."

Buck gave a dry laugh that wrenched a cough from him. "It will cost you, honey."

Silverheels bolted up and glared at him. He gave her a faint smile. "Kiss me, Gerta," he said. "A big kiss and your everlasting love. That will be the price if you want to know my secrets."

She stared, horrified. He laughed again. "We're both gamblers, you and I. Well, Silverheels, the chips are down. I'm calling your bluff. What's my claim worth to you?"

Ever naive, Sefa blundered to the bedside with a cup of her horrid tea just then. "We must get him to drink this. It will save his life," she said.

"I'll do that. Why don't you bring in more firewood," Silverheels replied. "We mustn't let him get cold." She and Buck had not let go of each other's gaze. Sefa mistook the look for true love, so she gave the cup to Silverheels and did as she was told.

When they were alone, Silverheels gave Buck a cold smile. "I don't think all the chips are down just yet, Buck. The real question is, what is *life* worth to you." And while he watched, she raised the cup to her lips and drank the tea that could save him.

When Sefa came in with the wood, Silverheels hurried her back outside. "He's resting. We shouldn't disturb him," she whispered. They went together to visit Wilbur and Stephen. Both men were dead, so Silverheels went to Wilbur's trunk and threw it open.

"What are you doing?" Sefa asked.

"He's dead. His gold's no use to him now," Silverheels said.

"I already took it, and the Bible," Sefa said.

Silverheels stared at her. "The Bible?"

"It had the address."

"What address?"

"For his mother and sister. I promised him I'd send them his gold."

Silverheels smiled. "Of course you did," she said. "Good, sweet, Sefa. What would we do without you?"

Silverheels crossed to the trunk at the foot of Stephen's bed and opened it, too. "We might as well do it for both of them, right? Ah, here we are." She straightened up, a bag of gold dust in one hand and a packet of letters in the other. "We can send this home for him, too, once the mail is running. I'll just keep them safe till then."

When they returned outside, Mr. Herndon was shoveling the snow away from the door of the dance hall. Sefa and Silverheels went to him and told him of the deaths.

Herndon nodded grimly. "They won't be the only ones. We're going to need a hospital, and I won't be doing any business until this is all over. We'll treat the sick ones here."

By the end of that day, two feverish men were already

sleeping in the dance hall. The next day they were joined by four more. Buck, however, was not brought in. Silverheels insisted that she alone care for her true love, and sent Sefa to help Herndon. So many sick men needed Sefa at the dance hall that she could not return even once to Buck's cabin. So it was that Sefa got no chance to say good-bye to the man she loved more than life itself.

After three days, Silverheels finally came into the dance hall. She announced Buck was dead, gave a theatrical sob, and ran to her cabin, where she locked herself in. Sefa wished the fever would take her, too, but it would not. So she worked on, through exhaustion and grief, administering her curing tea to any who would drink it.

She was mopping the brow of a young boy a week later when he said, "I'm going to die, aren't I?"

"Hush. Save your strength to get better," Sefa said, coaxing a little tea into him.

"I want to see Silverheels before I die. Will you get her? I want to tell her that I love her."

"I've got other men to tend to," Sefa said. But Herndon was nearby and overheard.

"I'll keep watch here, Sefa. You fetch her. Maybe it'd help all these boys to have their sweetheart here with them. Lift their spirits to see a pretty face."

Sefa went to retrieve Silverheels. In the dancer's cabin, several bags of gold dust sat on the table, along with the letters from Stephen's trunk. Silverheels glanced at them, then agreed to Sefa's request. She put on her prettiest dress and pinned silk roses into her golden hair, and Sefa knew how it would be. Her beauty would lift the men's spirits, while Sefa's tea saved their lives. And it would be Silverheels they would remember. But what could she do, the lump of mud in the wake of the goddess?

Days dragged by. Sefa gave out medicine, mopped brows, spooned broth into the living, closed the eyes of the dead. Silverheels, glowing and beautiful, sang and spoke to the men, listened to their secrets, and piled their gold ever higher in her cabin.

It took a month for the epidemic to run its course, a month that left nearly half the men dead and stacked frozen in the graveyard, where the bitter weather kept the bodies until the graves could be dug. At last, however, the day came when no new men arrived sick and none died, and those in the makeshift hospital had the fever behind them and the slow but hopeful days of recovery ahead.

"I think we're through the worst of it," Herndon announced one night as Sefa and Silverheels headed off to bed.

But Herndon had been wrong. Silverheels showed up the next day, her whole face flushed with fever.

"I feel so tired," she announced, as she stumbled in and collapsed against the piano, the back of her hand pressed to her forehead.

"No," a man sobbed from a bed nearby. "Not Silverheels!"

Jack Herndon went to her side, full of concern. When he

was near enough, she swooned gracefully into his arms. He swept her up right away.

"Sefa, help me get her home. Bring some of that brew of yours," Herndon called. He carried Silverheels all the way to her cabin and laid her on the bed. Sefa mopped her brow and cheeks with a damp cloth and was surprised when pink rouge came away. It surprised her too, when Silverheels was suddenly alert, slapping the cloth away.

"Just let me rest," Silverheels said. "I'm sure that's all I need." She batted her lashes at Herndon and he did as she said, taking Sefa with him.

Sefa returned that evening with supper, and Silverheels reluctantly opened the door. In the dim light of the fire Sefa could see Silverheels was more flushed than before, with bright red spots appearing on her cheeks. She also saw Silverheels's fancy kit of stage makeup open on the table, alongside all that gold.

"It's the pox for sure," Silverheels said, pointing to her face, but staying in the dim light and not letting Sefa get too close. "I'll be scarred! My beauty will be ruined!"

"It doesn't look like the pox," Sefa said, suspicious. She glanced again at the gold.

"Of course it's the pox," Silverheels snapped, "and it will make me ugly! I don't want to be seen if I'm ugly. Get out!"

Sefa wondered if she should tell anyone of her suspicions, but who in town would believe her? They were all blinded by love for Silverheels. Besides, Sefa was a good girl and didn't like to speak ill of anyone.

She returned in the morning but found the door was locked. She called, but got no answer. She tried again at supper time, but it was the same. When no response came the next morning, Sefa went to the dance hall and told the men of what Silverheels had said and how there was no sign of life at her cabin.

As one, the recovering men rose from their beds, dressed, and tramped through the bright, cold morning to Silverheels's cabin. As they walked, they vowed to give her all their gold if that's what it took to console her. At her cabin, they knocked and called out sweet sentiments, but she did not answer. At last, two burly men broke the latch and burst in. The whole crowd of besotted men rushed inside, with ugly, forgotten Sefa in their wake.

The cabin was snug and tidy as always. And empty. Silverheels was gone. And so too, Sefa noted silently, were the piles of gold from the table. In their place lay only a worn pair of dancing shoes with silver filigree on the heels.

CHAPTER 22

I sat staring at the pages long after I'd finished reading them. What had Josie meant by printing them up like this and giving them to me? And how many other copies had she made? Did she have the proof of what she was telling me—perhaps a relative of Jack Herndon or Sefa Weldon? No, I reminded myself that the wife and daughter of Eli Weldon were both inventions; Josie had made them up right in front of me. I found my list of names from the graves and looked at it again. There was no Wilbur or Stephen, so she had made them up too. So her whole story was a fabrication—characters and slander and all.

The problem was, it was convincing slander. If she had printed a whole stack of them and intended to sell or give them to tourists, it would ruin my chances of enticing them into an outing to Buckskin Joe. Who wanted to go visit a place where wretched things had happened to wretched people? The beauty and romance of it was all lost.

I vowed to find out what her plans were the next morning, but I didn't get the chance. Mrs. Crawford called another meeting, and it was once again in the café. Most of the same ladies as before were there, with the exception of Mrs. Schmidt. Mrs. Crawford appeared to have recovered from the terrible headache the picnic had given her, and arrived at the café with a look on her face that meant business.

George came too, and gave me a big warm smile. He apparently felt better about our kiss than I did, because he sat down and invited me to sit beside him, as if everything between us was perfect. Under the table, he put his hand on my knee, and I let him.

When everyone was settled, Mrs. Crawford began the meeting. "Due to the unfortunate circumstances at yesterday's picnic, we were unable to tally up the pledges for the Liberty Bond drive. When I call your name, you can bring up your money, and George will record how far you are toward your fifty-dollar subscriptions."

The ladies in the café glanced around at each other nervously, but none of them said anything.

The first name Mrs. Crawford called was Mrs. Engel. Mrs. Engel looked back at her in surprise. "Now, Phoebe, you know I don't have anything."

"Nonsense. You raised eighteen dollars before the picnic, and raffle tickets were still selling."

"But the hat was ruined," Mrs. Engel said. "By the time the Larsen boys fished it out of the mud, it had been half eaten by a cow. I'll have to refund the money for all the tickets."

Mrs. Crawford frowned at the idea. "That won't do. You

simply must replace the hat with another, Mrs. Engel, and move forward with the raffle."

Mrs. Engel's mouth fell open. "I can't do that! That hat cost me twelve dollars, and it was as much as I could afford. To donate another—"

"Of course you can afford it. It's for the war effort. Remember the sacrifices our boys over there are making. Surely you will not shrink from making a sacrifice for their sakes. To see them home safely into the arms of their wives and mothers."

"I'll see what I can manage," Mrs. Engel muttered, her brow knitted.

Mrs. Crawford gave a satisfied nod and started down the list again. One by one, the ladies reported what they had made— two dollars from the bake sale, and four from the knitting, but once spread among all the ladies who had contributed, no one had even made their initial one-dollar commitment, and none knew how they would complete a fifty-dollar pledge.

Imogene and I had made $1.30 together, since Imogene had kissed a few boys at the dance and then made them pay up. It seemed Imogene had found a way to make money that suited her perfectly.

"And George still owes Pearl at least a dime," she added loudly as she set our money on the table in front of Mrs. Crawford.

"My pleasure," George said with a grin, and added a dime to our earnings as my face went scarlet.

When all was said and done, there were only fifteen dollars on the table, and many women were saying they couldn't pledge to a bond at all.

"This is not nearly enough," Mrs. Crawford said. "Mr. Merino down in Fairplay has already collected thirty-five dollars toward pledges, on twenty bonds."

"There is another option if you want to collect a bigger sum," my mother said. With my father working in the kitchen, she was able to attend this meeting. "Mr. and Mrs. Schmidt did a lively business selling their franks after the rainstorm, and I believe Mrs. Schmidt is eager to use the proceeds for the war effort."

There was a murmur of approval around the room.

Mrs. Crawford's eyes narrowed and the line of her mouth hardened. "They had the nerve to serve their Hun food, after I expressly forbid it?"

"I think they saved the picnic," Mother said.

Under the table, George removed his hand from my knee. I bit my lip and prayed my mother would go back to the kitchen without saying anything more.

"I think it's a fine idea," said Mrs. Sorensen. "What would we have to do to convince Mrs. Schmidt to donate the money to the Liberty Bond fund?"

"Oh, I don't think it will take much convincing," Mother said. "But I think it would have to start with an apology."

Mrs. Crawford's face turned red and she began to splutter. If she'd been a train, she'd have probably had enough steam to get over the pass and all the way to California. Unfortunately though, she was Mrs. Crawford, and she wasn't going anywhere. "I will not go crawling to a German to ask for money, if that is what you are implying, Margaret Barnell. The fact that she even sold German sausages at a Fourth of July picnic is a slap in the face to our boys over there. If she were a true patriot, she'd be here donating the money for herself. I blame her entirely for this disaster!"

"I hardly think it's Mrs. Schmidt's fault that we had a gullywasher in the middle of the picnic," Mrs. Abernathy said.

"But she profited from it, and as a result, no one had money to spend on anything else." Mrs. Crawford got to her feet and looked around at everyone. "I could not take her blood money and sleep at night, and I am surprised that those of you who paid good American dollars for German food can. And I certainly hope that you can all find an equal amount to spend on Liberty Bonds. I think the governor is very interested to know, these days, who is supporting the war effort and who is hindering it."

With that, she marched out of the café. Without a word to me, George stood and followed her. There was a mutter and buzz of conversation as others gathered their things and left as well, some looking worried, others angry. No one was smiling anymore.

As the café emptied, my father stepped out of the kitchen, where he had apparently heard the whole thing. "I don't know, Maggie. I don't like it. When Phoebe Crawford has a bee in her bonnet, there's sure to be trouble."

"I'm not going to sit by and let her ruin good people," Mother said. "And I'm not going to let her scare me."

"Maybe I should stay for a while. Till things settle down," he said.

"Nonsense," Mother said. "You know as well as any of us, you don't have many months up at the mine before the snow flies. And with tourism down this summer, we need the money. Especially if Phoebe Crawford is going to pressure us all into buying those Liberty Bonds."

So it was settled. The next morning Father left for the mine, and things went back to normal in Como, or so it seemed at first. In the afternoon I went to the post office, hoping for a letter from Frank. While Mrs. Abernathy checked, I watched Mrs. Crawford trying to sell a Liberty Bond to one of the zinc miner's wives, a small woman with a baby on her hip. The woman was trying to explain that she had spent all her spare money for the month on yarn.

"It's the duty of every American," Mrs. Crawford replied unsympathetically.

Mrs. Abernathy returned to the window and reported there was no letter. Then her eyes fell on Mrs. Crawford and she shook her head. "She's determined to sell those bonds," she muttered. Then she leaned closer and whispered, "She talked big to Mr. Merino at the Fairplay Mercantile, so it's a matter of pride to her. She can't stand to be showed up."

I glanced back at the miner's wife and knew I had better

get out before Mrs. Crawford got her hooks into me, or before George came in and found me. It made no sense, but ever since the kiss in the rain, George felt like a shoe on the wrong foot. I knew it was my fault. I hadn't been romantic enough; I had listened too often to Josie and had been thinking the wrong thoughts. I *did* want to be with George—I had dreamed of it for years! I wanted to set things right with him, but I had no idea how.

As I left the store, I saw Mrs. Engel across the street, putting a second hat in her window for the raffle—not as nice as the first, but still a worthy prize. She looked worried.

I set off toward home, only to see George loitering in the street a block ahead of me. A little flutter went through me when I thought he was waiting outside the café for me, but then I realized that he had his clipboard and a money can to collect people's Liberty Bond pledges. Plus, he wasn't looking toward the café, or toward me at all. He was looking toward the platform at the depot.

I followed his gaze. A train to Denver had only just pulled out, and Josie was standing on the platform watching it go. I remembered her National Women's Party friends at the picnic. I guessed she had just seen them off. Her attention on the train, she didn't see George as he approached slyly along the street, looking like a cat stalking a bird. In this case, I hoped he knew she was a very big bird, with a sharp beak and talons.

I had stopped walking, still about a half block away, but I

couldn't leave. The fascination and dread of what was about to happen rooted me to the spot.

Josie turned at last, only to find herself face to face with George. He flashed his most spectacular smile. Josie scowled.

"Good day, Mrs. Gilbert. It's come to my attention that you haven't yet begun your subscription for a Liberty Bond. And we all know how much you support liberty. How much can I put you down for?"

"Not a red cent," Josie said. "Now leave me alone, boy." She tried to push past him, but he stepped in front of her.

"Now Mrs. Gilbert, you know it's in your best interest to buy one."

"And how do you know what's in my best interest?"

"These are dangerous times," George said. "It wouldn't hurt to own a little protection."

At that Josie gave him a look that could have scorched the whiskers off the devil himself. "I wouldn't buy a rope from you Crawfords if I was dangling off a cliff," she said.

His smile disappeared. "Well you just might be, Josie Gilbert. And we Crawfords might just have enough rope to hang you," he said. He turned as if to go and caught sight of me. At once his smile came back, but I felt no flutter this time.

"What about you, Pearl? You're a true patriot, right? You'll support the war effort."

"Of course I'm a patriot. But I don't have much money."

"What about the money you made taking that city boy on tours a few weeks ago? Every little bit helps the fund. Unless your loyalties lie elsewhere," George said. He glanced at Josie.

"Of course not," I said. I reached into my apron pocket, where I carried a little money for making change in the café, and took out a nickel. I couldn't tell George I didn't have the money from taking Frank on tours. If he thought I'd done it for free, he'd think I was sweet on Frank. "Put it toward my mother's subscription, please."

"I knew my girl would come through," he said, giving me a bright smile and a peck on the cheek before writing down my contribution on his list. Then, whistling a tune as if nothing unpleasant had happened, he strode off toward his family's store.

"And here I'd hoped you were finally getting a spine," Josie said when he had left. "He'll keep taking as long as you give, you know."

"You should contribute too," I said.

"I prefer to put my money into something I believe in."

"If you knew what they were saying about you—"

"You think I don't know what they're saying? I've got ears, girl. But I've got a conscience, too, and I do what it tells me." With that, she stumped off in the opposite direction from George, leaving me feeling ashamed for no good reason at all.

For the next two weeks, the Liberty Bond drive continued everywhere people in town gathered. It seemed like you couldn't step out of your front door without being accosted by George or Mrs. Crawford. George had taken to asking for contributions on the platform when the noon train came through, always approaching the pretty girls who couldn't resist his charm. Mr. Orenbach didn't like it, but he didn't dare oppose the Crawfords.

The only person in town who resisted them outright was Josie. She hadn't contributed at the picnic, and she hadn't bought so much as a penny's worth of Liberty Bonds. While Mrs. Crawford seemed to have everyone else in town cowed with accusations of un-Americanism and the threat of writing the governor, Josie only became more stubborn and more vocal in her opposition. She wouldn't support a president who didn't support the rights of citizens, and she made sure everyone heard her say it.

While a small part of me admired her courage, a larger part of me wished she would give in and buy a bond, or at least be a little quieter with her opinions. I didn't want her to get into serious trouble, and I didn't want to end up in trouble through association, since she was back to campaigning daily in the café. I still hadn't asked her about the story, either. I couldn't risk a private conversation and the gossip it might start.

More than ever, I was anxious for a letter from Frank. If he could get the truth from Tom Lee, I could put an end to the wager and get Josie and her seditious talk out of the café once and for all. My other clues had produced nothing, and I'd come only to dead ends in my search for whoever had been at Buck Wilson's grave.

I looked nightly at the photo I had received from Mae

Nelson, hoping it held a secret I hadn't seen before—a shadowy lady in the distance or in one of the windows of the dance hall. I even imagined that the blurred schoolmarm in the photo was Silverheels. Perhaps Silverheels had come back to Buckskin Joe, disguised as a humble teacher, just to be near her beloved Buck, and she had avoided being captured in the photo to keep her secret. That seemed too far-fetched even for me to believe. I thought it would have made a fine, tragic ending for a penny dreadful, but I knew it would only make Josie laugh.

Josie did not ask about my search, or say anything at all about Silverheels. As the weeks progressed, she fell into an increasingly foul temper, until her mood could no longer be ignored. One evening she stormed into the full café and slammed the newspaper down on the counter hard enough to slosh coffee cups two seats away.

"What's eating her?" Orv said to his associates at the old-timers' table. Josie spun on him instantly.

"What's eating me? I'll tell you what's eating me! It's living in a country that's willing to send men to die in the name of freedom overseas, but doesn't grant that same freedom at home to its own citizens. That's what's eating me!"

"Now, Josie—" Russell said in a reasonable tone, but she cut him off.

"Don't you patronize me, Russell! I say we impeach Wilson if he doesn't support the principles at home that he claims we defend abroad!"

A gasp went up from several tables.

"Impeach Wilson!" Mrs. Crawford said in horror. Even Mr. Crawford came out from behind his newspaper and gave Josie an angry frown.

"You don't really mean that, Josie," Russell said.

"You can't impeach the president when there's a war on," said Harry. "We've got to stand behind him. Stand united to win the war."

"I will not stand behind a president who arrests his own citizens for fighting for freedom!" Josie shouted.

"I won't have you spreading sedition in front of my child! It's indecent. Cover your ears, George," Mrs. Crawford said.

George did not cover his ears. On the contrary, he seemed to be taking in the whole spectacle with delight.

Josie glared at the Crawfords, but Russell stepped between them.

"Come on, Josie. I know you have strong feelings, but folks are eating their supper now. Let's sit down, you and I, and we can discuss this between ourselves."

He took her elbow politely, but she jerked out of his grasp. "I've told you before, Russell, I'll not be silenced by you. If you all won't listen, I'll find those who will."

She stomped toward the door.

"Good riddance!" Mr. Crawford said. George nodded.

"You forgot your paper," Orv called after her.

Josie's only response was to slam the door on her way out.

"What's got her on the warpath?" Tom said.

Russell looked at the newspaper. He gave a low whistle and read:

"'Suffragist Alice Paul and six of her so-called National Women's Party have been arrested once again from the picket line before the White House. Officials tell this reporter that there will be no leniency this time. Prosecutors will be asking for the maximum sentence, six months to two years in prison, if convicted.'" He shook his head. "No wonder she's spittin' nails."

He set the paper on the counter and I could see the picture—a line of well-dressed ladies standing before a large gate, holding American flags and a banner that read *Mr. President How Long Must Women Wait for Liberty?* I knew there was a war, but this still didn't sit right with me. Wives and mothers to be sent to prison, when all they had done was stand before the White House with signs and flags? For doing what Josie did daily in our café?

My thoughts were interrupted by George. "I think it serves them right, don't you?" he said. He was talking to me. I bit my lip and looked away.

"Of course, we all do, George dear," said Mrs. Crawford. "That's why everyone around here is supporting the Liberty Bond fund, except that awful woman. Now, Pearl, bring George a piece of that cherry pie. And I'd like another cup of coffee."

I did as I was told in silence. After so many months of wishing I could get rid of Josie and her campaigning, why did I feel outrage at this news? And why was it making me worry so much about Josie, when she refused to worry about herself?

CHAPTER 23

Frank's letter was waiting at the post office the next day when I checked after lunch. Relief swept through me. With the proof it contained, I would be able to stop Josie from campaigning in the café, which would be best for all of us. Of course, Josie wouldn't see it that way, but I couldn't shake the growing fear that Mrs. Crawford could do real harm. Josie needed to lie low for a few weeks, until the Liberty Bonds were all purchased. I rushed home, sat down at the first table I came to, and tore open the letter. My heart pounding, I read.

Dear Pearl,

How delighted I was to receive your letter! With the fes-tivities for the Fourth of July and Robert shipping out for training, you must forgive my delay in responding. Robert, you will be glad to know, was a perfect gentleman and very good to Annie until he left, though I still do not trust him. Annie has not breathed a word to Mother of what happened, nor have I. After all, Robert has gone off to war now, and we all must pray every day for his safe return, along with all the other boys who have gone to France, as Mother reminds us daily.

I wrote Mr. Lee at once after other matters were dispensed with. He is in frail health, but was eager enough to tell his story. Last Wednesday I went to his daughter's house, where she takes care of him, and he told me what he knows.

I have been trying since to think what to write you. Pearl, I am sorry to say he says the whole story as you know it is not true.

I drew in a sharp breath in shock. This was the worst possible news, but I could not stop reading now, so I plunged ahead.

Mr. Lee first came to Buckskin Joe in 1868, so he was not there during the epidemic, but he says that tales of it have been greatly exaggerated. Silverheels never had smallpox, nor did she disappear from town. She had many suitors after the epidemic, but she chose Jack Herndon, the saloon owner. Miners were leaving town after the free gold played out, and the saloon business was drying up, so they staked a homestead claim in the valley and settled into ranching. They built up the finest spread in South Park, and had a pretty little baby girl named Marian. They stayed on a few years after that, until Mr. Herndon's father passed on in Kentucky and they inherited the family farm down there. They sold their spread to Mr. Lee and haven't been back to Colorado since.

Are you very disappointed, Pearl? I hope I have done the

right thing to tell you this. It is not really a very exciting story after all the rest, but I suppose the truth of life is never quite as thrilling, is it?

Please write me back and tell me what you think. I suppose there is not much to think if Mr. Lee actually knew her. He must be right. But do write me back all the same. Has Orv recovered from his fall? How is Russell? Have you seen Mrs. Nelson again? I want to know everything that goes on there and hope every day for a letter from you or Willie. Things are dull here in Denver without you.

Sincerely, your friend,

Frank Sanford

I stared in disbelief at the letter. I was defeated! Now I saw the secret clue in Mae Nelson's photograph that I should have seen all along. The picture was taken in the 1870s, and Tom Lee was only a child. He could not have remembered the epidemic of 1861. The only way he could have known Silverheels would be if she had stayed on. And if she hadn't disappeared, chances were the rest of the story was false too. There was nothing at all to the story I had believed all my life. How could Silverheels have been just an ordinary person—a ranch wife—who had led an ordinary life? This was worse than Josie's version of the story. At least Josie had allowed her to be clever and conniving. A ranch wife? I'd never get Josie to stop campaigning now!

I was still staring at the letter, trying to decide what to do, when the front door burst open and Mrs. Crawford came thundering through, shouting my mother's name. Mother came out of the kitchen, her eyebrows raised.

"Margaret Barnell, how dare you!" Mrs. Crawford said.

Mother calmly wiped her hands on her apron. "How dare I what, Phoebe?"

"Don't pretend you don't know! I was just down in Fairplay, where I ran into Mr. Merino from the mercantile."

"Oh?"

"He tells me that he has sold all of his Liberty Bonds. He's collected over one hundred dollars. And some folks are well on their way to fulfilling their subscriptions. Well, of course I wondered how he had managed that feat so quickly, and you know what he told me? He told me that the butcher's wife from up in Como came down with thirty-five dollars. Not only did she buy her bond, but she contributed to the subscriptions of some of her friends in Fairplay!"

Mother smiled. "Well, that's fine news. I'm glad to hear that so much has been raised for the war effort."

"Don't pretend innocence with me," Mrs. Crawford spat back. "I know you talked her into selling her frankfurters at the picnic, after I expressly forbid it! And as if that wasn't bad enough, you told her to take the money down to Merino's store. You are both traitors to this town."

"It seems to me, Phoebe, that you said you wouldn't take Mrs. Schmidt's money. Besides, what difference does it make where we buy our Liberty Bonds? They all support the same war effort, don't they? Aren't we supposed to be thinking first of our boys over there?"

Mrs. Crawford's eyes narrowed. "I am writing the governor, letting the authorities know you conspire with the Germans and with the National Women's Party. Mark my words, Maggie Barnell. There are two sides to this war, and you'll be sorry you picked the wrong one!" With that, she turned and marched out the still-open door.

Mother watched her go. Then she sighed and turned back to the kitchen.

"What are you going to do?" I asked, following.

"Start supper," she said.

"No, I mean about Mrs. Crawford. She thinks we are traitors!"

Mother looked me in the eyes. "Are we traitors, Pearl?"

"Of course not!"

"Then we have nothing to worry about."

"But she's writing to the governor! And she has evidence. Everyone knows you told Josie she could campaign in here at lunchtime. And now you are helping the Schmidts?"

"Mrs. Gilbert," she corrected. "And if I wasn't standing by the Schmidts, I really would be a traitor."

"But—"

Mother held up a hand to stop me. "Pearl, listen to me. These are hard and confusing times. The best I can do is to be true to what I know is right. It's the best any of us can do." She touched me over my heart. "What's right in here is more important than what someone like Mrs. Crawford tells you is right. Try to remember that."

I understood what she meant, but I knew that it wasn't practical advice. After all, the suffragists at the White House were doing what they believed in their hearts was right, and they had ended up in jail. I couldn't let that happen to my mother, so I slipped out the back door and went looking for George.

I found him relaxing on the front steps of the mercantile, and I asked him to take a walk with me. He agreed, taking my hand in his as we set off toward the creek. When we were out of sight from town, he pulled me to him and kissed me on the lips. I let him, reminding myself it was what I'd always wanted, even if his lips felt like they were smothering me and his breath smelled like onions.

To my relief, George pulled back for air and I was able to speak before he could trap my mouth again. I told him what had happened in the café that afternoon. He wasn't a bit surprised.

"Can you talk to your mother?" I asked him, after I had told him of her threat. "Ask her not to write to the governor about my mother?"

"But Pearl, you know it's all true. Your mother has invited Josie to spread sedition in the café, and she did conspire with Mrs. Schmidt."

I remembered the day my mother went to talk to Mrs. Schmidt about the picnic, and I knew he was right. "But that was all harmless."

"That's for the governor to decide." He brought his lips close to mine for another kiss. "Don't worry, Pearl. I don't blame you."

I pulled back. "Don't worry? How can I not worry when your mother is trying to get my mother arrested?"

He stared at me for a moment with a small smile at the corner of his mouth. Then he slid his hands around my waist and pulled me close, imprisoning me in his strong arms. "Maybe they will let your mother off easy, since your father wasn't here. She hasn't had much guidance this summer. And you're so sweet and naive, no one will blame you."

"I'm not a child, George!" I said, annoyed.

He smiled a mischievous smile. "I know," he said and pressed his lips to mine again. I jerked away, breaking his grasp and stepping out of his reach.

"What? Isn't this why you brought me here, out of sight from town?"

"I brought you here to talk, George! Your mother is trying to cause us trouble when my mother hasn't done anything wrong, and you know it! How can you think of kissing at a time like this!"

I ran back to town and into the café. I didn't look back to see if he followed, and he didn't try to stop me. I hoped he would see reason and come make up with me that evening, but he didn't. In fact, virtually no one came in for supper. I was certain Mrs. Crawford's threats were keeping everyone away. The next morning, however, the usual group of old-timers was there, minus Josie. She didn't come in for lunch, either. A tiny spark of hope kindled in me. Perhaps Josie had heard of Mrs. Crawford's anger and had decided to go easy on us until things smoothed over. Mother suggested we take her breakfast when she didn't come the next day, but the old-timers insisted she was in a snit, and it was better to leave her alone.

When she still hadn't surfaced for breakfast for the third day in a row, it could no longer be ignored.

"It's not like Josie to stay away so long," Russell said. "I reckon it's time we checked in on her."

"Maybe Pearl could go over after we eat," Mother said, coming out of the kitchen with our breakfast.

"I'll go with you," Russell said.

I loafed over my breakfast, in no rush to visit Josie in broad daylight, but at last we had to go. Her house was closed up tight as always. Her boots sat outside the back door, but there was no sign of life from within.

"Her boots are here, so she must be home. Unless she's gone out barefoot," Russell observed. He rapped gently on the door, but there was no answer.

"Russell, look," I said, pointing to the boots. A spider had built a web across the opening of one of them, as if it had been sitting there undisturbed for a while. All the lines of Russell's face tightened and hardened with worry. He raised his hand, and this time when he rapped on the door, each knock was loud and crisp.

"Jo, are you in there?" he called. There was no answer.

"Josie?"

No answer.

Impatiently, he called louder. "Josephine Gilbert! Open this door!"

Still, there was no answer.

Russell took the doorknob and jerked the door open. Together we rushed inside.

The house was neat and tidy—the bed made, the dishes all washed and put away, the table wiped clean. Even the old printing press in the corner, which had been cluttered by stacks of leaflets when I had last been here, was tidy. The papers themselves were gone, and so too, apparently, was Josie. Just like the Silverheels of legend, she had disappeared without a trace, leaving only her tidy cabin and her shoes behind.

CHAPTER 24

The news that Josie was gone did not really cause much of a stir back at the café. Perhaps if it had been winter and the weather posed a danger, or if there had been signs of feeblemindedness it would have been different. As it was, they all figured Josie could come and go as she pleased, which of course was true. And most of them really preferred the idea of her going to the idea of her coming, so there was no fuss there. The problem was, she had never gone before, not like this.

Mother, Russell, and I were the only ones who felt that we should look for her. We inquired with Mr. Orenbach, but he hadn't sold her a train ticket or seen her board a train. We inquired with Mr. Johnson at the livery, but Josie had not been there either. She had apparently left town on foot without the boots she always wore, but no one had seen her, or if they had, they'd paid no attention.

While no one else cared to look for her, everyone arrived at the café that evening to gossip and speculate about where she might have gone. Even the Crawfords came, all three of them looking smug. Mr. Crawford had the newspaper under his arm, but for once he didn't bury himself in it. He seemed more interested in watching the festivities along with his wife. George hadn't spoken to me since I had left him by the creek. I feared everything was over between us, so I was surprised when he turned his radiant smile on me. Angry as I was, that smile still made my heart give a little hiccup.

"Maybe a dashing young gambler swept her off her feet and they ran away together," Orv suggested, to a wave of approving laughter.

"Maybe she's gone off to enlist," suggested Harry.

"There is the nurses' corps," Russell said in all seriousness. "They do need women to sign on as nurses."

"Josie, signing up to help people?" Orv said.

"I think I'd rather die of my wounds," Harry muttered, and once again the laughter erupted.

I didn't find their jokes funny. I remembered her standing silently in the moonlight with her gun, watching the hotel the night Robert had gotten drunk. She did help people, sometimes.

The chatter and speculation quieted when Mr. Orenbach entered with a slip of paper in his hand.

"Telegram for you, Pearl. From young Master Frank."

"For me? From Frank?" I took it with a trembling hand. Telegrams hardly ever came to Como. There was a telegraph machine in the railroad office, but it was used almost entirely for railroad business. The only time anyone else received a telegram was when there was bad news, so of course, every eye in the room turned to me. Mother even came out of the kitchen.

"It's about Josie," Mr. Orenbach said.

"Josie?!" I took the telegram, more confused than ever.

"Read it to us, Pearl," Orv said. "We all want to know."

I unfolded the piece of paper and read.

> *TO Pearl Barnell*
> *Como, Colorado*
> *Josie Gilbert in jail STOP See July 19 RM News p3*
> *STOP Please advise what to do STOP Frank Sanford*

"Anyone got a copy of the *Rocky Mountain News*, July 19th?" Russell called out.

Mrs. Crawford smiled triumphantly and took the paper from her husband. She brought it to the counter, already flipped open to the article on page three. George sauntered over behind her. Other folks gathered around to read as well.

RALLY FOR ARRESTED SUFFRAGISTS TRIGGERS MORE ARRESTS

I read through it quickly. The Colorado Chapter of the National Women's Party, led by a Miss Josephine Gilbert, had organized a rally on the steps of the state capitol to demand the release of their sisters in Washington. When they were asked by police to disperse, a scuffle ensued. I didn't have to read the details farther down the page to know how it had happened. I could see it clear enough in my mind. After all, I had seen Josie scuffle with the security men on the platform. The article ended with unsympathetic commentary about those who put their personal causes before patriotism in war time. It was exactly the sort of thing Mrs. Crawford had been saying all summer.

I looked up from the article, taking a deep breath to calm myself.

"Looks like she's dangling off that cliff after all, doesn't it, Pearl, and without a rope," George said, smiling. He slipped an arm around my waist. "Now do you see why I've been trying to protect you? I'm glad you weren't involved with her."

I ignored him and turned to Russell. "What are we going to do?"

"Don't see as how there's much we can do," said Mr. Orenbach. "If she insists on making her bed, she's going to have to lie in it."

"But she's in jail!" I said.

"I'm sorry, Pearl," Mr. Orenbach said, and walked away.

"She got what she deserves, Pearl," George said. "I tried to warn you."

My back stiffened and I stepped forward, away from his encircling arm.

"Now, son, it's best not to judge a person until you've walked a mile in their shoes, as they say," Russell said.

George smirked, and I wondered what I had ever found

handsome about his hard, mean face. "A mile in her shoes?" He waddled back and forth in front of the counter, imitating her lopsided gait and snorting like a donkey. Then he laughed and said, "I hope Sufferin' Josie stays locked up forever, the traitor!"

"Mrs. Gilbert," my mother corrected him. "Please respect your elders when you are in my café."

"Actually, it's Miss Gilbert," I said. "She's proud to have never taken on a man's name, or his laundry."

Russell gave a surprised hoot of laughter. "That's Josie, all right."

George's eyes narrowed. "So you were working with her then."

"No, but I know she's never hurt anyone in this town, and she's been better to her neighbors than the Crawfords have been!" I said. There was a collective intake of breath around the room, then all eyes shifted to George's parents.

"Don't hang yourself with the rest of them, Pearl. We have all the evidence, and we've already sent it off to Denver to prove our case. Josie Gilbert is going to stay in jail, and there's going to be a full investigation of everyone who's been helping her," George said.

"That's right," Mrs. Crawford said. "We've been keeping track of all the sedition around here. Mr. Orenbach letting Josie attack the president in front of all those soldiers. The Schmidts selling their Kaiser Dogs at the picnic. Your mother helping hand out Josie's slander rags in here at lunch!"

George nodded and looked me square in the eye. "It's

about time we cleared out all the traitors and Germans from this town. Do you really want to side with them?"

"Get out!" I said.

"Pearl." He reached for me, as if he could melt my resolve by being near me. It had worked for him in the past, but not this time. As his hand closed on my arm, I pushed him away angrily. Surprised, he stumbled backward, caught his leg on a stool, and crashed to the floor in a clatter of furniture. Several people nearby could have caught him, but they stepped out of the way and let him fall.

"Pearl!" said Mrs. Crawford. "How dare you!" She turned on me instantly and slapped my face, hard. Just like that, Willie was between her and me, his fists clenched. I could see the hair on the back of his neck bristling, like an angry bulldog.

My mother caught her by the arm and began walking her toward the door. "Mrs. Crawford, I'd like you to leave."

Orv stepped to the door and held it wide.

Mrs. Crawford yanked her arm free from my mother and glared around at everyone. "You'll all be sorry when that investigation comes," she said. "Don't think I don't know about all of you. I know everything that happens in this town!"

"Out," my mother said.

"And don't ever touch my sister again," Willie growled at George.

"You're making a very poor business decision," Mr. Crawford said. He was trying to stare Mother down, but she didn't budge. "If your husband were here, he'd set you right."

"Come along, George," said Mrs. Crawford. She turned up her nose and marched out the door as if she were the Queen of Sheba, and George followed behind as if he were the Queen of Sheba's momma's boy. Which is what he had turned out to be. Why hadn't I seen it sooner? Mr. Crawford followed and closed the door behind them, and everyone in the café let out their breath.

I turned to my mother when they were gone, rubbing my stinging cheek. "Do you really think there will be an investigation?"

"We'll cross that bridge when we come to it," Mother said.

"Would they really shut down our café?"

My mother shrugged. "The thing is, Pearl, sometimes you just have to do what you believe is right, and trust that good will prevail. It usually does, somehow."

"But not always," I said. "It hasn't for Josie. Someone's got to go to Denver and get her out of jail!"

There was a silence after that. Most folks wouldn't look my way. No one wanted the responsibility, or the risk.

Anger surged in me all over again. "Well, if no one else will, I'll go!" I declared. "I'll go if I have to walk every inch of the way!"

"My, my," said Russell, a smile pulling at the corner of his lip. "Ol' Josie *has* been teaching you a thing or two, hasn't she."

I looked at Mother. Her brow was knitted. "I'm sorry, Pearl, but I just don't see how we can manage it. I would have to close the café."

"Then I'll go alone," I said.

"No. That is out of the question."

"But you're the one who said we had to stand up for what we believe in. You're the one who insists neighbors do for neighbors!"

"Pearl." Mother's tone was reproachful, which would normally have been enough to silence me, but not this time. I was finding strength in knowing I was right, and it felt good to stand my ground. Russell was right, Josie had taught me a thing or two.

"I'll go, Mrs. Barnell," Russell said, stepping forward and undoubtedly getting me out of trouble by doing so. "I've been trying to talk sense into that woman for two decades, so there's no point in me stopping now."

"And I'm going too," I insisted. "If she won't listen to Russell, she might listen to me. Please, Mother?"

"I'll wait tables while she's gone," Willie said. He gave me a little smile and nod that warmed me right through.

Mother was still frowning, but she looked me in the eye. "This is what you believe is right, Pearl? You feel that strongly about it?"

I straightened my shoulders and nodded. "I do."

Mother let out a big sigh. "Well, then. I suppose we better get you packed."

CHAPTER 25

I t took all the next day for Russell and me to get ready to go. During that time, a curious thing happened. Various people who hadn't said a thing to Mrs. Crawford in Josie's defense now came forward with offers of support. The miners' wives offered to help mother run the café in my absence, and the old-timers agreed to look after Russell's ranch. Willie assured me he'd do a good job of washing the dishes, even if it was women's work. Several other folks came forward offering cash to pay Josie's bail, if needed. I knew many of them complained about Josie, but as more than one of them said, she was a neighbor.

I helped my mother through breakfast and lunch, then went upstairs to pack. We planned to catch an evening train so we could arrive in Denver midmorning the next day. As I gathered my things, I saw the old tintype on the dresser. It hardly mattered anymore, but I put it in my bag all the same. Perhaps Frank would like to see the young Tom Lee, since he had met the old man.

That evening Russell and I said good-bye to Mother and Willie and boarded the eastbound train to Denver. The journey took all night. Russell and I couldn't afford sleepers, so we tried to sleep in our stiff seats. It was no use. Even if I had been comfortable, I was too nervous about going to Denver, seeing Frank again, and seeing Josie in jail.

By the time we stepped off the train the next morning, I was stiff, tired, and rumpled. Unlike our little platform in Como, the station in Denver was crowded. I looked around for Frank. I had wired him, but had received no reply before we left, so I wasn't sure what to expect. I certainly hadn't expected the way my heart soared when I spotted him at the back of a big crowd, waving his arms in the air to catch our attention. I waved back. He broke into a huge grin, and once I made it through the crowd, grasped me in a hug that left me breathless.

He and Russell carried our suitcases out of the station into the busy streets of Denver, and for a moment, I forgot about Josie. Streetcars clanged by, running on electric wires down the middle of the street. People crowded the sidewalks and motorcars whizzed past. Of course, I had seen cars before, but I hadn't imagined there would be so many. And the buildings! Every one was brick or stone, and some had as many as four or five stories!

Frank took my hand and smiled at me. "So what do you think of Denver?" I could see in his eager face how badly he wanted me to like it, but I was too amazed to even speak.

As soon as we were out of the crowds in front of the station, Russell set down our suitcases and asked about Josie. I felt a little guilty that I had been gawking like a tourist instead of asking after her myself.

"Josie's in the city jail on ten dollars bond," Frank told Russell. "I did go see her yesterday and told her you were coming."

"How is she?" I asked.

"A little angry."

Russell chuckled. "I bet she is. Madder than a tomcat in a pack of hound dogs, I'd wager. When does she have her hearing?"

"She goes before the judge tomorrow," Frank said. "It's a misdemeanor, so if she pleads guilty, she just has to pay a fine and she'll go free. If she pleads innocent, I think they set another date for a trial."

Russell frowned. "Sounds like we got here just in time. Now if we can just talk some sense into her."

"Can we go see her?" I asked.

Frank nodded again. "Visiting hours at the jail are at one o'clock. That's when I saw her yesterday. Mother says I should bring you home and let you settle in. We don't have a spare bedroom, but you're welcome to stay with us. Russell can have my room, and you can sleep with my sisters, Pearl. After lunch, you can go see Josie."

Frank's mother greeted us graciously and we spent the morning resting and freshening up after the long train ride. After lunch, Russell and I set off for the jail.

I had never been to a jail before. I tried not to think of all the criminals that might be in there as we climbed the big stone steps and entered the building. I stayed as close as I could to Russell as he filled out papers at the front desk and we followed a policeman into a big room with a long table down its center. Several other visitors, mostly women, already sat on our side of the table, as the policeman now instructed us to do. We sat down and waited, listening to a clock on the wall tick out the minutes. At last a door on the other side of the room opened and five prisoners filed in under the watchful eye of a guard. Josie was the only woman in the group and the only one wearing street clothes instead of a striped prison uniform. I suppose they didn't have prison uniforms for women, or maybe they just hadn't been able to wrestle her into one.

I stared at her as she entered. She was well dressed, in a dark suit and shiny black ladies' boots. I had never seen her dressed so respectably before. She could have passed on the street as a regular citizen of the big city, completely lacking the small-town manner that I knew marked Russell and me, no matter how we might dress.

She carried her chin high and her back straight as she approached the table. Her eyes flashed defiantly at everything around her, but when her gaze met mine, I saw fear there.

I couldn't believe it. Josie—who defied everyone, who did as she pleased, who made an effort to get herself into trouble—was afraid. And yet she had to have known when she came to Denver that it could lead to this. Had she been afraid before she had been arrested too? Had she put herself in danger, even as she feared doing so? And all the while I hadn't even been brave enough to acknowledge my friendship with her. With a pang of guilt, I saw now how unworthy of that friendship I had been.

"Well, don't sit there gawking, girl. You don't want everyone in Denver to think you are a complete hayseed, do you?" Josie said, breaking the spell of admiration as she settled her broad backside into the chair on the opposite side of the table from us. "Don't know what the two of you think you're doing here, but if you just dragged me in here so you can gawk at me, I'm going back to my cell."

"Good to see you too," Russell said. "Honestly, Jo. You are the most infuriating creature on God's green earth!"

Josie gave her usual donkey snort.

"We came to get you out," I said. "We collected money back home for your bail. Everyone chipped in."

Josie raised her eyebrows. "Everyone? Good thing your mother isn't here to hear you tell that whopper."

"Well, a lot of people. My mother, Mrs. Abernathy, the old-timers, Mr. Orenbach . . ."

"Well, you can take their money right back to them. I'm not having you bail me out."

"Dagnabbit, woman! For once in your life, listen to reason!" Russell's usually mild face was contorting and quickly turning red.

"I'm staying, and I'm saying my piece in court," Josie said.

"Well, we're not leaving this town without you!" Russell said. The two of them glared at each other across the table like two rams about to butt heads. I wouldn't have been surprised if either of them had started pawing the ground.

"But, Josie," I said, not caring if she heard the fear in my voice, "don't you want to get out of this place? You can still say your piece in court."

"If you bail me out, they'll think they've broken me. I'm staying right where I am. I'm not going to let them forget about me for a minute." She glared again at Russell, challenging him to try and stop her.

Russell leaned back in his chair, throwing his hands up in frustration. "Fine. Rot in jail. Maybe it'll give you time to come to your senses and see that accepting help from your friends wouldn't hurt one little bit." He stood so suddenly his chair tipped over and clattered to the floor. "I'll be outside whenever you're ready to go, Pearl."

When he was gone, I looked back to Josie. She was glaring after him.

"We just want to help," I said.

"I don't need anybody's help." She sounded like a pouting child.

"Is there anything you do need?" I asked.

She looked up at me. A little smirk curled one corner of her mouth. "You never told me what you thought of my penny dreadful, girl."

"Penny dreadful?"

"The True Account of Silverheels. I've kept the plates. I'm thinking of sending it off to the *Denver Post*, or the *Rocky Mountain News*. Who knows, maybe the *New York Times* has room for a new serial."

I stared, blinking. I couldn't believe she was bringing that up, of all things, when she was in jail! Besides, it didn't matter anymore. Not since I'd gotten the letter from Frank.

"Well?" she snapped. "Cat got your tongue, girl?"

I sighed, feeling trapped, even though she was the one in jail.

"We're both wrong. Frank talked to a man, Mr. Lee, who lived in Buckskin Joe and knew Silverheels. None of it is true. She was just an ordinary person."

Josie rolled her eyes. "Tom Lee was a fool. I wouldn't trust him as far as I could throw him."

"You know Tom Lee?"

"Stories get around the park, you know that."

"But he remembers her," I said.

The guard at the prisoners' door called out that visiting time was nearly over.

"Josie, we came to help you get out of trouble. The Crawfords say—"

"Honestly, Pearl. The Crawfords? When are you going to stop bothering with those busybodies?"

"But what about your defense tomorrow? They sent evidence against you!"

Josie stood and looked down at me. "Can you disprove my version of events in Buckskin Joe or can't you, girl? If you can't, I claim the victory."

A guard waved her into line with the other prisoners. She sneered at me over her shoulder as she was marched out.

Russell was waiting for me outside on the steps of the jail. He took one look at my face and grinned.

"Looks like she got to you, too."

I nodded, still too frustrated to speak.

"Well, let's go back and see Frank. He'll cheer you up."

Frank was waiting for us on the porch steps, tossing a baseball lazily into the air and catching it in his bare hand. He set it down and got to his feet when he saw us.

"You didn't get her out?" he asked, but I could see he wasn't a bit surprised.

I shook my head. "What do you think will happen when she goes to court tomorrow?"

"Don't worry, I suspect they'll let her off with a fine and a slap on the wrist," Russell said.

"Come on," Frank said. "Supper's not ready yet. Let me show you around."

Russell said he preferred to sit out the hot afternoon on the shaded porch, but I could tell from the smile he gave us he was letting Frank and me have some time alone.

We wandered together down the sidewalk toward the busy streets of downtown, where Frank pointed out local landmarks. I tried to pay attention to what he was saying, but I was distracted by his nearness as we walked. His skin radiated the warmth of the July day, and gave off a clean, city-boy scent. He might not be as good-looking as George Crawford, yet being near him felt so much warmer and more comfortable.

After a while we came to a patch of green grass with a shaded bench. We sat, and Frank took my hand.

"Pearl, are you angry with me?" he asked.

I turned to him in surprise. "Of course not. I'm so grateful you told us about Josie. She didn't tell anyone in town where she was going. We wouldn't have known without your telegram."

"I don't mean about that. I mean about talking to Mr. Lee."

"Oh." I hoped my disappointment didn't show on my face, but it must have, because Frank lowered his eyes from mine.

"I'm sorry, Pearl. I ruined everything. I didn't want to tell you, but I didn't want you to think I'd forgotten about you either."

I squeezed his hand and smiled. "I'm glad you wrote me."

"But what Mr. Lee said did spoil things, didn't it."

I shrugged and looked away at the cars again. It was the only way I could make myself look like it wasn't important.

"I don't know. Josie says Mr. Lee is a fool. That he can't be trusted."

"You told Josie about my letter?"

"Sort of . . ." I said. "She asked me for . . . She's interested, that's all."

"She didn't seem that interested when I was up in Como. She said the story was cockamamie."

"She just sees things differently." I hadn't told anyone about what I had been doing with Josie, but suddenly I wanted to. I wanted to tell Frank. I took a deep breath. "Josie thinks Silverheels was a thief."

"What?"

"She thinks Silverheels only stayed so she could claim the gold that belonged to all those dying miners. They were all so in love with her that they believed her when she promised to send it to their families. Then she only pretended to get sick and ran away with all the gold."

Frank looked at me, his expression sour. "I think I like Mr. Lee's story better. How does Josie know that? She told me she came to Como about twenty years ago."

"She did. She just made it up."

"Why does she want to ruin the story?"

It was a good question—why had Josie started the competition with me? I thought back to how it began. It was the day Frank had first come to Como and I had just told them the legend the way I had always heard it.

"She doesn't like the idea that Silverheels did it all for love. That she sacrificed herself out of love."

"What's she got against love?" Frank said. "I think love is a fine reason to take action, don't you?" He leaned in close to me, an invitation.

"I do," I said, and taking the invitation, I kissed him.

CHAPTER 26

I t was a perfect kiss. His lips were soft and warm, and felt like sunshine on my mouth. Even after the kiss ended, the sunshine lingered, warm and glowing under every inch of my skin.

I floated on clouds all the way back to his house, my hand in his. I should have been thinking about Josie and her court date tomorrow, but all I could think about was love, and Frank's kiss, and the giddy joy of being near him.

At supper I met Frank's whole family—his mother, father, and five sisters. Annie, the oldest, was warm and friendly to me, as if we had been dear friends in Como. Here with his family she put on none of the airs I had seen when she was with Robert. I liked this Annie much better.

After supper the whole family went out onto the porch with iced tea. All the girls were knitting socks and caps for the Red Cross to send to soldiers.

"Frank tells me he had a fine time with your family in the mountains," his mother said to me, her knitting needles clacking steadily.

"Yes, ma'am," I said. "At least, I hope he did. I had a fine time with him." As soon as I said it, I had to turn away so she wouldn't see me blush at how it sounded.

Mr. Sanford smiled. "He couldn't stop talking about that wonderful mystery of Silverheels you told him. He's been trying to figure it out since he got back."

"Say, did you bring that picture Mae Nelson gave you?" Russell said.

"A picture?" Frank said, sitting up straighter. "Of Silverheels? You didn't tell me you brought a picture."

"No, it's not Silverheels. It's Tom Lee's old school picture." I retrieved the old photograph from my suitcase. Back out on the front porch I handed it to Frank. He bent close over it, examining it carefully, from the woman in the back to the blurred children in the front.

"That's Tom Lee," I said, pointing to the boy. "And this beside him is Eliza Carlisle, Mrs. Nelson's mother."

"Say, she lives in Denver now too, doesn't she?" Frank asked.

I nodded.

"So she must remember Silverheels too."

"I don't think so," I said. "Mrs. Nelson never said anything about that."

"But Mr. Lee says that when he was growing up, Silverheels still lived in South Park on her ranch. And if they grew up together, Mrs. Carlisle must have known her too."

"I hadn't thought about it that way," I said, looking again at the photograph. "They are the same age."

"We have to go talk to her, Pearl. Tomorrow, while you're still here."

"But Josie's hearing is tomorrow."

"Not till the afternoon. We could go see Mrs. Carlisle in the morning. It will be fun."

I wasn't sure how fun it would be. I didn't want to hear more about how uninteresting the truth was. But I agreed, because it would mean a morning with Frank.

The meeting with Mrs. Nelson's mother was quickly and easily arranged, since Frank's family had a telephone, and so, apparently, did Mrs. Carlisle. Russell wanted to spend the morning learning all he could about Josie's hearing, so Frank and I had two hours on our own to visit her.

We took the streetcar across town to Mrs. Carlisle's neighborhood. Frank sat close to me and held my hand the whole way.

"I've been thinking about what we should ask her," Frank said, and he began to list off the questions. I was grateful that he would do the talking. I hadn't been thinking clearly since he kissed me the day before, and now that his hand was in mine, I couldn't seem to think at all. Was this why people risked so much when they were in love? I had always thought love made them heroic, but maybe it just addled their brains. With a shock, I realized that was just what Josie would say. I jerked my hand out of Frank's. He stopped listing off the questions and looked at me, his eyebrows raised.

"What's the matter?" he asked.

"I—, I—" Blood rushed to my face. "I just had an awful thought about Josie," I said. Not exactly the truth, but it was the best I could do under the circumstances.

He smiled. "Don't worry, Pearl, she hasn't been in trouble before. They will let her off easy. She'll be back in Como with you in no time."

I nodded and gave him a weak smile in return. "I hope you're right. Maybe you better do the talking at Mrs. Carlisle's house," I said. "I can't seem to keep my mind on anything this morning."

Frank took my hand again. "Sure."

Mrs. Carlisle lived in an older neighborhood with tiny frame houses, in the tiniest house on the block. The woman who opened the door introduced herself as Mrs. Carlisle's daughter, Miss Marjorie Carlisle. She was a tall boney woman who looked as if she'd been gritting her teeth for too much of her life.

Mrs. Carlisle came from the kitchen and greeted us. A softer-looking woman than her daughter, she put us at ease with a kind smile. We sat down together in the front parlor, and Frank got right to business.

"We're interested in the story of Silverheels and what happened in Buckskin Joe. Your daughter, Mrs. Nelson, was very kind to tell us what she knew."

"Oh, of course," said Marjorie, rolling her eyes. I was surprised by her tone, and I could see Frank was too. "My sister never gets enough of telling about seeing Silverheels with her

very own eyes. She told you that, right? Twice in the cemetery. No one else in town ever saw her, but Mae saw her twice.
What a lucky girl she was."

Mrs. Carlisle let out a heavy sigh. "I'm sorry. My girls were
always competitive, I'm afraid."

"Mae got the best of everything," Marjorie muttered.

"Now that's not true, dear. You got the high school educa-
tion while Mae dropped out to marry. And you went to the
Fourth of July barn dance with that boy you both liked. What
was his name?"

"Thomas. And as you may recall, I went to the barn dance
with him, but Mae *left* the barn dance with him."

Mrs. Carlisle looked at us with a tired smile. "Whatever you
say, dear. I'm sure these children aren't here to hear about all
that."

"No, ma'am," Frank said. "We also learned about Mr. Lee,
who grew up in Buckskin Joe, and I've talked to him about
what he remembers."

"And now you want to talk to me, too," said Mrs. Carlisle
with a pleased smile. "What can I tell you? My mind's like a
steel trap, even at my age."

"We wanted to know what you remember about
Silverheels."

"Oh, she was long gone by the time I can remember,"
Mrs. Carlisle said dismissively. "But Silverheels wasn't the
only important person in Buckskin Joe. Horace Tabor had
a store there with his first wife, Augusta, before he made his

fortune in Leadville and left her for that hussy Baby Doe." She shook her head. "Always the way with rich men, a good, hard-working woman like that abandoned for a pretty face."

Frank glanced at me, his eyes begging for my help.

"Mrs. Carlisle, your daughter lent me this picture. I was wondering if you could tell me what you remember about it—or about any of these people."

I held the old tintype out to her. She put a pair of spectacles on and examined it, running her finger along from person to person as she did.

"Lordy be! I haven't seen this picture in years. That's me there, and that's Tom Lee." She gave a little chuckle. "Look at him, love struck as always for Emma Clark. Who could have blamed him—she was a pretty little thing, wasn't she."

By now we were all gazing at the girl with the bow and the ringlets, the same girl the ten-year-old Tom was admiring in the image.

"I don't recall you ever talking about an Emma Clark, Mother," Marjorie said. "Did she stay on in Buckskin Joe?"

"For a time. I suppose I never much talked about her because I was jealous, along with every other girl in town. Every boy who cast eyes on Emma had no eyes for any of the rest of us, and you know how that is. Nothing blinds a girl like jealousy. Just look at my two daughters, both thinking the other had it better than them."

"Mae did have it better than me," Marjorie said. "She was always everyone's favorite."

Mrs. Carlisle looked back down at the picture. "Poor Tom. He was smitten."

"What happened to Emma Clark?" Marjorie asked. "Did Tom marry her?"

"She married a farmer who came up from Kentucky. They claimed homesteads in South Park, side by side so they could put them together as one. Once they proved up on those, they claimed a few more. Eventually had one of the finest spreads in Park County. When his pa died back in Kentucky, they pulled up stakes and headed back down south. As I recall, Tom bought their spread. I think he was still secretly in love with Emma, though she had a husband and child by then. He couldn't have her, so he bought up her ranch to remember her by."

Frank's brow was all scrunched up by now. She stopped and looked at him.

"Something the matter, son?" she asked.

"Not exactly. It's just that Mr. Lee said that it was Silverheels who had that ranch and who left for Kentucky and sold it to him."

Mrs. Carlisle laughed. "Tom Lee's gotten mighty confused in his old age. In those days there was a big Fourth of July pageant down in Fairplay every summer, and we kids from Buckskin Joe put on a little play about Silverheels. And every time, pretty little Emma, with her blond curls, got the part of Silverheels, while the rest of us girls had to be dying miners, all covered with ugly pox. Poor Tom was so in love with her he probably came to think of her as the real Silverheels."

I didn't realize I was smiling until I looked at Frank and saw him smiling back. I turned to Mrs. Carlisle.

"Well, if Mr. Lee didn't know the real Silverheels, was there anyone in Buckskin Joe in your day who did?"

"A couple of old miners," she said. "One fellow whose face was all scarred with pockmarks would sit outside the saloon and tell his story to anyone who'd buy him whiskey. The poor old drunk." She shook her head sadly and looked back down at the old tintype. Then her face lit up with surprise.

"Oh, there was her!" she said, jabbing her finger at the woman holding the child.

"The school mistress?" I asked.

"I'd forgotten about her. She wasn't really a school mistress. The year this picture was taken we didn't have a teacher. She was the oldest girl in the school, so she taught the little ones their letters and did what she could for us older ones. Mostly, we read the books left behind by the previous teacher."

"And she knew Silverheels?"

"She never talked about it, but apparently her pa died in the epidemic, when she was about twelve, and she was orphaned."

"What about her mother?" Frank asked.

"Her ma was an Indian, but I don't really know what happened to her. Some folks said she ran off with her tribe and never came back. Some folks said the child was so homely not even her own mother wanted her. You know how vicious rumors can be. Folks said Silverheels had been the child's only true friend in town and she was heartbroke when the dancer disappeared. She went up into the mountains with a search party, looking for Silverheels, but they got caught in a blizzard, nearly froze to death. She lost all her toes on one foot to frostbite. Never did walk quite right, even when I knew her."

I was staring at Mrs. Carlisle, my pulse thundering in my ears.

"What was her name?" Frank asked.

"Good heavens, I haven't thought of her in years. Let me see, what was her name?" Mrs. Carlisle pursed her lips and thought. "It was something Spanish or French as I recall."

"Sefa?" I asked.

Mrs. Carlisle looked at me, her eyebrows popping up in surprise. "Why, yes, that's it. Sefa Weldon. It was short for Josephine, but since there were several Joes in town, folks called her Sefa, to keep them straight. She left Buckskin Joe not long after this photograph was taken, I think. After we got a real teacher. I wonder what ever became of her."

I said nothing in reply, but I was pretty sure I knew—or would by the end of her hearing that afternoon.

CHAPTER 27

How did you know her name, Pearl?" Frank demanded as soon as we left Mrs. Carlisle's house and headed back toward the courthouse. He sounded annoyed, and I couldn't blame him. After all, we had both promised to share whatever we learned with each other, and now he thought I had been holding back. But I hadn't. I hadn't known Sefa was real, hadn't known Josie had ever been in South Park before she took over the Como newspaper office twenty years before.

"I didn't know," I said.

"Yes, you did."

"Josie told me—but I thought she made it up."

"Josie told you?" Then the shock of recognition swept over his face and he froze on the sidewalk.

"Good heavens! You don't mean—Josephine? Josie?!"

"And she says Silverheels was a cheat and a thief and a liar!" I said, walking faster. I didn't want to talk about it or even think about it.

Frank scrambled to catch up to me again. "So she's bitter—no wonder, if she felt abandoned by Silverheels. It's another lead we should follow. We have to talk to her and get the whole story from her."

"I don't want the whole story. I just want to go home," I said.

"Pearl, I don't understand. Why are you so angry? Please, talk to me!"

I heard the hurt in his voice, and the anger and humiliation ran out of me. Frank did not deserve my anger. I apologized, and once we were back on the streetcar, headed downtown, I held his hand once again. As we rode, I told him everything about Sefa—her unrequited love for Buck, her helplessness when he died, and how she nursed the dying without thanks while Silverheels stole their hearts and their gold.

Frank shook his head when I finished. "No wonder she's such a bitter old woman. No wonder she hates Silverheels so much."

I nodded. "It's like Russell says. You can't know someone until you've walked a mile in their shoes. I guess if it had been me, I'd hate everybody too."

"She doesn't hate everybody," Frank said.

I surprised us both by snorting like a donkey. I guess that's what bitterness does to a person.

"She doesn't," Frank insisted. "She just—I don't know. Wants to be right more than she wants to be liked, I think."

I was quiet then, thinking about that. It was what the whole exchange between us had been about. She had wanted to win. Maybe she hadn't been laughing at me the whole time. Maybe she just wanted to be right. To be heard. To be vindicated.

Frank smiled to himself. "At least we know now who's been fixing up Buck Wilson's grave."

I nodded. "I guess we do."

The courthouse was a busy place when we arrived. Lawyers and judges were scurrying around with stacks of paper and books under their arms. Families, friends, and enemies were sitting in the hallways on benches or filing in and out of courtrooms.

We found Russell on a bench outside a tiny courtroom on the second floor of the courthouse. He was dressed in a suit and tie and his hair was neatly slicked down, but unlike Josie who cleaned up real slick, Russell still looked like a hayseed, as Josie had called us. I'm sure I did too.

"It's a fairly simple hearing," he explained when he saw us. "She's waived her right to a lawyer—says she'd rather speak for herself."

"I wish she had taken a lawyer," I said, and Russell and Frank nodded.

"You know how Josie is," Russell said. "I just hope she doesn't get herself into worse trouble. There's no jury. It's just her and the judge and the policeman who arrested her. I doubt we'll really have a chance to do or say anything to help her, but we can at least sit in there and let her know folks are pulling for her."

Frank and I nodded. It wasn't much, but it was something.

An hour later, Josie, escorted by a policeman, approached down the hallway. I looked hard at her, harder than I had ever looked before. I guess I was searching for some sign of the brokenhearted, rejected little girl, or the aching loss that would bring her back to clean Buck Wilson's grave nearly sixty years later. She did look a little worse for wear after several days in jail, but otherwise she was the same Josie I'd always known. Tough, cranky, outspoken Josie, ready to take on anybody for her cause. Josie who was proud to have never taken a husband, who refused to be beholden to anyone.

We followed her into the courtroom. The judge entered and took his place at the bench. He read the charges—obstructing traffic, creating a public nuisance, and resisting arrest. I was relieved to hear no mention of sedition. He asked Josie for her plea.

She said clearly, "Not guilty." My relief evaporated.

The judge cleared his throat. "Miss Gilbert. Allow me to clarify your position. Four other women were cited for obstructing traffic and creating a public nuisance along with you. Those ladies pled guilty to the charges, paid their fines, and have gone home to their husbands where they belong. Their acceptance of the charge will be used as evidence against you should you deny guilt.

"These are not serious charges, and if you are willing to pay the fine and return home to"—he consulted the paper in front of him—"to Como, we are willing to drop the resisting arrest charge, which is more serious."

"I will not!" Josie said, her back straightening. "We have a constitutional right to assembly and to free speech. There was no obstruction of anything but justice."

"And the charge of resisting arrest, madam? We have a police officer here with some mighty big bruises on his shins that I am willing to admit as evidence. Plenty of witnesses were on hand. I'd say the state has a clear case against you."

"I was resisting false imprisonment on false charges. Your police force does not have the authority to ride roughshod over my constitutional rights just because the exercise of my free speech is an embarrassment to them," Josie said.

I closed my eyes and tried to calm myself. She was doing exactly what I had feared she would—arguing and insisting she was right against something that was too big for her. Fighting a battle she couldn't win just because it was the right thing to do. But there was no point to it. She couldn't win this war from inside a prison cell. She'd be locked up and forgotten. No one would even know she was there, sacrificing her freedom.

The judge cleared his throat and shuffled his papers again. "Miss Gilbert, I don't think you fully understand the gravity of your situation. Should this go to trial, the prosecution's case against you will be watertight. When you are convicted of resisting arrest and of assaulting a police officer in the process, you will find the consequences severe—a steep fine and quite probably a lengthy stay in jail."

"Are you saying you've found me guilty already, without due process, Judge Gifford?" Josie said. "I don't believe that's legal either."

The judge's eyes narrowed. "Due process will not be denied you, Miss Gilbert. I am simply trying to advise you of the folly of your current course of action. You have elected to dispense with legal representation, so I want you to clearly understand. As far as I can tell from the facts of this case, there is ample evidence against you and very little that supports your claim of innocence. The state, in bringing this case forward, has admissions of guilt from your associates, witnesses, the physical evidence of injury to the police officer and his possessions. They even have here a letter from a concerned citizen in Como, recounting a similar assault made by you on railroad personnel there, and the public danger of your ongoing seditious activities. It is, madam, a solid case against you. The court is willing, however, to let you off with a lesser fine and a warning, should you elect to plead guilty."

"You are awfully eager to get rid of me quietly," Josie said. "Afraid a public trial will shine an embarrassing light on the public servants of Denver, are you?"

"Dagnabbit, woman, just plead guilty and pay the fine," Russell said in a low voice. The judge looked in our direction for the first time.

"Do you have something to say on behalf of the defendant?" he asked.

Russell stood slowly. "We are her friends, your honor, from Como."

The judge glanced back to Josie. "Well, it's good to see you have some friends with good sense. This letter from Como in your file says otherwise. What is your relationship to the defendant, sir?"

Russell shuffled his feet a little and glanced at Josie's stiff back. He cleared his throat. "She's my wife, your honor."

Frank and I both turned and stared at Russell, our mouths hanging open. I'd never heard Russell tell a lie before. The judge's eyebrows popped up.

"These documents say *Miss* Gilbert. Is there a mistake?"

"My common-law wife, your honor. We've shared"— Russell glanced uncomfortably down at me before continuing—"shared marital relations, if you take my meaning, for fifteen years. I've asked her plenty of times to make it proper, but she won't have any part of that."

"I see," the judge said. I could see what he was thinking, that us country folks were about as backward and uncivilized as a pack of wolves.

"You see, your honor, Miss Gilbert is about as stubborn as a mule with a stone in its shoe, and sometimes she can't see what's best for her when it's hitting her in the face. But the other thing you've got to know about her is that she cares a good deal about doing the right thing. She cares about women getting the vote and being able to take care of themselves. She may be stubborn and wrongheaded in how she tries to get those things, but its always about the greater good. Folks like whoever wrote that letter, they only see things in terms of their own comforts in the here and now. Josie, there, she don't care about her own comfort if she can ensure what's best for future generations."

"Well, you make her out to be a very noble woman, but you claim to be her husband. I am going to have to see your testimony as biased."

"It's true, sir," I said, jumping to my feet. "Josie—Miss Gilbert has put the needs of others before her own for her whole life."

"And who are you, miss?" the judge asked.

My cheeks warmed, but at the same time I felt my back stiffen, just like Josie's. "I'm Miss Perline Rose Barnell," I said. "I'm one of those future generations, and Miss Gilbert is my friend."

"And you can vouch for this lifetime of good deeds you claim she's had?"

"Yes, sir. Back in the early days of our county's history, she nursed the sick through a terrible epidemic of smallpox. When others fled, she stayed to help the sick, even though she was just a girl."

"Hearsay," the judge said. "Do you, yourself, Miss Barnell, have personal experience with this altruistic spirit of hers?"

"Why yes, your honor. That's what this is here today. She could stay safely at home and mind her own business. After all, women have the vote in Colorado. But she's fighting for everyone, no matter the consequences to herself."

"Hmm," the judge said. He didn't seem convinced by that. I was racking my brain for another example, when Frank got to his feet beside me. The judge gave a little sigh, but nodded to him to speak.

"My name is Franklin Sanford, your honor. I live here in Denver. I met Miss Gilbert and these other folks a few weeks back, when I visited Como with my sister and her new husband." From there, Frank went on to tell the judge of the drunken scene in the street with Robert, and of my mother and Josie coming to our aid. He embellished it a bit, giving Josie a bigger role than she'd had, but none of us contradicted him.

When he finished, the judge turned back to Josie. "I hope you see, madam, that you have some good friends and supporters here. Have you considered how they would feel if you got yourself convicted to six months in the women's workhouse?"

"Six months!" I gasped.

The judge glanced at me, then back at Josie.

"Six months is a long time in the workhouse for a woman your age," he said. "This court will take a fifteen-minute recess for you to reconsider your plea, Miss Gilbert, now that your situation has been made clear to you. I urge you to talk to your friends and listen to their advice."

With that the judge turned and left the courtroom, and Josie spun to face the three of us.

"I've never seen such a bunch of lying, groveling, cocka-mamie fools in all my life!" she shouted. "Your wife! Never, Russell McDonald! And you!" She jabbed a finger at me. "Get your head out of that silly story already! I am not your Silverheels!"

"You're welcome," Russell said. "Now shut up and listen to sense for once in your life." He gave her a little push to make her sit down in the chair behind her, but before he could say anything else, a policeman entered the room and called him away. We watched with a sinking heart as Russell followed the man out of the room. He might have had a chance of convincing Josie to change her plea, but I didn't see how Frank and I could.

"Please, Josie. Please plead guilty and pay the fine so you can come home with us," I said.

"You can do more for your cause out of jail than in it," Frank added.

"They are scared of having me in jail," she said. "Look at all the press my sisters in Washington have gotten. They don't want all that trouble here. I've got them right where I want them. If they acquit me, they've admitted cases like mine are frivolous, and I'll take it straight to Washington. If they convict me, they will have all the mess and controversy on their hands that they've been trying to avoid."

"And I'll have nothing," I said. "If they convict you, you'll be in the workhouse and you won't come back to Como."

Josie snorted. "They'll probably have a picnic in Como to celebrate being rid of me."

Tears welled up and spilled from my eyes, and I brushed them away furiously. "No they won't! Como needs you. I need you! We'd all just die of boredom without you in town. If you only knew all the folks that put in money for your bail."

"Pull yourself together and stop blubbering, girl," Josie said gruffly. "You're talking nonsense."

"It's not nonsense," I insisted. "Can't you see that Russell loves you, and I do too! We want you back in Como."

"Nobody loves me, girl, and that's how I want it," she said.

She got up and walked away from me, and I could see it was no use. She wouldn't bargain—not for her freedom, not for her life, and especially not for love. It was hopeless. I'd only realized how much I cared for her just in time to lose her. The tears came faster and I could not stop them. Frank put his arm around my shoulder. I leaned my head against him and sobbed.

"Gosh, Miss Gilbert. Have a heart," Frank said. He offered me his handkerchief and I wiped my eyes, but the tears kept flowing.

Though it hadn't been fifteen minutes, the door opened behind the bench and the judge came back in. Russell was not with him. He had a smug look on his face as he sat down at the bench. He banged his gavel once to let us know we ought to sit down and pay attention.

"Miss Gilbert," he said, "the case against you has been resolved in absentia."

"In absentia?" Josie repeated.

The judge gave her a condescending smile. "That means in your absence."

"I know what it means, but I'm not absent. I'm right here, you old fool. You can't do that!"

The judge banged the gavel again. "Order in the court. The court may rule in absentia when the defendant has proved belligerent in the courtroom, or at a conference regarding sentence reduction. Your charges have been reduced to obstructing traffic and creating a public nuisance, and your husband has paid the fines. All other charges are being dropped on the condition that you accompany your husband back to Como immediately upon leaving this court and do not return to Denver for six months. Your husband—"

"He's not my husband!"

"The nature of your relationship is sufficient for this court to accept his authority over you under common law. I am releasing you into his custody. He has agreed to accompany you home to ensure that you abide by the agreement. If you return to Denver you will be sentenced to six months in the county workhouse, and your husband will face charges for aiding and abetting you in your criminal activity."

"You can't do that," Josie said. "He can't do that. I'm an adult and he has no authority over me!"

"The court has ruled. The case of City and County of

Denver versus Josephine Gilbert is now closed." The judge banged his gavel one more time and strode form the room without a glance back at the defendant, who stood blustering uselessly before his bench.

CHAPTER 28

A police officer escorted us out of the courthouse.
Russell was waiting on the steps with our traveling
bags as well as a beat-up carpetbag that apparently
belonged to Josie. She glared so murderously at him when
she saw him that he took a step back from her. I was glad a
policeman was on hand, just in case.

Russell had a car waiting at the curb. The police officer was
to escort us to the train station and onto the first passenger
train headed west, so I only had a brief moment to say good-
bye to Frank. He kissed me lightly on the cheek and told me to
keep his soggy handkerchief. I kissed him back and promised
to write, hoping he didn't think me such a silly, weepy sap that
he was glad to be rid of me.

Then we were in the automobile headed to the train station. It was the first automobile I had ever ridden in, and I
would have loved it, but traveling with Josie and Russell was
like traveling with a thundercloud that might burst at any
moment. No one said anything. No one wanted to be the one
to burst it open.

At Union Station the policeman and Russell stayed close at

either side of Josie as we navigated through the crowds to the ticket window and bought our tickets. We had to wait nearly two hours for the train. The whole time anger scorched the air around us. At last an attendant came through ringing his handbell and announcing our train was boarding. We found our compartment and closed ourselves into it, still silent as the train lurched and pulled away from the station. I started to think that if someone didn't say something soon the whole compartment might just explode into flame, like old dynamite left at an abandoned mine too long. Russell must have felt the same way and wanted to keep me safe, because he dug into his pocket for a dime and suggested I go to the dining car and get us each a bottle of Coca-Cola.

I found the dining car two cars forward from ours. I took my time getting the soda pop and making my way back to our closed compartment. When I got back, the explosion had occurred. I could hear the shouting from the aisle, and I was glad that Russell had paid the extra for a compartment. Josie would have been impossible in a regular seat, surrounded by strangers.

"I don't care!" she was screaming as I approached the closed compartment. "I still say you had no right!"

"And you have no sense!" Russell countered. "And there's no way I was going to sit by and let you get yourself thrown into jail when there was something I could do about it. So I did it. You ought to thank me!"

"Thank you? Thank you for undermining all my hard

work? Thank you for treating me like a child? Like a *possession*? What exactly am I supposed to thank you for?"

"For loving you for twenty years no matter how stubborn and selfish you can be sometimes," Russell said. "Lord knows why I do!"

"You don't own me, Russell McDonald! And don't think a sappy speech like that will get you back in my good graces, either. It's over between us!"

"I figured it would be. I knew I ran that risk when I made my deal with the judge. But I couldn't let you go to jail, Jo. Not when there was something I could do—even if it meant losing you."

"You had no right!" Josie said again, but she wasn't shouting now. Good thing, too, since folks on either side of our compartment were sticking their heads out into the hall to see what was going on.

"I didn't ask for your help, and I certainly didn't need it! I had the situation under control—I had them by the throat."

"Someday, Josie, I hope you'll come to realize that *everybody* needs help at some time or other, and there ain't nothing wrong with accepting it when that time comes."

I felt foolish standing in the hallway with three bottles of Coca-Cola and all those people staring, so I slid open the compartment door. I nearly collided with Russell coming out.

"Sorry, Pearl," he said. He took the bottle I held out to him without looking at it. "I'll be in the dining car if you need me. Or if you just need to be somewhere else too." With that, he squeezed out past me and I was alone with Josie. She plopped down on the seat and glared out the window. I sat down in the seat opposite her and looked out as well. Anyone glancing in on us at that moment would have thought the flatland farms around Denver were the most interesting things in the world from the way the two of us were studying them. I was the one who eventually broke the silence.

"I think I've found the truth about Silverheels," I said. "I think I can finally prove it."

Josie looked at me, then back out the window. "Planning to take that victory away too, are you?"

"I just think there's more to the story. A lot more that needs telling." She said nothing, so I continued. "Sefa was deeply hurt by Silverheels leaving, but more than that, she was hurt by the miners who gave Silverheels all the credit and none to her. She was tired and heartsick and alone, and little more than a child herself. What they did was wrong, but she was too miserable to say so.

"Still, she didn't give up hope. She hoped for her mother and little brothers to return, and she hoped for a good man of the town to notice her and love her for all she had done.

"So, refusing to let despair overtake her, the brave Sefa joined the miners who searched the mountains for the missing dancer. But she was caught by the cruel weather and the toes on her left foot froze and had to be cut off. She recovered from the injury, but her broken heart would not heal. And when winter turned to spring and spring to summer, and her mother did not return to Buckskin Joe, she began to listen to the cruel rumors folks were whispering. That a no-good Indian wife wasn't the type to come back. That Sefa was unwanted, unloved, and unlovable. And then and there, Sefa vowed she'd never love again, or let anyone love her. Am I getting this right?"

Josie glanced at me, then turned back to the window. "I thought you said you wanted to tell Silverheels's story. I don't know why you're so interested in Sefa."

"I want to know what happened to her. I know she stayed on for a time, probably working Eli Weldon's claim. I doubt she would have accepted charity from the townsfolk, so she must have had some way to make a living."

"I don't see as it matters—the story was over by then, already making its way into that sappy legend you feed the tourists."

"It matters to me," I said. I took out the photo and handed it to Josie. She took it reluctantly and looked down at it. Her expression was unreadable, but she looked for a long time.

"So she stayed in Buckskin Joe until she was grown up," I said. "She worked as the schoolmarm when the teacher left and they couldn't get another. But then she left Buckskin Joe and Park County altogether."

"Did Mr. Lee tell you that?"

"Eliza Carlisle did," I said. "Mae Nelson gave us the picture."

A little smile pulled at the corner of Josie's mouth. "Eliza was one of the few pupils who ever paid much attention to her teacher."

"Except she called you Josephine *Weldon*. But you told me you'd never married."

"I never did."

"Then how did you get the name Gilbert?"

"Gilbert has always been my name, from my real father, the French fur-trader who gambled away my mother and me in a card game," she said. She pronounced it *Geel-bear*, and now I could see it was French, though I had never thought about it. "I never knew him, but my mother liked the name, so she remembered it. She said the bear was strong medicine."

"Why do you think she didn't come back?" I asked.

"She was dead. She only made it as far as Fairplay before the smallpox caught up to her. Indians have no immunity to it, you know. She died before anyone knew who she was or where she'd come from. The townsfolk shipped her boys off to the Indian School in Pennsylvania. I don't know what became of them."

"Oh, Josie, I'm so sorry."

She shrugged. "It was a long time ago. They are all gone now, even Sefa. All just lost in the legend."

"Please tell me. I want to know."

Josie looked back out the window. "Sefa taught the school, read the teacher's old books, gained a taste for knowledge. She discovered that learning, not just beauty, could get you what you needed. So, she scraped together her savings and the last little bit of gold she could squeeze from Eli's claim and left Colorado. Went back east and applied to the new Wellesley College for Women in Massachusetts. Graduated top of her class, but still, being an ugly old boot, and not quite white, she found no work. The good jobs were all reserved for men, and the secretarial positions were given to the pretty girls."

"But the women's suffrage movement saved her?" I guessed. "Took her in, gave her a job and a cause to believe in?"

"You're a smart girl, Pearl, and pretty enough. You could go far if you'd just get your head out of those silly daydreams and start standing up for yourself. If you weren't always hiding behind your polite 'yes, ma'ams' and 'no, ma'ams' and daydreaming about romantic cockamamie like Silverheels."

We sat a moment in silence before I spoke. "I've ended things with George Crawford," I said. "And while I was standing up for you, I sort of knocked him down."

Josie's eyes darted away from the window to my face at that, and I might have seen a trace of a smile on her lips. "Did you, now?"

"But I don't think the story is cockamamie," I said.

Josie snorted and turned back to the window. "Just when I thought you were showing some backbone. Even now that you know I was there, and you've heard the story from my own lips, you still prefer to believe in your pretty little Silverheels?"

"It's something else Mrs. Carlisle said, something about her daughters. Jealousy blinds a girl, she said. Both her daughters think the other had it better. They can't both be right, can they? I think Sefa was jealous of Silverheels and couldn't see the truth."

"Silverheels took everything I had when she left town! When she killed Buck!" Even all these years later her words were sharp with bitterness and anger.

"You don't know that she killed him—you weren't there. And you were just a kid. Buck Wilson was a grown man. I can't see that he was ever yours, except in daydreams. I don't blame you for seeing Silverheels as a thief, but I think in the end, you robbed yourself by deciding to never love again, or to let anyone love you."

"Love!" Josie spat out the word as if it tasted bad. "Women in love throw their lives away for men—look at that fool sister of Frank's. I suppose you think she's a romantic heroine too. Love is what makes us the weaker sex."

"No! You're wrong!" I said, surprising myself with my sudden anger and certainty. "Don't you see? Love makes our sex strong! Not the love men give us, but the other way around. Our ability to love others." Josie rolled her eyes, but I continued. "It was love that made my mother strong enough to face down that drunk with nothing but a spoon, and love that gave her the strength to feed all those soldiers. It's love gets her up at four o'clock in the morning to fix the food that brings together our whole town, no matter how tired she is. It's the love of all these mothers and wives and sisters that keeps the country strong while the men are away fighting the war."

She sneered and opened her mouth. I cut her off.

"And if you were really so strong, Josie Gilbert, you'd be brave enough to let Russell love you! You're just a big coward when it comes to love. You're not strong enough to face it!"

There was an icy silence after that in which she glared at me, and I realized how badly I was behaving, talking to my elder like this. I took a long, deep breath.

"I'm sorry," I said quietly.

"Your mother is a good woman, and a strong one, and I'll say nothing against her. But I'll thank you to keep your pert little nose out of my business, Perline Rose Barnell," Josie said.

With that, we both went back to staring out the window in silence. After a long while Russell came back with sandwiches, and sometime after that we all slept. No more than a dozen words passed between us the rest of the trip.

The next morning we rolled into Como at last. Russell and I headed straight for the Silverheels Café to let everyone know we were home. Josie stormed off to her newspaper office, without a word to anyone.

CHAPTER 29

I dreaded stepping into the café. I hadn't thought about the Crawfords' threat while I was in Denver, but now that I was home, I feared that I would find the café shut down, or worse yet, taken over by the Crawfords. Stepping through the door, everything was as usual, except Willie was serving the customers in my place, and sloshing coffee everywhere as he did. I rushed through to the kitchen to see Mother.

She was getting pies into the oven, but stopped to welcome me home with a hug.

"What's happened while I was away? Has there been an investigation?" I asked.

Mother laughed. "All is well, Pearl, but it's too much to tell now. Let's just say I don't think the Crawfords have as many friends as they used to. After lunch, I want to hear all about your trip!"

I went to my room to change my clothes and clean up, then I served the customers off the noon train. By the time the train pulled away again, word had spread that we were back, and about half the town gathered to hear what had happened in Denver. Of course, I was more interested in hearing what had happened in Como, so I told only what I had to—that Josie had only had to pay a fine, and that Frank sent his greetings. Beyond that, there was little I wanted to make public. My feelings for Frank and Russell's for Josie seemed best left unspoken.

When I had finished my tale, I asked again about the investigation. At once, my question was greeted by laughter and cheerful expressions all around.

"Oh, there's an investigation, all right," Orv said. "The governor sent the county sheriff up from Fairplay to find out why that busybody Mrs. Crawford insisted on writing him daily."

"What did the sheriff do?" I asked.

"He no sooner got off his horse than Mrs. Crawford accosted him in the street and demanded that he shut down the café and the butcher shop. Seems she had done some reading and found out the government can seize the property of traitors, and that other folks can buy that property from the government."

"Oh no! They aren't going to seize the café are they?"

"You have nothing to worry about," Mrs. Engel said kindly. "When folks heard that the sheriff was here to take the café from your mother, the whole town showed up to protest. There's not a one of us here who hasn't felt Maggie's kindness, and we weren't going to let anything happen to her. When we started explaining everything to the sheriff, it started coming out what we had all put toward the Liberty

Bonds. Phoebe Crawford would have been better off not calling in the sheriff."

Several people in the café laughed, and most everybody looked pleased.

"Turns out, we'd all been turning in money toward our pledges, but the Crawfords had been putting most of it toward their own pledges, in their names," said Mrs. Abernathy.

"So it looked like they were the only ones giving?" I asked.

"And so they would be the ones to collect the dividends once the war is over," Mrs. Engel said.

"Which is fraud *and* theft," Orv finished. He leaned back in his chair, a satisfied grin on his face. "So you see, Pearl, there will be an investigation. But I don't think you or your mother need to worry."

"Mrs. Crawford will be the county's guest down in Fairplay for a spell, until they get it cleared up, I reckon. And Mr. Crawford and George have gone down there too. I'm sorry you didn't get to say good-bye to George, Pearl. I hope you won't be too lonely without him," Harry said.

I laughed with relief, but Mother hushed me, reminding me of the golden rule. She said if the Crawfords repaid the money or put it toward the bonds in the correct names, no real harm was done, and that we should hope it could be cleared up without them being ruined themselves. I nodded, but secretly I hoped it would take a good long while to settle things, at least long enough to keep George out of Como for the rest of the summer.

Willie hung back on the edge of the crowd, looking nervous. After most folks had gone home, he asked if I wanted to walk down to the creek with him, and I agreed. I could see he had something on his mind and needed space to tell me. When we were alone, he finally spoke.

"Imogene stopped by the café yesterday."

"What did she want?"

He fidgeted for a moment. "She came to tell me she didn't think things would work out for us. Her and me."

"Oh, Willie," I said. "I'm sorry."

He shrugged. "She's a nice kid and all, but I'd rather go fishing. But the thing is, Pearl . . ." He paused again, kicking at the stones on the edge of the creek.

"What?"

"George Crawford asked her to the barn dance down in Fairplay, and she's accepted."

He finally ventured a glance up at my face to see how I would take this news. I stared at him for a long moment before I burst out laughing. His eyebrows popped up.

"You mean, you're not heartbroke? I know he's the handsomest fellow in the county."

"Handsome isn't enough for me," I said. "If it's enough for Imogene, she's welcome to him."

Willie nodded, then got a knowing grin on his face. "Because of Frank, right?"

I opened my mouth, then closed it. "I like Frank," I admitted. "But Denver's awfully far away."

"But you can write him. Distance makes the heart grow fonder, folks say."

I didn't know if that was true. Love somehow seemed a lot more complicated than I had ever before imagined it. Or maybe it was people who were more complicated. I intended to keep up the correspondence with Frank and just see where it took me.

Willie flopped down beside the creek and tossed a pebble into the water. "Would you want to leave here, Pearl? Would you want to be a city girl some place like Denver now that you've seen it?"

I shrugged. If I had learned one thing in my search for Silverheels, it was that none of us could say where life would take us. Why, Josie had even gone to college, all the way out in Massachusetts! There seemed to be a whole range of possibilities I had never thought of before. The world was an open book—and no mere dime novel or penny dreadful, either. I was ready for whatever was in its pages.

Willie leaned back and looked up at the sky. "I don't ever want to leave here, where we can go camping and fishing anytime. We've got it nice and easy here," he said.

I just smiled and hoped that would always be true for him.

I couldn't wait to write to Frank and tell him all that had happened in Como. I tried to tell him how much his kiss had meant to me too, but that part wasn't so easy to put into words. Frank wrote back right away, sweet letters full of news and telling me how much he missed me. I savored every letter over and over, and hoped he'd come back to Como. He had wanted to come for a job cutting hay in August, but that was not to be.

Though Robert's battalion had not yet been in battle, there had been an accident in the boiler room of his ship. He was badly burned, and word was he had lost a leg in the explosion. Robert was due to be shipped back home within a month, and Frank would stay in Denver to help Annie. She would have her hands full with the invalid for some time.

"I think Annie has had second thoughts about her marriage since the incident in Como," Frank wrote, "but this seems to give her a new resolve to work everything out. That's the thing about Annie. She never gives up hope, so I know she'll get Robert through this, no matter how bad it is. But, oh, Pearl! I wish it were different for her!"

I wished it too. Somehow, tragedy was not as beautiful in real life as it was in stories. Yet I knew Annie would be every bit as heroic as I had always believed Silverheels to be.

In Como things were settling back into place, but not necessarily the same places they had been in before. Josie quit coming into the café entirely. Russell came in daily, but I could see he was still suffering from a broken heart. I didn't know what to do for him, so I offered him what kindness I could, and I kept his secret.

As for me, I was back to serving food, clearing plates, and selling maps to the occasional tourist. I wasn't telling them the Silverheels story so much now, though. I guess I couldn't quite decide what the truth of the story was. I hadn't given up on it. I just decided it needed a rest until I could settle on what to tell.

Toward the end of the fifth week after our return, Josie showed up at the café for the first time. She wasn't on foot as usual, and she didn't come in for coffee. She was driving the trap from Johnson's Livery, with good old Strawberry hitched to it. The lunch train had been gone for nearly two hours when she arrived.

"Good afternoon, Mrs. Barnell. I'm wondering if Pearl would be free to accompany me on an errand this afternoon?" she said politely. I almost dropped a stack of plates in surprise. My mother looked a little surprised too, but she smiled and nodded.

"If Pearl would like to go, I'll finish the washing up."

"Where are we going?" I asked as I climbed up onto the seat beside Josie in the trap.

She cracked the reins and "gi'yad" to Strawberry before she answered.

"Buckskin Joe," she said. "I've got a score to settle."

"A score to settle?" I repeated, wondering if I should have asked before agreeing to go with her.

"Ghosts to put to rest," she said.

We rode in silence for a time. The afternoon sun shone brightly, and it didn't seem like the right time to be seeing ghosts, but I figured for Josie they would be everywhere in

Buckskin Joe, whether anyone else could see them or not. I thought again about what Frank and I had talked about so often, about how terrible it must have been for all those young men, dying alone, far from home. Now I thought it might have been more terrible to have lived.

"I am sorry about what I said to you on the train, Josie," I said.

"But you still think I'm a cowardly old woman, don't you."

"No," I said, remembering what I had seen in her eyes in the jail. "I think you're brave to stand up and fight for what you believe in. I never had the courage to do that until I got to know you."

She looked at me suspiciously. "You've known me all your life."

"I guess so, but I never bothered to understand you until now. I stood up to George because I finally understood how brave you were, and I was ashamed of myself in comparison. You were right about me, hiding behind my good manners so I didn't have to stand up for what I wanted."

She chuckled. "You may grow a spine yet, girl."

"Pearl," I said. "My name is Pearl."

"Pearl," she agreed.

We rattled on in silence for a few more minutes before she spoke again. "You weren't wrong about me on the train," she said. "About me and love. I suppose we all have our ghosts and demons, and the longer we let them haunt us, the harder they are to dispel. Mine have been with me for nigh on sixty years, but no more. We're putting them to rest today."

"I think that's brave too," I said. "Mighty brave."

By the time we arrived in Buckskin Joe, the sun was riding low over Mount Silverheels, and the sunlight was falling in rich golden shafts between the trees. Josie brought Strawberry to a stop and set the brake on the trap. We sat for a long moment in the silence. I was glad no one was there but Josie and me. It seemed right that it should be still and peaceful, slipping back as it was into nature. Great sadness and tragedy had happened here, and for Josie great pain had hardened into bitterness. It was right that the place should welcome her back now in peacefulness, as she came to put those feelings to rest.

She took a deep breath, and, reaching under the seat of the trap, she pulled out a big bundle of daisies. She gave a few to me, then clambered down to the ground. Together we walked through the silent grassy field that had once been the center of town. Josie did not turn her head to look at the dance hall or the old store, or the old cabins, where men had once died and she had once lived. She walked straight for the creek, her eyes on the broken-down fence beyond. Of course that's where we were going, I thought. Where else would we find the ghosts of Josie's past.

She only paused once, right on the edge of the cemetery, just outside the leaning picket fence. I stepped through first and seeing her pause, extended my hand back to her, but of course, she refused to take it. She straightened her shoulders, took a deep breath, and stepped over the threshold into that hallowed ground.

Carefully, she picked her way through the tangle of weeds and leaning markers to the back. She did not pause to read names or to orient herself. She walked directly to Buck Wilson's grave and stood before it, her jaw set, gazing down hard at the cross with the name freshly scratched into its crossbar. I could not bear to look. I wished I wasn't there, intruding on her private grief. As quietly as I could, I stepped back from her and moved away through the cemetery. I laid a few daisies on each one of the graves of the men who had died so long ago in that freezing, lonely winter. Josie just stood, staring down at the ground where Buck Wilson lay. The sun dipped down behind the peak, and with a sigh of cool air, the rays of sunlight died from between the trees. That's when Josie spoke at last.

"I came to say good-bye, Buck. To say that I forgive you. But I can't."

My heart fell. She had come all this way, but in the end it was too much to give up the bitterness that had imprisoned her heart for so long.

"I can't because there's nothing to forgive." She bent and put the flowers on the grave. "You never did anything wrong, Buck Wilson, except to die. And in that, you wronged only yourself, my friend. So I guess I'm just here to say good-bye, and to let you go, fifty-six years too late."

I stepped up beside her, looking at the white flowers, bright on the ground as dusk began to settle around them.

"What about Silverheels?" I asked. "Have you forgiven her, too?"

Josie frowned. "One thing at a time," she said. "Some wounds are deeper than others."

"I guess we will never really know what happened to her," I said.

"She went off into legend," Josie said. "Where she could be anything to anybody."

"But in real life? What do you suppose really happened? She could have taken all that gold she'd collected and sent it to their families like she promised, you know."

"Doesn't matter, does it? Maybe you're right and she was a hero, made strong by love. Maybe she was a charitable angel of mercy."

"Then you do forgive her," I said.

Josie looked at me with a spark of challenge in her eyes. If I had thought she was going home from this a sweet old lady, I was sorely mistaken. "Or maybe she was a money-grubbing thief and a liar, who lived out her days like a queen in Paris or New York."

She looked up toward the summit of Mount Silverheels and shrugged. "Or maybe she just froze to death in the hills before anyone even knew she was gone."

"I don't think she froze to death," I said. "She had love, like my mother, and brains and determination, like you. She wouldn't have frozen to death."

Josie shrugged. "Then we can each live with our own

convictions about the truth, can't we."

We turned and walked from the cemetery and back down toward the creek.

"What about Russell?" I asked as we walked. "He seems mighty brokenhearted since we got back. He's miserable."

Josie nodded. "Someone needs to put him out of his misery. And since I can't shoot him, I guess I'll have to marry him."

"Oh, Josie! That's wonderful! We can have the wedding feast at the café! I'm sure my mother would—"

"Hush up, girl! Honestly, I only just faced Buck for the first time in fifty-six years and you're already pushing me into the arms of another."

"That's not true. I know you've come up here every spring to clean Buck Wilson's grave, Josie."

She looked blankly at me. "I have done no such thing."

"Sure you have," I insisted. "You cleaned it and freshened his name on the cross in June, just before I brought Frank up here."

"Don't be ridiculous," she snapped. "I haven't been up here since 1875, when I left and vowed I would never come back. I'm not a romantic ninny like you, Perline Rose Barnell." With that, she splashed grumpily across the creek and lumbered up the slope toward the waiting trap.

I froze, the hairs on my neck prickling. Josie hadn't been the one to clean the grave?

Slowly, I turned and looked back toward the cemetery.

She stood tall and slender in her black gown and veil, barely more than a shadow at Buck Wilson's grave, gazing down at the flowers Sefa had left there. When she sensed me looking, she raised her veiled face, and through the filmy cloth, her eyes met mine.

I recognized her at once, because I had seen those eyes before. They were my mother's eyes, gleaming with love. They were Annie's eyes, hopeful despite her regrets. They were Josie's eyes, shrewd and defiant.

I knew then that I would tell her tale again, to anyone who would listen, to anyone who dared to call women the weaker sex. She knew it too, and she smiled as she faded into the twilight shadows among the graves. I turned and hurried back to the waiting trap, knowing that I had at last found the spirit of Silverheels, only to realize it had been with me all my life.

Author's Note

I grew up in Colorado and spent many hours of my child-hood camping and exploring around the old mines and ghost towns in the mountains. I can't say where I first heard the legend of Silverheels—I have known it for as long as I can remember. As a child, I loved the romantic ideal of the tragic, self-sacrificing angel of mercy, as Pearl does. I hadn't thought about the legend in years, when I heard it again recently and found myself wondering why, if they had loved her so much, the miners did not know her name. I realized a cynic might interpret the story very differently, and thus this novel was born.

Various historians and old-timers alike have tried to learn the details of Silverheels's story, but, as Josie says, she has gone on into legend, and no one really knows for sure. The names Gerda/Gerta Bechtel or Gerda Silber have been attributed to her, as well as the name Josie Dillon. Likewise, in various versions her lover has been identified as Buck Wilson or as Jack Herndon, who owned either the dance hall or the saloon. While various communities in and around South Park have claimed her story, most place her in the town known as Buckskin Joe, which was officially named Laurette, in honor of Laura and Jeanette Phillips.

A manuscript by Albert B. Sanford, preserved by the Colorado Historical Society, records Tom Lee's version of the story. As Frank gets the story out of Mr. Lee in my book, I let him borrow Mr. Sanford's last name. Lou Bunch was the last famous madam in the Central City red light district. Sefa Weldon and her family are my own creations and do not appear in any version of the legend. Likewise, with the exception of Tom Lee, the people of Pearl's time, and the organization of Como, are all fictional. Como, Colorado, is a real town and was a key stop on the railroad lines connecting Denver to Fairplay and Breckenridge, Colorado, but I have taken liberties to make the town what I needed it to be in my 1917 version. I have also placed Buckskin Joe considerably closer to Como than it really is, to make Frank's visit a little more convenient.

Because the various interpretations of Silverheels's story raise questions about the traditional roles of women and their sources of strength, I felt the World War I era was a time that threw those issues into sharp relief, and so I chose it as the time period to tell this story. As many women were sending their sons, husbands, and sweethearts off to war, others were fighting for the vote. The National Women's Party was a radical suffragist organization that split from more traditional suffragists in 1913, when Woodrow Wilson was newly elected. Rather than fighting for the vote in individual states, they believed the fight had to be for a national constitutional amendment, and so they picketed the White House. When the United States entered the war in 1917, they publicized the hypocrisy of Wilson's claim as a champion of civil rights in Europe while opposing women's right to vote at home. Their message, which had been tolerated in a time of peace, became considered seditious in wartime, and their arrests in the summer and fall of 1917 led to harsh treatment. These are the real national events alluded to in my story that drive Josie's actions. The rally and arrests in Denver, however, are fictional.

Liberty Bonds were first issued in the spring of 1917 and were not widely accepted by the general public. A variety of strong-arm tactics were taken up across the country to sell the bonds, among them suggestions of un-American behavior for those who didn't subscribe. Bond subscriptions were made starting with a pledge of one dollar, but requiring payments totaling fifty dollars over six months, which, in rural communities, was a large sum of money.

Today, the town of Como, Colorado, has only a handful of residents, though the historic hotel, railroad depot, and roundhouse remain. Little remains of the town site of Buckskin Joe, but you can still walk through its cemetery. Who knows, you might even see a woman there, in a black veil and silver dancing shoes.

You will certainly see her namesake, Mount Silverheels

(elev. 13,829 feet), one of the most beautiful mountains ringing South Park. It is Colorado's 99th tallest mountain. Of the hundred tallest mountains in the state, it is the only one named for a woman.